THE DEAD CAN'T TALK

Ivan Sage

To Judy
with love

1

Saturday, 29th August, 1987.

IT WAS one of the worst cases of murder that DCI David Shepperton had seen. The girl in undergrowth adjacent to the Blackwater Canal towpath, he assumed, was probably no more than 15 or 16 years old. Her body bore multiple stab wounds, mostly to the chest but several more wounds were apparent on her arms suggesting the poor girl had been trying to protect herself from what appeared to have been a frenzied attack.

Shepperton had worked on – and solved – at least a dozen murder cases while serving in the Metropolitan Police but, since relocating to the relative sleepy market town of Somersley, this was the first time he had worked on such a serious incident. With no immediate evidence of a sexual motive – the girl was fully dressed – the intensity of the attack suggested the killer harboured a personal grudge against his or her victim.

Shepperton began to allocate various roles for his officers and prioritised measures to secure the crime scene. Sitting in the back of a nearby panda car was the extremely distressed middle-aged woman who, while walking her dog, had discovered the body and alerted the police to the scene.

Within the hour the entire area was swarming with police forensic officers while other officers were tasked with interviewing local residents in the hope that someone may have seen something out of the ordinary that may offer some clue as to who may have been responsible for this horrific crime.

Sadly, despite extensive enquiries over the following days and weeks, no useful leads had been established. As Shepperton sat in his office late one evening he had to admit to himself that this could turn out to be one of the most difficult cases to date in his career.

This one, he feared, might never be resolved.

-o0o-

13 months later.

Wendy Brown sat nervously in her car, her clammy hands tightly gripping the steering wheel. She looked in the rear view mirror and noticed the beads of sweat gathering on her forehead. It was the first time in more than a year that this once bubbly, confident and popular teacher had parked her vehicle in the staff car park of Somersley Secondary Modern School.

After a few moments she turned off the engine and placed her head between her shaking hands. Could she really do this? Could she really pluck up the courage to go through that door and face her colleagues once again? And what about the kids? Her mouth felt dry. She felt clammy, almost sick. Her heart was racing as she fumbled to open her door. She clambered out of her green Vauxhall Viva and looked around.

Although she had arrived early she noticed that most of her colleagues' vehicles were already present. As she locked her car door she realised just how much her hands were shaking. She took a deep breath and closed her eyes. 'Come on Wendy. You can do this. It's now or never,' she muttered to herself.

Under normal circumstances the first day of term after the summer holidays would have harboured no fears for Wendy. In fact, the 44-year-old dedicated teacher had always been more than ready to return to the busy routine of school life.

Being a single parent since her husband Brian had left her for another woman three years previously, Wendy had since immersed herself completely into her career – a position that had given her little time to dwell on the rejection she had felt since Brian's infidelity had come to light. But this was no normal return to work. This was a day she had been dreading for weeks – and with very good reason.

She placed her car keys in the side pocket of her handbag and walked towards the heavy black-painted door bearing the words MAIN ENTRANCE across the top in large white capital letters. She took another deep breath, opened the door and made her way along the long, wide corridor towards the staff room.

Her footsteps echoed as she neared the staff room. She could make out the muffled voices of her colleagues. She reached for the door handle then had a sudden change of heart. She turned around and hurried into the ladies' washroom. On arrival she looked into the mirror above the washbasin. The flushed, watery-eyed face looking back at her did little to improve her demeanour.

Perhaps this was too soon. Looking again in the mirror she was convinced. Yes, it was far, far too soon since *IT* happened. She grabbed some tissues and wiped her face then fumbled in her handbag as she searched for her car keys. As she did so the door behind her opened.

'Wendy! Oh Wendy, it's *so* good to see you back again! How are you doing?' No sooner had she uttered those words, Felicity du Beke, one of Wendy's closest colleagues, wished she hadn't opened her mouth. The short, rather plump English teacher with a kindly face gasped in embarrassment.

'Oh Wendy, I'm *so* sorry. What a dumb question!' She stepped forward and gave Wendy a comforting hug.

'It's okay Felicity. To be truthful, I was just having a moment. Gotta be honest I'm really not sure I can do this after all.'

'It was never gonna be easy love, was it?' said Felicity as she cradled Wendy's face reassuringly between her hands. 'You've just gotta remember that you're amongst friends here. *Good* friends. We're all gonna be here for you. We'll help you get back into the groove as much as we can.'

Felicity disappeared behind the cubicle door.

'I guess you'll have to make a few allowances for us all though. I know some of 'em won't really know what to say to you in case they put their foot in it – just like I did just now!'

'I guess you're right,' replied Wendy. 'I suppose it'll be best to get it over with.'

The toilet flushed. Felicity reappeared.

'That's my girl!' she said as she washed and dried her hands.

'Come on then Wendy, I'm gonna be right with you.'

The two women walked back along the corridor towards the staff room door.

'Ready?'

Wendy nodded nervously. Felicity opened the door and announced: 'Look who's back everyone!'

Without exception everyone stood up, turned to Wendy and welcomed her back with open arms. Several hugs and kisses later Wendy dried her eyes and opened her locker. Felicity was right – she had some very good friends. As she was putting away her handbag Felicity tapped her on the shoulder.

'Geraldine's asked that you come to her office.'

Wendy nodded.

'Thanks.'

Wendy made her way to head teacher Geraldine Abbott's office. She gently tapped on the door which was immediately flung open. Geraldine embraced Wendy and kissed her on the cheek. The women had known each other for years and had formed a very close friendship. Indeed Geraldine had been a tower of support to Wendy throughout the most difficult time of her life, having regularly visited her at home and frequently telephoning to check if she was okay.

The women were unlikely friends, Geraldine being of a much larger stature than the demure Wendy. Geraldine was a rather stocky fitness fanatic while Wendy liked nothing more than to curl up on her sofa reading a good book. Yet, despite their differences, the two women had been close friends from the early days of Wendy's career at the school.

'It's so good to have you back,' she gushed. 'You've been missed so much. Not just by me and the staff but the kids too. I wanted to catch you before the bell rings. It's important you know that we're all here for you. Any problems, don't hesitate to come to me. Anything at all. Okay?'

'Thanks Geri. That means a lot. Everyone's been so nice, so supportive, especially you. I know it'll take a while but, hopefully, I'll get there. One step at a time eh?'

Geraldine hugged her again.

'Exactly! Like I said, it's so good to have you back in the fold. I really wondered at one time if we'd ever see you head up a class again after *IT* happened.'

It appeared that Geraldine still felt uncomfortable to express out loud in words what *IT* was.

'It was a terrible shock for us all,' she continued. 'God only knows how you've managed to come through the other side but I'm so glad you have.'

IT happened to be something that had turned Wendy's life upside down. One moment life, with the exception of her marriage, had been going reasonably well until the evening of Saturday, August 29 the previous year. Wendy had become concerned that her 16-year-old daughter Heather had not returned to her home, No23 Coriander Drive, at her usual time. Heather had been such a responsible and reliable girl. She had certainly grown up fast since her father had turned his back on her and her mother. In fact the teenager's bond with her mother had become so much stronger that Wendy would often joke that Heather had become more like a sister since the break-up of her marriage.

Wendy had good reason to love her daughter. Early on in her marriage to Brian she had given birth to a baby girl who, sadly passed away just three days later owing to complications surrounding the birth. The grieving parents had been informed that it would be highly unlikely that Wendy would be able to carry another child so, when Heather arrived, it was as if a miracle had occurred.

Most Wednesdays and Saturdays during the school summer holidays Heather would head off into town with her best friend Maureen Robson. The girls loved to tour the department stores looking at clothes and fashion accessories before meeting up with school friends around teatime in the Wimpy Bar in the High Street. Normally Heather would be back home by 7.30. However, it was now 8.30 and Heather had still not returned.

At first Wendy had not been too concerned but, by 9.30 she was beginning to feel a little uneasy as it would soon be getting dark. She knew Heather would always go to a telephone box and call to let her know if there was any reason to cause her to be late home but even at 10 o'clock the 'phone had remained silent. Something must surely be wrong.

By 10.30 Wendy was becoming frantic. She began to telephone the parents of Heather's friends, asking if they had any idea where she might be. Her first call was, obviously, to Maureen's parents but there had been no answer. After Wendy had exhausted all the other contacts she tried once more to contact Maureen's parents. To her immense relief Maureen's mother picked up the 'phone.

'Somersley 3630, Deborah speaking.'

'Hi Deborah, it's Wendy. I'm rather worried. I don't suppose Heather's with you?'

'No, she's not. I'd have thought she'd be back home with you by now.'

Wendy's heart sank. 'Is Maureen there now? Can I speak to her?'

'Sure, though I don't know what's up with her. I heard her go straight to her room the moment she came home. I didn't even see her. I hope they haven't had a row.'

'Oh Deborah, that's hardly likely is it? Those two are practically joined at the hip.'

Wendy heard Deborah call out.

'Mo! Can you come down a minute? It's Heather's mum. She needs to speak to you.'

Wendy heard footsteps coming down the stairs.

'Er, hi Mrs Brown, what's up?'

'It's Heather. She's not come home and I'm getting worried. Have you any idea where she might be?'

'Sorry, no. I assumed she'd be coming straight home as usual. I left her at the bus stop in Priory Street.'

'What time would that have been?'

'Dunno. Around 6.30. 6.45 maybe. Are you sure she's not upstairs in her room?'

Wendy had, of course, already checked Heather's room — several times. Besides, she would have heard her coming through the front door.

'She's not in her room Maureen. I don't know who else to call. She always lets me know if she's gonna be late.'

'Have you tried ringing her dad?'

Wendy was sure her daughter had not gone to her father's. Heather had very little time for Brian or for Stella – *'that woman'* as Heather and her mother always referred to her. Besides, apart from the rejection she felt from her father, Heather had been further hurt by his apparent fondness for Stella's daughter Gemma. She could not help feeling she had been replaced by Gemma in her father's affections. A double rejection in Heather's eyes. Despite receiving many letters from her father, Heather had binned them all unopened so she had never read his pleas for forgiveness and a reconciliation.

'No Maureen,' replied Wendy, 'I haven't rung him.'

There was a pause.

'Perhaps you should. I doubt if she's there but it's gotta be worth a try. For what it's worth I don't think she has any more time for him than you but you never know. If she's not there I reckon you should call the police. I mean, it's just not like her is it? You will let me know if you hear anything won't you?'

'Yes of course. Thank you Maureen.'

Wendy put down the 'phone. Close to tears she looked for the piece of paper bearing *'that woman's'* telephone number.

'Somersley 3647.'

'Is Brian there?'

'Who is this?'

'It's Wendy.'

'What do you want?' replied Stella curtly.

'I want Brian,' replied Wendy exasperatedly. 'If he's there tell him I need to speak to him urgently.'

'Charming, I'm sure!'

'Oh for God's sake just get him to the 'phone. It's Heather, she's not come home!'

'She's a teenager,' replied Stella dismissively. 'She's most likely out with friends.'

'She's only 16. It's almost midnight and it's dark outside. If it was your Gemma you'd be frantic by now. I want to speak to Brian now – right now!'

Stella sighed.

'Alright, alright. I'll fetch him.'

Wendy heard Stella lay the receiver down on the table.

'Brian! Telephone call for you!'

'Who is it?' she heard Brian ask in the background.

'*The wife*,' came the whispered, rather sarcastic reply.

'Wen, what do you want? It's late and I only got home from work an hour or so ago,' he said irritatedly. 'What couldn't wait until the morning?'

By now Wendy was in tears.

'What's happened?'

'It's . . . it's Heather! . . .'

Wendy began to sob almost uncontrollably.

'Heather? What about Heather? For God's sake Wen pull yourself together. What's going on?'

'She's missing,' blubbed Wendy. 'She's not come home. I've rung all her friends and their parents. No-one's seen her since she was at the bus stop in town around half six. Brian, I'm going out of my mind with worry.'

There was another pause as Brian gathered his thoughts.

'Right. Okay. I'll come straight over. If she's not home by the time I get there I reckon we should call the cops. I don't like this any more than you.'

'Okay.'

'Right,' he added, 'and until all this is sorted we oughta put all this other stuff behind us and just concentrate on getting our girl back home safe. You agree?'

'Course I do. Just hurry up will you?'

Ten minutes later Wendy heard Brian's bright red MGB GT sports car pull up on the driveway. She peered through the curtains as her estranged husband awkwardly extricated himself from the car.

He looked so different these days. He'd dyed his greying hair black and had grown it longer. He was dressed in clothes befitting a much younger man – he was 45 – and, as for the car – well that exemplified the fact that, in her mind, her husband was going through a mid-life crisis. However, this was not the time to dwell on such trivial matters. She rushed to the door to let him in.

'No rush Wen, I've still got a key.'

'I know but I've had the locks changed.'

'Why?'

'Why do you think?' she snapped.

'I thought you'd agreed,' he said. 'Let's have none of that tonight. Is she back yet?'

'No.'

Wendy began to sob again. Instinctively Brian moved to reassure her but she pushed him away.

'We'd better get down the cop shop,' said Brian. 'Have you got a recent photo of her?'

Wendy nodded and rummaged through her handbag.

'I've got this one.'

'That'll do. Come on, let's get going.'

'Just a minute.'

'What are you doing?'

'I'm leaving a note for Heather in case she turns up while we're out. She'll need to know where I am.'

Wendy hurriedly scribbled a note and left it on the bottom stair. She then locked up and joined her estranged husband in the MGB GT. Within minutes they entered the police station and presented themselves at the front desk.

The duty sergeant, Ray Smith, looked up from his *Daily Mail* sports pages and took one last sip of his tea.

'Good evening Sir, Madam,' he said cheerily. 'What can I do for you?'

Wendy retrieved the photograph from her handbag.

'This is Heather Brown. She's our daughter. She's 16 and she's missing. She should have been home hours ago. We're both extremely worried.'

Smith took the photograph. His hitherto carefree expression seemed to dissolve.

'Er, would you please excuse me for a moment?' he asked rather awkwardly.

Brian nodded.

'I'll just take this photo with me,' said Smith. 'I'll try not to keep you waiting any longer than necessary.'

He turned and disappeared through the door behind him. Brian looked at Wendy, now looking just as worried as her.

'Did you see his face?' he asked.

Wendy nodded.

'I don't like this. I don't like this one little bit,' said Brian.

Meanwhile, Smith headed straight for the incident room. The DCI was in deep conversation but Smith decided to interrupt.

'Sir, you'll want to see this.'

DCI David Shepperton turned around.

'What is it Ray?'

'There's a Mr and Mrs Brown at the front desk. They're saying their daughter's missing.'

Smith handed over the photo.

'Could this be the girl whose body was found earlier this evening?' he asked.

Shepperton looked closely at the photograph.

'Jeez Ray, it looks awfully like her doesn't she?'

He continued to peer at the photograph, then shook his head.

'No,' he said. 'No, it's not her. The girl by the canal has a tiny scar on her left cheek. The girl in this picture doesn't.'

'Phew,' replied Smith, 'that's a relief. I didn't fancy having to tell them their daughter's been slashed to death by some vicious psycho.'

Shepperton frowned.

'I wouldn't celebrate yet if I were you Ray,' he replied. 'The similarities between the two girls are disturbing. Look, they're both around the same age and they both have blonde shoulder-length hair. The girl next to the towpath had been brutally murdered – a real case of overkill if ever I've seen one. I just hope to God this missing girl doesn't turn out to be another victim of some crazy knife-wielding nutter.'

'Perhaps it'll be best not to mention that to the couple in reception,' ventured Smith.

'Of course. They've got enough to worry about already,' agreed Shepperton, 'but I've got a nasty feeling that this young lady,' he said tapping his finger on Heather's photograph, 'might well have come to a nasty end. As you know, I don't believe in coincidences.'

Smith nodded. 'I'll go see them,' he said. He returned to the reception desk.

'Sorry to keep you waiting,' he told the worried parents. 'Normally, we would suggest waiting a few more hours before we begin to search for missing youngsters but, in this instance, bearing in mind the time of night, I think we'll instruct our patrols to keep an eye out for your daughter straight away. May I keep this?' he asked as he held up the photograph.

Brian and Wendy nodded.

'I'll ensure our officers receive copies of this as soon as possible,' said Smith. 'In the meantime I'm gonna need the names and contact details of as many of your daughter's friends and acquaintances as possible. We'll need to know all the places she likes to go to and establish as much information as you can possibly offer us in regards to Heather's routines and habits.

'We'll also need to know if she's expressed any worries over the past few days or weeks or if she has had any upsets with anyone. Anything you can tell us could be of vital importance to us no matter how insignificant it may appear at this moment.'

The door behind Smith opened and a smartly-dressed man appeared. He introduced himself.

'Hello Mr and Mrs Brown. I'm DCI Shepperton. I understand your daughter is missing. If you'd like to accompany me to the interview room we can get started. Hopefully we can find her quickly and bring her home safely to you.'

It was 4.15 in the morning when Brian and Wendy left the police station. Both emotionally drained, they climbed back into Brian's sports car and headed back to the former marital home. Wendy unlocked the front door and removed her shoes.

'You'd better come in I suppose,' she said. 'I'll put the kettle on.'

They sat in silence as they sipped their tea. Wendy yawned.

'You look shattered,' said Brian. 'Why don't you go upstairs and lie down? I'll stay down here and try to kip on the sofa.'

'No way,' said Wendy. 'I'm staying downstairs. I want to be right here in case she comes through that front door.'

Brian sat at one end of the three-seater sofa. Wendy sat at the other. Within an hour both of them had drifted off into a restless sleep until Wendy was woken at 6.45 by the ringing of the hallway telephone. In an instant she jumped up and rushed to pick up the receiver. She heard a woman's voice, apparently very upset.

'Is Brian there? It's Stella.'

'Stella, you need to get off the line. I need to keep it clear in case Heather tries to get in touch.'

'Wait! Please, don't hang up! I really have to speak to Brian. It's Gemma. She's not in her room!'

'Oh I wouldn't worry if I were you,' replied Wendy sarcastically. 'She's probably out with friends – after all, that's what you reckoned when I was panicking over Heather last night.'

'I'm so sorry Wendy. Is she still not home?'

'No. We've been to the police. They're looking out for her.'

'*Please* Wendy, let me speak to Brian. I'm *so* worried.'

Wendy recognised the fear in Stella's voice. As a mother she could understand her fears. In spite of everything this was no time to start trying to score points off each other.

'Okay, I'll get Brian now. Gimme a sec.'

Brian was stirring as she returned to the lounge.

'Was that the 'phone?' he asked, rubbing his eyes.

Wendy nodded.

'Heather?' he asked hopefully.

'No, it's Stella. Gemma's missing.'

Brian rushed into the hall to pick up the receiver. Moments later he rejoined Wendy.

'I've gotta get back. Gemma's bed's not been slept in. Seems she's been missing all night. I'm gonna pick up Stella and take her to the police station. Are you gonna be okay?'

Wendy nodded, albeit unconvincingly.

'I hope she's okay. Let me know, eh?'

Brian hugged her awkwardly. Seconds later he was driving away. Wendy watched from the front door as he disappeared from view. Duty sergeant Ray Smith had finished his shift by the time Brian and Stella arrived at the police station, Sgt Roger Everett now being tasked with manning the reception desk. Stella rushed up to the counter.

'We need help. My daughter's missing!''

Everett's ears pricked up immediately.

'Okay Madam. Try to calm down. Can you tell me her name and how long she's been missing?'

'She didn't come home last night. She's 16. This is her photo. Her name's Gemma Gooding.'

Brian noticed an immediate concerned expression on Everett's face. The officer took the photograph and, in what seemed to be a case of *déjà vu*, excused himself and disappeared through the door leading to the incident room. DCI Shepperton was still on duty. The tall, balding 45-year-old policeman, with his shirt sleeves rolled up and his collar undone, looked mightily weary. He noticed Everett approaching.

'Roger, what's that you've got there?'

'There's a couple outside. They say their daughter's missing. They gave me this photo.'

Everett handed over the picture. Shepperton took once glance at it. His heart immediately sank.

'What's her name?'

'Gemma. Gemma Gooding. She's 16.'

Shepperton turned to his fellow detectives and announced solemnly: 'Gentlemen, it seems, pending a formal identification, that we now have a name for the deceased young lady.'

He held up the photograph.

'This,' he said, 'is Gemma Gooding. I want no stone left unturned until we find out who is responsible for her death. I want every available officer, whether they are on duty or not, to join me in the debriefing room in one hour. With another girl missing I'm fearful we might have a serial killer on our hands.'

2

Wendy's return to work followed the most traumatic time for her and Brian. Meanwhile, Gemma's untimely, tragic and brutal death had placed an unbearable strain on Brian and Stella's relationship not least because of Stella's continued refusal to accept Brian's grief for his own daughter. Brian and Wendy, she claimed, were lucky. They were still able to harbour some degree of hope that Heather might still, somehow, be alive whereas her daughter was already dead and buried.

Shepperton, leading the investigation into Gemma's murder and Heather's disappearance, appeared a dejected detective at subsequent press conferences as time passed by. He and his team had worked tirelessly, night and day, following up on dozens of leads and tip-offs that had ultimately amounted to nothing of any real value.

Any hopes that Brian and Wendy had clung on to that Heather might still come home crumbled when Shepperton, under immense pressure from reporters, felt obliged to admit that, owing to the time that had passed, it was 'highly unlikely' that Heather would now be found alive although 'we must never lose hope.'

Brian had since moved out of Stella's home and was now living in cheap rented accommodation on the far side of town which, as a self-employed gardener, proved to be all he could afford. At one point he had intimated that in order to support each other through such trying times he might eventually move back into the marital home but this was a suggestion Wendy had been swift to dismiss. 'That ship sailed a very long time ago,' she insisted.

Her demeanour had been a cause for concern amongst her friends, colleagues and family. A lack of sleep exacerbated her fragile state of mind. Geraldine had been a regular visitor and had been at pains to assure Wendy that her job was safe and that she should take as long as she needed before returning to work. Felicity, she said, could fill in as the school's French teacher until Wendy felt able to come back.

Following the morning assembly of Wendy's first day back at work she waited nervously in the classroom for her pupils to appear.

'Let's face it Wendy, the newbies will be just as nervous as you – perhaps even more so,' joked Geraldine. 'Just remember, you're the best French teacher we've ever had. They'll be lucky to have you.'

While Geraldine's assurances failed to quell Wendy's apprehension at first she was pleasantly surprised to find by lunchtime that first day that most of her earlier nerves had eased. The tension began to subside and, slowly but surely, her enthusiasm and passion to introduce young children to the wonders of the French language grew markedly as the day wore on. That said, once the home time bell sounded at 3.50 no-one had been more relieved than Wendy to retreat to the sanctity of the staff room.

'Well,' asked Felicity as they sat down for a much-needed cup of tea, 'how does it feel to be back in the saddle?'

Wendy smiled.

'In hindsight, I guess it's just what I needed,' she admitted. 'Let's hope tomorrow goes just as nicely.'

It did. So did the next day and the next. At last Wendy felt she was beginning to rediscover her purpose in life and, although nothing could allay her fears for her daughter's welfare, she realised the importance of regaining some form of routine.

Brian, on the other hand, was struggling – mostly with his conscience. He was now regretting the way he had walked out on Wendy and Heather. He had treated them both badly and the thought that his girl may have ended her days believing he did not love her as much as he should was something he could not get out of his head. Looking back he realised he'd been a poor father and husband who did not deserve any form of forgiveness from Wendy.

A few weeks later, with all these thoughts racing around in his head and having lost one of his main gardening contracts to a competitor, Brian went home and sought to end it all with a bottle of Jack Daniels and a handful of aspirins. Had it not been for the swift action of a concerned neighbour and the skills of medical professionals, he would not have survived.

He did, however, have one visitor at the hospital – Wendy. Despite all the past acrimony between them she could not find it in her heart not to do the right thing when she heard the news.

'It wasn't a cry for help,' he insisted when she arrived at his bedside. 'I truly wanted to end it all. I'm sorry for the way I left you,' he admitted tearfully, 'but even more so because Heather washed her hands of me. I can't honestly say I blame her either. That's something I'm gonna have to live with for the rest of my life I suppose.'

Wendy's response was not as conciliatory as he might have hoped.

'Doc told me you'd had a very lucky escape. Reckons another hour or so and you'd have copped it,' she replied coldly.

'Might have been better if I had. Better for everyone.'

'Oh shut up will you? Don't be so pitiful. You're alive so you should be thankful. What about *'that woman'*, has she been in to see you?'

Brian shook his head.

'I've not seen or heard from her. To be honest, things had been rather strained between us long before Gemma's death – money issues really. My wages couldn't compete with what her ex-husband earned so I couldn't keep her in the manner she'd been accustomed to. I guess she's thinking the same as you now – that that ship has already sailed.'

'Well,' said Wendy coldly, 'you'd better sort yourself out quick 'cos Shepperton 'phoned this morning. He's asked if we could come in to speak to him.'

Brian sat up expectantly.

'Really? Have they found something?'

'I don't think so. I told him you were in here. He said there was no rush and that I was to call him when you're up and about to arrange a meet-up.'

'No rush, eh? Doesn't sound like he's got anything positive to tell us then, does it?'

'Guess not. He was on the telly again last night, being quizzed about the investigation. Doesn't sound like there's been any progress at all.'

A meeting with Shepperton five days later proved Wendy's theory wasn't far off the mark.

'Thanks for coming in,' said Shepperton bearing a very solemn expression. 'I thought I should speak to you both face-to-face rather than over the telephone.'

Brian looked at Wendy.

'I don't like the sound of this,' he said.

'Have you found her?' asked Wendy desperately.

'No Mrs Brown, we haven't. Believe me, if we had we would have informed you both immediately.'

Shepperton fidgeted on his chair and wrung his hands together.

'Look,' he said, 'there's no easy way to tell you this. To be brutally honest the investigation into Gemma Gooding's murder is making incredibly slow progress. At this moment in time we have very few leads remaining to follow up on. As for the investigation into your daughter's disappearance is concerned we seem to have exhausted every line of enquiry to date. We've come to a dead end.

'You have to understand that, without a body, we cannot continue to assume that harm has come to Heather. For all we know she may have disappeared of her own volition. For that reason we are now concentrating our rather limited resources on the Gemma Gooding investigation.'

'But Heather would never just disappear! She's not that kind of girl. She'd never do such a thing!' Wendy protested. Brian seemed devastated. He sat rocking on his chair, his head clasped between his hands.

'I dreaded something like this,' he said.

Shepperton looked sadly at the two desperate parents sitting in front of him. As a father himself, he could fully appreciate their despair.

'I can quite understand your point of view Mr and Mrs Brown, really I can. I'd feel just the same if it were a child of my own but, as my Chief Constable insists, it's a fact that Gemma was murdered and the public must be reassured that we are utilising every resource available to us in order to catch the person or persons responsible for her death.

'It's out of my hands I'm afraid. I'm dreadfully sorry but that's just the way it is. We will, of course, follow up any leads as to the whereabouts of Heather if and when they present themselves to us.'

It seemed pointless to protest. As Shepperton had said, it was out of his hands. Stunned, Brian and Wendy left the station. They made their way to Brian's car, got in and sat staring into space, neither of them speaking a word. Brian eventually broke the silence.

'It's just not fair! This ain't right!

He banged his fists against the steering wheel. Wendy looked across at him and noticed he had begun to weep. Subconsciously she reached out and gently squeezed his hand. Seconds later they were both in floods of tears with their arms around each other. Wendy was the first to pull away. She took a tissue from her handbag and dabbed her eyes.

'Come on,' she said, 'let's get out of here.'

Brian wiped his eyes with the back of his hand, fumbled around in his pocket to find his keys and started up. A few minutes later he parked up outside Wendy's front door.

'I'll come in with you Wen. I don't wanna leave you here like this.'

'No, it's fine,' replied Wendy firmly, adding: 'I just want to be on my own.'

It was immediately clear that any hopes that Brian may have had of reconnecting with his estranged wife following their brief embrace were not reciprocated. He watched sadly as she got out of the car and put her key in the lock of her front door. Without looking back or even saying goodbye, she opened the door and disappeared inside.

Some time passed with no news from Shepperton. Brian had begun to put his life back together having replaced the gardening contract with a more lucrative one which enabled him to relocate to a small rented cottage which was much nicer than the tiny flat he had been living in since leaving Stella.

Thanks to the unwavering support of her colleagues Wendy was now getting back into the swing of things at Somersley Secondary Modern. Of course she had down days – several of them – but, all things considered, she was getting by reasonably well on a day-to-day basis. Sadly though, one morning, all that was to change.

September 12 would have been Heather's 18th birthday so, naturally, her missing daughter was uppermost on Wendy's mind. The new school term had only just resumed after the six-week summer holiday period and was a particularly busy time. Wendy coped as well as she could by throwing herself full-on into her work.

Over the first few months of Heather's disappearance Shepperton had, at least, telephoned both Wendy and Brian with updates but those calls had since dried up. Nevertheless, Wendy had made a point of calling the detective once a week, not particularly expecting to hear of any new developments but to remind him, should it be needed, that a young girl remained missing, possibly murdered.

It was Friday, the last day of the first week back at school. Wendy had called in at the local fish and chip shop on her way home – she was far too tired to cook that evening. After her meal she washed up and was about to settle down to watch *Blankety Blank* on TV when the telephone rang.

'Wen, it's me.'

'Brian, what's up?'

'I really need to speak to you. Can we meet up?'

'When?'

'Tonight?'

'Oh Brian, I was just gonna watch a little telly, have a bath and have an early night. What's it about? Can't it wait?'

'I really need to see you. Please Wen, meet me at The Dog and Duck in an hour.'

The line went dead. Wendy was puzzled – and somewhat curious. Brian had sounded upset. Had he heard something? News maybe of Heather? It seemed there would be only one way to find out. She went upstairs, had a quick dip in the bath, changed and set off. Brian's car was already parked up outside The Dog and Duck when she arrived. Although it was only eight o'clock the pub was already busy, the bar being practically full, the lounge slightly less so.

Wendy peered around the smoke-filled bar but could not see Brian. She wandered through to the lounge and found him sitting forlornly at a table for two in the far corner, looking down at his half-full glass of Guinness. As she neared the table he looked up.

'You came! Oh thank you!'

He stood up and hugged her, obviously greatly relieved.

'I really didn't think you'd come,' he said.

'I nearly didn't,' replied Wendy. 'What's all this about?'

'First of all, let me get you a drink. What'll you have?'

'Oh I dunno . . . a Snowball perhaps.'

Brian returned to the table and placed Wendy's drink in front of her. He sat down, his hands shaking. Wendy looked into his eyes. They were reddened. He had obviously been crying.

'You're worrying me now Brian.'

'I think I might be going mad,' he said. 'I can't sleep or even think straight these days.'

'Hardly surprising I suppose,' said Wendy. 'If it weren't for my work I'd probably have cracked up completely by now.'

'Yeah but, with respect Wen, it's worse for me.'

'Oh really?' Wendy replied indignantly. 'Is that why you asked me here – 'cos you're feeling sorry for yourself?'

Brian realised his *faux pas*. He raised the palms of his hands.

'Oh no, no, no Wen. No! Not at all! I'm so sorry, that came out all wrong!'

'Why then?'

Brian took a deep breath.

'This is something I should have said a very long time ago.'

He looked directly into Wendy's eyes.

'I was such a fool. Leaving you the way I did was unforgiveable – and this is not me trying to worm my way back into your affections – but the more I think about it, the more I've come to regret the things I've said and done to you. You never deserved any such treatment and for that, I want you to know – I *need* you to know – that I'm really, really sorry.'

At first Wendy made no reply. She took a sip of her drink and sat in thought.

'Wen, please – say something – anything.'

He waited anxiously. Wendy took another sip of her drink and turned to face him.

'It's not me you should be thinking about is it? It's Heather. All that time and you never once got in touch with her. No 'phone calls, no letters, birthday cards. No wonder she had no time for you after what you'd done.'

'But . . . '

Wendy drained her glass and stood up.

'You're pathetic. That's it, I'm leaving.'

'Wen, no!'

Brian grabbed her arm but she angrily shrugged him off. One or two patrons turned around as Wendy strode out of the lounge, closely followed by Brian. As she was about to drive off Brian blocked her way by standing in front of her car, his arms outstretched. Wendy sounded the horn but he refused to move. She wound down her window.

'Don't be stupid Brian, get out of the way!'

'Not until you've heard me out! There's stuff I really need you to know!'

Two men approached. One held on to Brian's arm, the other bent down to speak to Wendy.

'This man bothering you, love?'

'It's okay thanks. He's my husband. It's just a silly row.'

The other man loosened his grip of Brian's arm. Brian angrily shrugged him off and glared at him.

'You sure, love?'

'It's okay, thank you both.'

The men turned around and walked back into the pub, leaving Brian and Wendy alone in the car park.

'Please Wen, just give me 10 minutes,' pleaded Brian, 'it's important.'

'Just stand aside Brian!'

Brian shook his head.

'Ten minutes Wen! Just give me 10 minutes!'

Wendy sighed. She turned off the engine.

'You'd better get in.'

Brian hurried round to the passenger door and got in quickly before she could change her mind.

'You've got it all wrong Wen. I *did* try to reach out to Heather – several times. I 'phoned several times and she hung up each time. And I *did* send birthday cards and I wrote to her loads of times but I never once heard back from her.'

'Can you blame her?'

'Guess not but you've gotta believe me, I did try to get in touch with her but she didn't want to know.'

'I never saw any letters or cards,' said Wendy.

'I don't suppose you did Wen. After all, you leave for work at half seven. That must be a good hour or so before the post arrives. I swear to you I *did* write to Heather – loads of times – begging her to forgive me but she never replied, not even once. That's why I tried a different approach.'

Wendy was intrigued.

'I asked Gemma to help me,' said Brian. 'She agreed to speak to Heather after school, to ask her to give me a chance to meet up with her.'

'Well,' said Wendy, 'there's no chance Heather would have agreed to meet up with her – she had no time for Gemma. After all, in her eyes, after you walked out on her you were more interested in Gemma.'

'But that's not true. If you remember, Gemma was one of Heather's first friends when she started at Somersley Secondary. That all fell apart when I moved in with Stella. I love Heather. I always have, always will.

'Look, I messed up big time. That's why I was so desperate. Nothing else had worked so I asked Gemma for help. Gemma agreed. I was so relieved. Gemma was my last hope of building bridges with Heather.

'Gemma's dad was a beast. He treated her and her mum real bad. I guess Gemma saw me as the father-figure she'd never had. I was missing Heather so much and felt bad that I'd let her down so badly. I guess that's why I tried so hard to be a father figure to Gemma if only to prove to myself I could be a better person.'

'Hmph!'

'It's true Wen. The trouble is, now I'm beginning to wonder if Heather's disappearance could be down to me.'

'How? What on earth do you mean by that?' demanded Wendy.

Brian looked distraught.

'A couple of days before Gemma was killed she agreed to try to arrange a meet-up with Heather. What if she did? What if they met on the day Gemma died? What if Heather had been with her when it happened? Gemma's killer couldn't have taken the chance to allow a witness to a murder to get away.'

Brian began to sob.

'Gemma was such a wonderful girl. We had a real connection. I really miss her. I loved her so much and now she's gone for ever. She was like Heather in so many ways. She loved art, she even stayed on at school after hours for private tuition. She was incredibly talented like that. Just like Heather.

'I can't bear the thought of losing Heather too. All this time I've been praying there's a chance Heather might still be alive, that she might walk back into our lives – but now . . .'

3

Having left The Dog and Duck Wendy and Brian both headed to the police station to update Shepperton. It was important that any shred of information should be forwarded to him even though, as Wendy suggested, it might be irrelevant to the investigation.

'I can't believe you'd have waited all this time before telling me this Brian,' she hissed.

'It only occurred to me last week,' he replied. 'I know it might be insignificant but it's been doing my head in these last few days. I had to say something.'

Wendy's already low regard of her husband had sunk even deeper since his revelation. Over that weekend she could think of little else. What if Heather had witnessed Gemma's brutal murder? Brian was right. If she had, there was every chance the killer would have eliminated her as potential witness too.

Shepperton shared Wendy's view.

'You should have told us this months ago,' he said.

'Like I said,' countered Brian, 'it's only recently occurred to me. Besides, after the way you interrogated me when Gemma was killed it's hardly surprising that coming back to speak to you wouldn't have been at the top of my to-do list. You took my car and my van for examination and you treated me like a suspect, a common criminal, asking me all sorts of questions – and very personal ones at that.'

'And with good reason,' replied Shepperton, 'because by your own admission you were working at the vicarage on the day Gemma was murdered – just a few yards from the canal where Gemma's body was found. In the vast majority of murders, the victim knows their killer. *All* family members have to be eliminated from our enquiries as a matter of course. Anyway, it wasn't just you was it? We questioned your wife and Mrs Gooding in exactly the same manner.

'One other thing. Mrs Gooding tells us she has been looking for a pendant of Gemma's. She can't find it anywhere. She believes Gemma may possibly have been wearing it on the day she was killed. Do you have any thoughts on this?'

'The one with her initial engraved on it?' asked Brian.

'That's the one,' confirmed Shepperton.

'Well,' replied Brian. 'I wouldn't be surprised if she was wearing it 'cos I know she was thrilled when we gave it to her on her 16th birthday.'

Coupled with Shepperton's admission that no significant progress had been made into Heather's disappearance it was a very unhappy Wendy who walked through the doors of Somersley Secondary Modern on the Monday morning. Her low mood was immediately spotted by Felicity who was the first to offer a comforting shoulder to cry on when they met up at the start of the day in the staff room.

'Here, have a fag Wen, it'll make you feel better.'

Wendy took a cigarette and Felicity flicked her lighter. Wendy took a deep breath and exhaled.

'That's it. It'll do you good. Feel any better now?'

'Not really. I didn't get much sleep last night.

'Perhaps you should go back home then,' Felicity suggested. 'Try to get some sleep 'cos you look exhausted. I could pop over to check on you tonight if you like.'

Wendy thanked her but insisted she would rather stay at work.

'I need to keep my mind occupied,' she said. 'No better place to do that than here. Besides, I'm still settling in with my new form.'

'They seem like a nice enough bunch,' said Felicity.

'They are,' admitted Wendy, 'though one of 'em, the new girl, Carly – Carly Mitchell – she makes me feel uneasy. I don't know why, it's probably just my imagination. Maybe it's the way she looks at me sometimes. She keeps smirking. I don't quite know what to make of it.'

'Carly Mitchell you say? I think her older sister was in Heather's class.'

'I don't think so. I don't recall a girl by the name of Mitchell.'

'You wouldn't. You knew her as Sarah Carter. Came from a bit of an iffy family. Their mum remarried. Their dad got locked up for some reason and the girls' names were changed to Mitchell by deed poll soon afterwards.'

'I remember Sarah,' said Wendy. 'From what I recall Heather didn't like her much. I'm not sure why.'

'She wasn't the most popular girl here,' said Felicity. 'She tended to rub people up the wrong way. A very clever girl though. One of the brightest, a bit short, but very pretty. All the boys seemed to like her.'

The school bell rang. Wendy stubbed out her cigarette and joined Felicity and the team and pupils for the morning assembly. Then it was into the classroom for Elementary French with Wendy's new form. All seemed to be going well until Wendy heard two girls giggling at the back of the classroom – one of them being Carly Mitchell.

'Perhaps there's something you'd like to share with the rest of the class Carly?' suggested Wendy.

Carly blushed and giggled.

'No Miss. Nothing.'

'Then perhaps you'd like to pay attention and not distract your friends.'

The lesson continued uninterrupted for the next few minutes.

'Okay,' said Wendy, 'let's try some basic vocabulary. Raise your hands if you know the answers. Let's start with the French word for brother.

One of the boys raised his hand.

'It's *frère* Miss.'

'Yes, well done Simon. How about the French word for cousin?'

'That'll be *cousine* Miss.'

'That's right Pauline.'

Wendy continued to ask for translations for the following five minutes.

'Okay, well done everyone. That was very good. Anyone got any questions?'

There was a giggle at the back of the classroom. Carly raised her hand.

'Yes Carly?'

'Please Miss, what's tart in French?'

'It's similar to the English Carly, *tarte*.'

'Thank you. And what's the word for pregnant?'

Wendy looked a little puzzled. A strange choice of words.

'Pregnant? Well, that's *enceinte*. Anyone else?'

Carly and the girl sitting next to her, Linda Powell, began to giggle again. Linda then raised her hand, having been egged on by Carly.

'Please Miss, what's the French word for scrubber?'

Before Wendy could answer Carly burst out laughing, setting off Linda in the process.

'That's enough!' snapped Wendy. 'I don't know what's got into you two but you can both stay behind afterwards. Perhaps a little extra work might remind you both not to mess about in my class in future.'

A mocking cheer emanated from the other pupils. Wendy, tired and fed up, continued up to break time without any further interruptions. As the bell sounded the pupils gathered their things and filed out, leaving Carly and Linda behind.

'Now then,' asked Wendy, 'are you two gonna tell me what all that was about?'

'Nothing Miss,' replied Linda, still with a smirk on her face.

'Really? Then why are you both looking so pleased with yourselves?'

'We were just having a laugh Miss,' replied Carly. 'No harm in it.'

'A laugh eh? What about?'

Carly suddenly began to fidget awkwardly.

'It was just something my sister told me,' she said.

'Then you'll tell me. Come on, if it's so funny you might make me laugh too.'

Carly was about to answer but Linda grabbed her arm and shook her head.

'What?' asked Carly.

'Best not,' replied Linda awkwardly.

By now Wendy had become tired of their fooling around.

'Okay,' she said, 'if you don't want me to keep you behind at the end of the day, you'd better tell me what's going on.'

Carly now appeared subdued. She hung her head and mumbled.

'What was that? Speak up!' demanded Wendy.

'Heather,' replied Carly. 'I said Heather.'

Wendy froze and the colour drained from her face. She grabbed Carly by the shoulders and shook her.

'What the hell are you on about? What about Heather?'

'I'm sorry Miss, let go!'

'Not until you tell me what's so funny!'

Carly began to weep, her lips trembled.

'It's not Carly's fault,' Linda chipped in, 'it was just something her sister said.'

'Sarah? Sarah has said something about Heather? Does she know where she is?'

'No! Of course she doesn't,' blubbed Carly.

'What then?' demanded Wendy angrily.

'She was only joking,' said Carly. 'She just said Heather ran off because she was a tart who'd got pregnant.'

Wendy, shocked to the core, could not stop herself. She slapped Carly's face as hard as she could.

'How dare you!' she cried before running, sobbing hysterically, from the classroom. Seconds later she burst into the ladies' washroom, entered a cubicle and slammed the door shut behind her. Her sobbing came to the attention of music teacher Joyce Payne who entered the washroom a few moments later.

'Hello? Who's in there?'

There was no answer, just sobbing.

'It's only me. It's Joyce. Are you okay? No, obviously you're not – stupid question. Who's in there? Can I help?'

'No, just leave me alone,' sobbed Wendy.

Joyce immediately recognised Wendy's voice.

'Er . . . I'm just gonna fetch Geraldine. I won't be a sec.'

Joyce hurried to Geraldine's office.

'Leave this with me,' said Geraldine who immediately made her way to the washroom.

'Wendy, it's me. Come on love, open the door. What's happened?'

The bolt on the door slid over and the door opened to reveal a dishevelled Wendy, her mascara running down her face, her hair a mess. Without saying a word Geraldine stepped forward and gave her a big hug. Wendy was shaking from head to toe, barely able to speak through her sobs. Geraldine decided to allow her time to compose herself.

When it appeared Wendy had calmed down sufficiently, Geraldine led her back to her office, sat her down and closed the door. She passed a paper cup filled with water to Wendy who, with shaking hands, raised it to her lips.

'Now then,' said Geraldine, 'what's going on?'

Wendy recalled what Carly and Linda had said.

'My goodness, no wonder you're so upset! What wicked girls!' exclaimed Geraldine. 'Well, they're not going to get away with that, I can assure you. I'll send for them. They can apologise and then I'll call their parents in. I think exclusions might be appropriate, don't you?'

Wendy shook her head.

'No Geri, let it go.'

'No way Wendy, they behaved disgracefully. I can't ignore that.'

'You don't understand Geri. I did something stupid. I slapped Carly. I slapped her really hard across the face.'

'Oh. Oh dear!'

'Exactly. You know what that means, don't you?'

Geraldine took a deep intake of breath and paced around her office, deep in thought. Eventually she came to a decision.

'Look Wendy, I don't wanna lose you. Let's just hope those girls wouldn't want their parents to know what they said or did today. I mean, I wouldn't if I'd behaved like that. I'd be too ashamed. Anyway, they wouldn't be the first kids to accuse a teacher of something would they? It's happened before if they had some kind of grudge. Just because an accusation is made, it doesn't necessarily make it true, does it? I'll say nothing. Let's see what happens. If it does eventually hit the fan we'll have to look at it again.'

'You'd really do that for me?'

Geraldine gave her another hug.

'You need to go home Wendy. Take some time off 'cos I reckon you've come back too soon. Everything's still too raw. I'll keep in touch with you as usual. Take as much time as you need but first things first my dear – get some sleep!'

Wendy felt fortunate to have such a good friend on her side. They had always got on well, even though they were as different as chalk and cheese. Geraldine simply oozed sophistication. Not only did she hold the top job at Somersley Secondary Modern, she was married to an eminent gynaecologist. She always wore the finest quality clothes, lived in an expensive and luxurious five-bedroom detached property and drove a new top-of-the range metallic green Ford Granada Ghia.

Unlike Geraldine, Wendy had never been one to draw attention to herself, preferring instead to adopt a more low-key profile and living on more modest means.

Once home Wendy curled up on her bed but, as tired as she was, she could not get the events of that morning out of her mind. How cruel, how spiteful some kids can be, having a laugh at the expense of someone else's abject misery.

But it was no use, she could not sleep. She went back downstairs, poured herself a cup of coffee and sat down on the sofa in the lounge. Then, eventually, she drifted off.

4

It had been a particularly warm day but, as the sun went down, it became increasingly muggy. Storm clouds were beginning to form and the wind began to gather. Most people in Somersley had spent the day making the most of the balmy weather but now it seemed wiser to stay indoors and to batten down the hatches. Weather forecasters had predicted thunderstorms and heavy downpours.

So it was that, by nine o'clock that evening, most areas were all but deserted, not least the secluded Roman Walk, the path adjacent to the canal where Gemma Gooding's body had been discovered.

This particular evening another teenager was in the vicinity. The rain had soaked her hair as were the hair and the clothes of the person with her. A few yards past the remote deposition site of Gemma's body was a patch of long grass. As the moon struggled to shine its light between the darkened storm clouds the two individuals dropped down onto the grass. Both drenched, one of them was gasping for breath.

The other couldn't. She was stone cold dead.

Her killer, with a racing heart, removed the eiderdown that had been wrapped around the corpse to reveal the teenager's heavily blood-stained clothing. Desperate not to be seen, and equally desperate not to leave any evidence, her killer hurriedly bundled the soggy eiderdown into a backpack then dragged the lifeless body further into the long grass.

Breathlessly, the killer was about to leave the scene when the sound of footsteps along the pathway were heard. The gasping killer, their heart pounding, laid flat in the long grass alongside the body desperately hoping the moon would remain behind the cloud until the stranger had passed.

Fortunately for the killer the stranger was in a rush, obviously not wishing to spend any longer than necessary in the pouring rain. As the sound of his footsteps subsided, the killer slowly sat up and parted the grass to ensure the coast was clear.

It was in the early hours of the morning that a fisherman made his way along Roman Walk looking for a good spot to set up for the day. By now the wind and rain had subsided and, as the sun rose, it looked as if another fine day was about to begin.

The man began to unpack his equipment, eagerly anticipating a productive day's fishing particularly as the water level, as a result of the heavy rain, had risen significantly. However, prior to casting out for the first time, nature called. Looking around to ensure no-one was around, he crossed the path and walked into the long grass before unzipping his trousers.

After he had relieved himself he zipped up and was about to return to his stool which he had placed on the bank of the canal. It was at this point he noticed the grass to his right had recently been flattened and, poking out from behind a small bush, was the unmistakable sight of a shoe. Worse still, it was still occupied.

The fisherman brushed back the branches of the bush to reveal the fully-clothed body of the young woman. She was obviously dead. Stunned, the fisherman reeled in horror, throwing up as he did so. He stumbled out of the grass and ran as fast as he could to raise the alarm.

Within 30 minutes police had cordoned off the entire area and a full-scale murder investigation was launched, DCI Shepperton being the senior investigating officer.

The discovery of the body ignited fears amongst the community that a serial killer had struck again.

5

Meanwhile, Wendy had been anticipating a call from Geraldine to inform her that Carly's parents had made a complaint against her. Surely one of her pupils must have told their parents about the classroom incident when she had slapped Carly.

Apparently not. Wendy was relieved that, at the time of the incident, the classroom had been empty apart from herself and the two girls. Linda had been the only witness. A week later, Geraldine called in after school. On arrival though she was shocked to see a large bruise on the side of Wendy's face and a cut on her top lip.

'Oh my goodness Wendy, whatever have you done?'

'Oh this?' Wendy replied, touching her face. 'It's stupid really. I felt thoroughly miserable last night and decided to drown my sorrows. I got a bottle of gin out of the cupboard and ended up drinking most of it. When I got up to go to bed I fell down in the bedroom and banged my head on edge of the chest of drawers.'

Geraldine brushed Wendy's hair back with her hand to take a closer look.

'Ooh, that looks nasty Wendy. Have you seen a doctor?'

'No. No need. I'll be okay. It was my own stupid fault. I hurt my pride more than anything else.'

Still unconvinced, Geraldine decided to drop the subject. She sniffed.

'Seems like you've been busy, Wendy. It smells really nice in here. Fresh. It's lovely.'

'Haven't got much better to do at the moment Geri, have I? Just trying to keep myself occupied. Come on through. I'll put the kettle on.'

Over coffee Geraldine appeared somewhat uncomfortable. Wendy picked up on it. She couldn't help but wonder if her visitor had been forced into a corner, that she'd come to notify her that she had been suspended.

'What's up Geri?'

'Well, I didn't know whether to say anything or not, to be honest,' she replied. 'Have you heard the news on the telly today?'

'I don't like to listen to it. It's always so depressing and I don't need any more negativity in my life at the moment,' replied Wendy. 'Anyway, what news?'

'I don't know then if I should mention it.'

'Come on Geri, take a chance.'

Finding herself on the spot, Geraldine reluctantly broke the news.

'They've found another girl, down by the canal. Murdered. Young, they reckon, about 16 to 18 years old. They're trying to identify her.'

Wendy gasped.

'Heather?'

'Oh no Wendy, it's not Heather,' said Geraldine placing her hand reassuringly on Wendy's knee. 'According to the police this girl is only around five feet tall and has long dark hair.'

'Are you sure?'

'Well, that's what they said on the news. I reckon . . .'

Geraldine was interrupted by the telephone. Wendy picked up the receiver. Her face dropped. Wendy recognised the voice instantly. It was DCI Shepperton. Wendy began to sob. Geraldine got up from the sofa and joined her in the hallway.

'Mrs Brown? It's DCI Dave Shepperton. Are you alright?'

'It *is* Heather isn't it?' she cried.

'No, no, no. Please Mrs Brown, I didn't mean to panic you. This is just a courtesy call. I guessed you'd heard the news and I wanted to reassure you that the girl found down by the canal is definitely *not* your daughter. I'm really sorry to have upset you. I should have called round, not telephoned.'

Wendy appeared to calm down.

'Sorry, sorry, I just panicked. Oh that poor girl. Have you any idea who she might be?'

'Her mother has just identified her. She's a local girl. Sarah Mitchell.'

Wendy heard a gasp from behind her. Geraldine had been listening in. The women looked at each other and simultaneously mouthed 'Oh my God!'

The discovery of Sarah's body naturally dominated the news. Now, more than ever, the belief that a serial killer could be on the prowl locally rose to the fore. Newspaper reports ensured that Gemma's murder and Heather's disappearance were prominently featured on the front pages which, once again, heaped pressure on Brian, Wendy and Stella. Three days later Wendy was writing out her shopping list when her telephone rang.

'Somersley 3677.'

'Wen, it's me, I need your help. I'm in trouble. Big trouble.'

'Brian? What's happening?'

'I've been arrested. They think I killed Sarah Mitchell.'

'What?'

'Wen, please don't hang up. I'm only allowed one 'phone call and I'm scared. I don't know what to do or who else to call.'

'Why on earth would they think it was you?'

'Shepperton suspected me after Heather disappeared when he found out we were not on good terms. He asked me where I was on Monday evening. I told him I was still working. That I was gardening at the vicarage.'

'The vicarage? But that's right by the canal!'

'Exactly. I've been working there a lot recently. Just 'cos Gemma was found nearby Shepperton's put two and two together and made five. I had no idea that it was where they found the Mitchell girl so when I told him where I was I played right into his hands.'

He began to sob.

'Wen, what am I gonna do?'

Wendy thought for a moment.

'Leave it with me,' she said. 'I'll give Eugene a call.'

'Who's Eugene?'

'He's Felicity's husband. He's a solicitor.'

'I didn't do it Wen, you do believe me, don't you?'

'Just hang in there Brian,' replied Wendy without answering his question. 'I'll give Eugene a call right away.'

Later that evening there was a knock on Wendy's door. A dishevelled Brian stood on the doorstep.

'They let me go,' he said tearfully. 'I was *so* scared.'

He noticed Wendy's bruised face and cut lip.

'Crikey. How did you do that?'

'It doesn't matter, I just slipped over. Tell me first what happened.'

'Reverend Palmer spoke up for me. He confirmed I never left the vicarage all day,' Brian explained, 'and the solicitor you contacted, Eugene, he was really helpful. He told Shepperton he had no evidence to hold me any longer. Shepperton didn't like it but he had no option other than to let me go.'

To Brian's astonishment Wendy burst into tears and flung her arms around him.

'Oh thank God!' she cried.

'I'm sure Shepperton's convinced I had something to do with Sarah's death but I swear to you Wen, I had absolutely nothing to do with it.'

'I know Brian. I *know* it wasn't you.'

Brian sighed with relief.

'Oh Wen, thank you. That means such a lot, knowing you believe me. I wouldn't blame you if you had your doubts. What makes you so sure?'

Wendy took a deep breath and looked him in the eye.

'Because it was *me* Brian,' she admitted tearfully. '*I* killed Sarah.'

6

Brian stood open-mouthed, completely flabbergasted.

'You can't be serious!'

'It was an accident Brian!' sobbed Wendy. 'I didn't mean to do it, really I didn't!'

Brian clasped his head between his hands as he paced around the hallway.

'I can't believe this! Is this some kinda nightmare? Why on earth would you do such a thing?'

'She came here.'

'Why?'

'It was a warm day so the back door was wide open. I was in the kitchen, peeling potatoes, when I realised someone was standing behind me. I turned around and it was Sarah. She started screaming at me, telling me she'd make me pay for slapping her sister and that she'd make sure I'd never teach again.

'Before I could react she punched me hard in the stomach. I fell onto the floor and she began kicking me. She was screaming at me, telling me she knew I'd hit her sister and that she was gonna make sure I paid for it. Then . . .'

'Whoa!' interrupted Brian. 'Just a minute! What's all this about you hitting some girl?'

'She said something rude in class about Heather and, before I could stop myself, I lashed out at her. That's why Sarah came here. After she got me down onto the floor she sat on my chest. She pinned me down and began slapping and punching me around the face. I was really scared Brian. I couldn't move.

'Eventually she seemed to run out of breath. She stopped hitting me and rolled off me. That's when I noticed the blood. She'd rolled over onto my hand. I was still holding the potato peeler and it was sticking into her side. She kinda gasped and staggered towards the kitchen door then fell face down in the hallway.

'There was blood everywhere Brian. I ran upstairs to get the first aid box but by the time I came down again she was unconscious. I felt for a pulse but couldn't find one. I was terrified.'

'Jeez,' said Brian. 'What happened next?'

'Well, I panicked. I didn't know what to do. I covered her up with the eiderdown and shut the hall door. I sat in the lounge with all sorts of thoughts going round my head. The girls at school – Linda and Carly – and Geraldine – knew that what Sarah had said upset me. What if someone had joined the dots? I couldn't risk anyone thinking I'd taken revenge could I? You have to believe me, it was a complete accident.'

Brian interrupted.

'Hang on a minute. You say she got breathless and rolled off you.'

'That's right.'

'So why should she roll off you? Are you sure the knife wasn't stuck in her side *before* she rolled off you?'

'Are you suggesting I actually stabbed her?' replied Wendy defensively. 'I've got a kitchen full of knives, including several big ones. Do you think if I'd intended to kill the girl that I'd have used a flippin' tiny potato peeler?'

'I don't know what to think,' said Brian. 'If she had you pinned down why else would she stop hitting you and just roll over?'

'Oh I don't know! It all happened so fast. I can't remember.'

She looked at Brian. His mind was obviously spinning. Without speaking he began to pace around the room.

'Say something Brian!'

'What can I say? I don't know what to think. I mean, you say Sarah threatened to ruin your career. How desperate would you have been to prevent her from reporting you?'

Wendy began to hyper-ventilate and held her head in her hands.

'Stop it Brian! You're confusing me!'

Brian was obviously unconvinced by her claims of an accident. Had she stabbed Sarah? Up until this point she had been sure that she hadn't – that it had been an unfortunate accident – but Brian had now planted the seeds of doubt in her mind. Surely she hadn't done such a terrible thing – or had she?

'You're confusing me!' she cried. 'I don't wanna talk about it!'

Brian grabbed her by both arms and shook her.

'Pull yourself together Wen. You need to tell me exactly what happened next – and I want the truth. I can't help you if you lie to me. Understand?'

Tearfully, Wendy nodded.

'You mean you'd actually help me?'

'If I don't, who will? Jeez! Look at us. What a mess!'

Once again Brian insisted she filled him in with all the details.

'I waited until it got dark,' she said. 'I wrapped the body in the eiderdown then backed the car up to the front door and put Sarah in the boot. I parked up near the canal and waited until I was sure no-one was around and then I dragged her into the long grass. A spot that was really remote.

'It was really windy and pouring with rain. I got soaked. Then I heard footsteps. Someone was hurrying along the canal path. I laid low and waited for him to pass by. I was absolutely terrified I'd be spotted.'

'Are you sure he didn't see you?'

'Positive – it was pouring with rain and he was in a hurry. He was looking straight ahead as he passed by.'

'Thank God for that,' said Brian. 'What did you do next?'

'I waited until he was out of sight and hurried back to the car. When I got home I stripped off all my wet clothes, put on some old clobber and began to clean up in here. It took ages to remove all traces of the blood. I ended up using bleach.'

Wendy looked at Brian, trying to gauge his reaction. Eventually he spoke.

'I dunno what to say Wen. This is beyond awful.'

Then came the realisation that Wendy had known the truth when he had called her from the police station.

'You knew! You knew when I called you. Why didn't you tell me then?'

'How could I Brian? I knew you were innocent so there was no way they would have been able to pin it on you.'

'But what if they had?' he demanded.

'Well, I'd have had to confess,' she said. 'I couldn't have let you take the blame for something I'd done, could I?'

'Who else knows?'

'No-one, I swear, though . . . '

Her voice drifted away.

'Though what?' demanded Brian.

'Geraldine called round the next day. She saw my bruises and commented on the fresh smell in the hallway. That's 'cos I'd been up most of the night cleaning up the blood but it's okay, I'm sure she didn't suspect a thing.'

'Oh well, that's alright then isn't it?' replied Brian sarcastically. 'And now,' he added, 'Shepperton and his boys are convinced Sarah's death is linked to Gemma's and possibly to Heather's disappearance. They'll be going down the wrong path. If we're to have any chance of finding out where Heather is or what's happened to her we're gonna have to tell him what really happened. We've got no choice.'

Wendy realised he was right. It had gone too far. If there was any chance that justice was to be served for Gemma and if there was any possibility of finding out what had happened to Heather, she would have to come clean. As Brian had said, she had no choice.

'Okay,' she whispered reluctantly. 'I'll get my coat. Will you come with me?'

Brian, in tears, nodded. They drove, in silence, to the police station and reported to the front desk.

'We need to speak to DCI Shepperton,' said Brian. 'It's a matter of the utmost importance.'

Duty sergeant Ray Smith seemed surprised to see Brian returning to the station so soon after his release.

'DCI Shepperton's not here at the moment,' he said, 'but I was about to ring you both. Perhaps you'd be so kind as to come with me.'

Smith led Brian and Wendy into a vacant interview room and summoned a Wpc to join them.

'Please, sit down. I have some information for you. It's not good news I'm afraid. DCI Shepperton's gone to arrest a young chap who's claiming to have killed Gemma and, I'm afraid to say, he's claiming to have killed your daughter too.'

'Oh my God!' gasped Wendy.

'Who? Who is he?' demanded Brian.

'I'm sorry, I don't know. Sgt Riley took the call and notified DCI Shepperton. They left immediately so I don't have any other details at the moment.'

Brian and Wendy sat in stunned silence. So Heather *was* dead. Their worst fears had, at last, been confirmed. The couple hugged each other, crying uncontrollably. Smith, who seemed close to tears himself, left them in the company of the young Wpc, a family liaison officer. She passed them a box of tissues and offered them each a cup of tea but Wendy, who was now in an extremely heightened emotional state, screamed at her.

'A cup of tea? Do you *really* think that'll make everything okay?'

Brian tried to smile sympathetically at the Wpc.

'I'm sorry,' he said, 'it's all been rather a lot to take in.'

'Of course,' she replied.

Half an hour later Brian and Wendy left the interview room, Smith having informed them that Shepperton had been delayed and that he had no idea how long it would be until they could speak to him. As they made their way out, Smith called out to them.

'I'm sorry Mrs Brown, there was something you wanted to tell me when you arrived.'

Wendy turned back to face him.

'Yes,' she replied. 'I needed to tell you . . .'

'It doesn't matter now,' interrupted Brian, taking her by the arm and firmly leading her towards the exit. 'Come on Wen, let's just get you home.'

It was early evening when the call came. Brian had remained with Wendy at her home, both of them desperate to hear from Shepperton. Three times the telephone rang and Wendy had raced into the hallway to answer but none of the calls were from the detective. By the time he did call both parents were at their wit's end.

'Has he told you where Heather is?' blurted out Wendy before Shepperton could begin.

'No, not yet, I'm afraid. We're still questioning him.'

'What's his name?'

'Bradley Winterton, he's an 18-year-old youth from Somersley. He's . . .'

'We know very well who he is,' interrupted Wendy. 'We've known him for years. I can't believe he'd ever hurt anyone, especially Heather.'

'He wouldn't,' chipped in Brian. 'He's a simple lad who wouldn't hurt a fly. You must have the wrong man.'

'Perhaps you could both come down to the station,' suggested Shepperton. 'We'd be very interested to know what you can tell us about Winterton and how he might have known Gemma and Heather.'

Yet again Brian and Wendy found themselves in the interview room, both of them equally convinced that Bradley could not have attacked either of the girls.

'You seem very sure of Winterton's innocence,' said Shepperton.

'Well, you seem equally sure of his guilt,' replied Brian.

'I am.'

'Well,' countered Brian, 'a few hours ago you were pretty sure that I was the guilty party. You were wrong then and we both reckon you are now.'

'Bradley's harmless,' Wendy insisted. 'We've known him for years. Okay, he's more than a little backward, but he's a harmless lad. Heather took pity on him 'cos he's a bit of an outsider. Some of the other kids taunted him, made fun of him 'cos he has a gammy leg and is a bit simple. He'd often come round ours and Heather would help him with his homework. No, it can't possibly be him.'

'I wish I had your confidence,' said Shepperton, 'but he was staggering around in town as drunk as a skunk. He was telling anyone that would listen that he had killed two girls. Most people reckoned he was just shouting his mouth off but one woman was so concerned that she called us.

'When we arrested him he was cautioned but all the way back here in the car he was claiming he'd killed Gemma and Heather.

'Trouble is, we can't use anything he said at that time because he was drunk and he hadn't had any legal representation. That's why it's important we speak to you – and Gemma's mother – as soon as possible to get any background information that you might be able to provide.'

'I still say he's innocent,' said Brian.

'Look, it's still far too early in the investigation,' said Shepperton. 'At the moment we have not been able to establish a link between Winterton and the Mitchell girl. In fact, he totally denies any knowledge of her killing.'

Brian and Wendy exchanged awkward glances. Shepperton continued.

'He's also rather vague about Gemma's killing, though he insists he was responsible for killing Heather.'

'And you believe him?'

'Yes, Mrs Brown. I think I do. Having said that, much of what he's told us about Gemma and how she was killed he could have read about in the press or, more likely, heard on the radio or telly.'

'But Heather? What possible reason would he have to kill the only real friend he's ever had?' asked Wendy.

'He claims Heather was pregnant with his child,' replied Shepperton, 'and that she was planning to terminate the pregnancy against his will.'

'That's ridiculous!' blurted out Wendy. 'Bradley's a sweet boy but he's always has been a bit simple. He's a fantasist. He can't help it. That's just the way he is. He's infatuated with Heather but she's never led him on. Ask anyone who knows him. It'll just be his way of gaining some attention. There's no way he and Heather would have, you know . . . Anyway, she was only 16. She wasn't – *she isn't* – that kind of girl.'

Brian sat silently. Wendy turned to him.

'Tell him Brian. Heather's not like that is she? Tell him she's not like that!'

Brian looked back at her, tears in his eyes.

'Wen,' he replied quietly. 'Can you remember how old we were when we first met?'

'I dunno. Er, you must have been around 16 I reckon. I'd have been 15. What's that got to do with anything?'

'Well, you know . . . '

'What?' demanded Wendy impatiently.

'Well, we were only Heather's age when we first . . . you know.'

'Oh stop it Brian, you're being ridiculous!' she snapped angrily as she tried to hide her embarrassment at his revelation.

'Look, I'm only saying that kids that age, they experiment don't they? It might be with booze or drugs – or sex.'

'But *not* our Heather!' insisted Wendy. 'She wouldn't!'

'How can you be so certain of that Mrs Brown?' asked Shepperton. 'I recall interviewing you when Heather first disappeared. You told me that she had seemed a little distant, rather quiet in the days leading up to her disappearance. It's possible she might have been pregnant. It could be that Winterton was telling the truth.'

Wendy shook her head emphatically, refusing to believe her daughter would ever have allowed Bradley to take advantage of her.

'No,' she said firmly, 'there's no way that could be possible.'

Shepperton stood up and paced thoughtfully around the room. He sat down again and looked directly at Wendy.

'Tell me Mrs Brown, did Heather have a birthmark?'

'Yes.'

'That's exactly what Winterton claims. It's under her left breast he says. How would he have known that if he had not seen her in a state of undress? He also claims she has another, smaller mark on her left buttock.'

The colour instantly drained from Wendy's face. Only now did she realise that the rumours spread by Sarah Mitchell may, after all, have had some substance to them.

'Look, said Shepperton, 'why don't you both head off home? I'll call you if there are any more developments.'

Brian and Wendy made their way to the car park. As they were about to get into Brian's car Wendy noticed Stella getting out of hers. She looked gaunt.

'Look Brian, over there, it's Stella,' said Wendy. 'Perhaps you should go in with her?'

'What's this?' asked Brian. 'I thought you hated her.'

'At the end of the day she's a mum who has lost her daughter,' replied Wendy. 'If Bradley really has killed our Heather we're both in the same boat.'

'Nah,' said Brian shaking his head. 'I don't think she's seen us so let's just go. I really don't think I can face her after all that's gone on. I'd rather stay with you.'

Up until Brian's 'mid-life crisis' as Wendy saw it, their marriage had, apart from the usual ups and downs, been a reasonably happy union. Heather had been a much-welcomed addition to the family and all had been well and good until the day Brian met '*that woman*' when dropping Heather off at the school gates.

Brian's preference to remain with Wendy was something she had never expected to hear from him. Having just been told that someone had admitted to killing their daughter Wendy put this into perspective – after all they were currently united in grief. That, for the moment though, was enough. After the events of the past few days she didn't want to be alone. Once back home she invited Brian inside.

'Do you really think she's dead?' she asked as she handed him a cup of tea.

'I don't know what to think at the moment. One minute I'm thinking Bradley would never do such a thing, the next I'm wanting to rip his head off.'

'I still don't believe Heather was pregnant,' said Wendy. 'At least I don't *want* to believe it but, looking back, she was unusually quiet in the days leading up to disappearance. I asked her if there was something worrying her but she just said it was her time of the month. If that was true she couldn't have been pregnant could she? What bothers me is how Bradley knew about her birthmarks if he hadn't actually seen them?'

'Maybe he was telling the truth after all,' ventured Brian, 'though, like you, I find it hard to believe.'

'It's all such a mess,' said Wendy. 'I should have handed myself in. Sarah's mother – she must be going through hell.'

'And what good would that do Wen, eh? argued Brian. 'Like you said, it was an accident, a tragic accident. If Sarah hadn't come here and attacked you in your own home it would never have happened. We should keep it to ourselves – at least for the time being.'

'But Shepperton – if he still thinks Sarah's death is linked to Gemma's – he'll be chasing shadows. If Bradley has killed our Heather but *didn't* kill Gemma, then Gemma's killer will have got away with it and I really don't think I could live with that on my conscience.

'Besides, if Carly knows that Sarah had planned to attack me it'll only be a matter of time before she says so and the police will be knocking on the front door.'

The stress that had been building up in Wendy suddenly erupted to the surface. She collapsed in tears. Brian hurriedly put down his cup and cradled her in his arms. He kissed her gently on the forehead.

'We need to keep all this to ourselves for now,' he said as he stroked her hair, 'because at this moment in time I reckon we need each other more than ever.'

Suddenly, a thought struck him.

'The eiderdown!'

'What?'

'The eiderdown. What did you do with it?'

'I brought it back here. I'm not stupid.'

'Back here? Where is it now?'

'In the dustbin.'

Brian was flabbergasted.

'You mean you've put a heavily-bloodstained eiderdown in your own dustbin? What did you use to clean up the blood on the floor?'

'Old towels and teatowels. They're in the bin too.'

'I thought you said you weren't stupid? Jeez Wen, that *is* stupid. I mean why don't you put a ruddy big sign up at the front gate saying *'Vital evidence here'*?

'I didn't think. I . . .'

'Obviously not,' interrupted Brian. 'We've gotta get rid of it – and quickly. What about your car? You say you put Sarah in the boot?'

'Yeah.'

'Okay, gimme your car keys.'

'Why?'

'Gotta get rid of the car too. There might be traces of blood or whatever in the boot. Can't risk hanging on to it.'

'Oh Brian, is that really necessary?'

'What do you think?'

She handed the keys over to Brian who hurried into the back yard and removed the contents of the dustbin and stuffed them into black plastic sacks which he then placed in the back of Wendy's battered Vauxhall. Moments later he drove off.

Two hours later the telephone rang.

'It's me.'

'Brian, where are you?'

'Blyton Common. I need you to come and pick me up. My car keys are on the hall table. Get here as soon as you can. I don't want anyone to see me here.'

Wendy replaced the receiver and grabbed the keys to Brian's MGB GT. In her rush to drive off she stalled the car twice. Once started she drove quickly the five and half miles to Blyton Common and parked up in the car park. Moments later Brian emerged from the bushes and got into the car.

'Just drive,' he said, looking all around to ensure they had not been seen.

As Wendy drove Brian filled her in.

'I drove to my allotment and chucked the eiderdown and the other stuff into my incinerator,' he said. 'There's just ashes there now. Then I drove over to the common and parked up on the far side. When I was sure no-one was around I poured paraffin over the seats and set it on fire. There's nothing left but a burnt-out shell now.'

'My car!' wailed Wendy.

'Sorry Wen, but that's a price you have to pay. When we get back you'll need to report it stolen.'

7

Shepperton had a self-confessed killer sitting on the opposite side of the table in the interview room and, this after a long and painstaking investigation that had not unearthed any significant evidence of the murder of Gemma Gooding or the fate of missing teenager Heather Brown.

Under normal circumstances he would have been pleased with this latest development but one significant question remained – had Bradley Winterton also been responsible for Sarah Mitchell's death and, if so, why had he been so willing to confess to Gemma and Heather's killings yet had been so adamant he'd had nothing to do with Sarah's murder?

Up to this point Shepperton had been convinced the same person had been responsible for the murders and Heather's disappearance. Now though he was not so sure. Despite his impressive conviction rate he now had to ask himself if he had he been guilty of tunnel vision as Bradley's interrogation was raising more questions than answers.

Shepperton's colleague Detective Constable James Clarke, on the other hand, had a more open mind. Unlike the local media and many of his colleagues and the public at large, 50-year-old Clarke remained unconvinced that the three cases were linked. He had found out the hard way that preconceived ideas rarely solved a crime. Although he had worked on a number of murder investigations he had witnessed at first hand early on in his career how one of his senior officers had fallen foul of jumping to conclusions. As a result Clarke was particularly wary of falling into the same trap.

Sitting alongside Shepperton, Clarke was becoming increasingly uneasy about the reliability of Bradley's confession. Much of what he related had already been in the public domain such had been the intense media coverage of the investigations. Clarke quickly realised that anyone could have offered up a similar account as that offered by young Bradley.

Furthermore, it soon became obvious that Bradley had significant intellectual as well as physical difficulties. Wendy was right – he certainly appeared to be a fantasist – a young man who, most likely, would have had challenges in establishing a meaningful relationship with a member of the opposite sex. Yet here he was boasting about his carnal exploits, not only with Heather but with several other girls from Somersley Secondary Modern.

Somehow, much of what Bradley claimed in this respect appeared to be nothing more than figments of his imagination. Nevertheless, he named names. Each of these girls would need to be interviewed in order to establish if any of Bradley's accounts had any credibility – and this was something that would need to be handled with great sensitivity for obvious reasons.

'I think we should take a short break,' said Clarke. Shepperton agreed. He stopped the tape and stood up. He addressed Bradley, his solicitor and his appropriate adult.

'We'll resume in two hours,' he said looking at his watch. Back in Shepperton's office the detectives took two cups of black coffee from the vending machine and sat down.

'Well,' said Shepperton, 'what do you think?'

'He's a fantasist,' replied Clarke. 'He's a good-looking lad but he's hardly a babe magnet is he? I can't imagine all the girls he mentioned falling at his feet.'

Shepperton nodded.

'I agree but we'll have to speak to them all, just in case there's any truth in what he's saying. Personally though, I'd put my pension on him trying to make a name for himself.'

'Ever heard of factitious disorder Dave?'

Shepperton shook his head.

'I read an article about it a while back,' said Clarke. 'Very interesting it was. There was this woman, she was a nurse, who deliberately injected a patient to bring them close to death and then played a pivotal role in bringing that patient back to a stable condition.

'As a result she was hailed as the patient's saviour when, in truth, she had been the cause of the emergency. It was only when she repeated the act a few times that anyone rumbled her. She was trying to gain attention and it certainly worked.

'Then there was a mother who gave her little boy some kinda medication that made him pass out. It happened again and again. Each time he was rushed to hospital where he was stabilised. Again, someone who wanted to be noticed. I reckon this Winterton kid may be doing the same thing.'

'The birthmarks suggest he's had an intimate relationship with Heather,' said Shepperton, 'but, quite honestly, I can't see him being a killer. Call it a gut feeling if you like.'

'In that case,' said Clarke, 'when we go back in we should press him harder – it's time we asked him specific questions about Gemma's deposition site and the state of her body when it was found – ask him for details that we've kept out of the public domain.'

Shepperton pondered over Clarke's proposition as he sipped his coffee. He lit a cigarette and offered one to Clarke who declined. As the senior investigating officer on the murder case Shepperton was only too aware of the importance of media assistance but he also was keen to withhold certain details that might be handy to keep in his arsenal for a later date. As he was taking the final drag of his cigarette he came to a decision.

'I don't want to give too much away,' he said. 'You know as well as I do that we need to keep back some of the information we've been able to glean so far but . . .' he stubbed out his cigarette in the glass ashtray on his desk, 'there's nothing stopping us feeding him a line. Let's see if he takes the bait.'

As the interrogation resumed Clarke and Shepperton continued to question Bradley in the same calm manner as they had started. Bradley continued to boast about his conquests with the young ladies, much to the discomfort of his advocates who, like the detectives, seemed to find his claims hard to believe.

Eventually Shepperton decided the time had come to turn the screw. He theatrically banged his fist on the table and declared:

'Okay, that's enough!'

Young Bradley almost jumped out of his skin, shocked at Shepperton's sudden change of attitude.

'Quite frankly young man, I think you are spinning us a tissue of lies – and neither I or Detective Constable Clarke have any more time to waste. You seem to have a very active imagination so now it's time we get down to more specific details. Let's start again with what happened to Gemma Gooding. I have three questions that I want you to answer right now.

'First of all, why did you find it necessary to strangle the poor girl before you stabbed her? Secondly, why did you stuff a handkerchief into her mouth and, thirdly, what did you do with her underwear?'

Clarke fidgeted uncomfortably on his chair. He, like Shepperton, wanted to press Bradley on details that only Gemma's killer would know but Shepperton's approach was to feed the suspect with three scenarios that were blatantly untrue. There had been absolutely no evidence that Gemma had been strangled, nor had a handkerchief been placed in her mouth.

Furthermore, she had been fully clothed when her body had been discovered.

Bradley sat shell-shocked, completely flummoxed by Shepperton's line of questioning. He looked towards his solicitor for guidance, then to his advocate. His solicitor whispered in Bradley's ear.

'No comment.'

'Oh come on now Bradley,' said Shepperton, 'why the sudden shyness?'

'She was screaming,' blurted out the panic-stricken boy. 'I had to keep her quiet.'

So much for 'no comment' thought the detectives. Shepperton pressed on.

'So you strangled her?'

Bradley nodded. His solicitor whispered once more in his ear but the boy, now in a most agitated state, seemed desperate to convince the detectives of his account.

'And the handkerchief?' asked Shepperton.

'Like I said, I had to keep her quiet.'

Shepperton raised his voice once more. He leant forward towards Bradley and demanded to know what he had done with Gemma's 'missing' underwear.

Suddenly intimidated, the boy replied: 'I threw it away.

'Where? Where did you throw it?'

'I . . . I dunno. I can't remember.'

Shepperton sat back down and turned to Clarke.

'I think we've wasted enough time here, don't you?'

Clarke nodded in agreement.

'The boy's a simpleton,' whispered Shepperton. 'I can't even be bothered with the paperwork to charge him with wasting police time.'

Clarke, in agreement, stood up and addressed Bradley's solicitor.

'We're done now,' he said. 'Bradley is free to go.'

Unlike most suspects, to the misguided Bradley, this was not good news as he wanted to be believed – to have his moment in the spotlight.

'But what about Heather?' he asked. 'You haven't even asked me about Heather and the baby.'

Shepperton chose not to waste his breath with an answer. He merely shrugged dismissively and, accompanied by Clarke, he returned, fuming, to his office. He slammed the door shut behind him. With his face, now crimson with rage, he turned to Clarke as his frustration finally boiled over.

'Sixteen – no 17 – murder cases I've successfully worked as the senior investigating officer but this one – this one's been a bloody nightmare. We're no closer to solving this than ever and today – today we've been wasting valuable time interviewing that imbecilic half-wit. Good God, if you gave that moron a knife, he'd be too stupid to know which end to hold it!'

'Hey, Dave, calm down will you?' Okay, he might not be the full ticket but that's hardly his fault is it?'

But Shepperton was obviously in no mood to simmer down.

'Well, you saw him – the lad's obviously brain dead. I mean, what use is someone like that? No use at all, that's what I say! People like him should be smothered at birth!'

Unable to control his temper, Shepperton lashed out with his foot, sending his paper bin flying across the office until it hit the wall, sending its contents all over the floor.

Clarke could barely believe what he was seeing or hearing.

'Dave, for God's sake, calm down. Have a fag and a coffee. I think I need some fresh air.'

Clarke left his incandescent senior officer and walked outside to the car park. He lit a cigarette and reflected on what he had just witnessed. He had known and admired Dave Shepperton for a good number of years and they had always got on well – and Shepperton was right – he was a brilliant detective with a superb clear-up record – but today he'd seen him in a totally different light. Shepperton had revealed a side to him that made Clarke wonder if he really knew him as well as he thought.

Thoroughly disillusioned, he decided to take a break. He got into his car and drove to The Dog and Duck. He sat alone in the corner, moodily drinking his pint and eating a bag of pork scratchings.

'Is there a DC Clarke in here?' called out the barman.

'Yeah.'

'Phone call for you Sir.'

Clarke put down his pint and walked over to the bar. The barman handed him the receiver. It was Shepperton.

'I thought you might be there,' he said. 'We need to talk. I'm sorry okay? Just come back, let's sort this out.'

Clarke reluctantly agreed but not until, he said, he'd finished his pint.

It was a sheepish Shepperton to greet Clarke on his return to the station.

'James, what can I say? I'm sorry. I let my emotions get the better of me and I know I said some terrible things about the boy.'

'You certainly did.'

Shepperton hung his head in shame.

'I didn't mean it when I said he should've been smothered at birth.'

'You said anyone like him should be.'

'Oh God,' groaned Shepperton, 'did I really? That's awful. No wonder you walked out. I was just so frustrated. We'd wasted so much time and I just felt we'd gone back to square one.

'It's not how I really feel, I hope you can believe that. I know it's no excuse but I can only apologise – and profusely. You and me – we work well as a team – and you're a good mate too. I'd hate to think throwing my toys out of the pram would come between us. I need you by my side if we're ever gonna have a hope of solving this case.'

He waited anxiously for Clarke's response, one his colleague appeared in no particular rush to deliver. When Clarke eventually held out his hand there was no way Shepperton could hide his relief.

'Okay Dave,' said Clarke, 'let's just concentrate on what's really important now shall we? Let's find the vicious bastard who's been killing these girls.'

-o0o-

'Gotta be honest with you,' admitted Brian some hours later after hearing from Shepperton, 'I really didn't think Bradley would ever have been capable of harming a mouse, let alone a young girl.'

Wendy sighed, nodding in agreement.

'He's such a disturbed, mixed-up kid,' she said, 'though whatever possessed him to make such ridiculous claims is beyond me. The poor lad. He must need some kinda professional help.'

'Attention-seeking, that's what it was I guess,' replied Brian. 'After all,' he continued, 'the lad hasn't got a lot going for him, has he?'

Wendy began to weep. She looked pleadingly into Brian's eyes.

'When will this ever end Brian? They'll never find out who killed Gemma or find Heather will they? Every way they turn seems to come to a dead end. I'm not sure how much more of this I can take. When I was in town yesterday I could have sworn I'd seen Heather. The girl looked just like her. I called out but she kept on walking so I ran after her and grabbed her arm. She looked so scared when she turned around. I felt such a fool.'

'I've done the same myself – a couple of times, in fact,' admitted Brian. 'I can't help it. I just can't accept she might be dead.'

As on so many times in the recent past, Wendy's emotions got the better of her and she collapsed sobbing into Brian's arms, her head resting upon his shoulder. As he held on to his grieving wife Brian gained some comfort from the unexpected renewed closeness between them. He stroked her hair gently, relieved she could not see the tears that were welling up in his own eyes.

'Something'll turn up Wen,' he replied, albeit rather unconvincingly. 'Shepperton will come up trumps eventually, I'm sure.'

Wendy stepped back.

'But what if he doesn't?'

'I dunno Wen. I don't really want to think about that. We've gotta hope for the best, after all, what other option do we have?'

He looked at his watch. Neither of them had had any sleep for at least 24 hours.

'I'd better get going,' he said. 'I've gotta be back at the vicarage in a few hours. Loads of pruning to get on with.'

'Do you have to? Can't you stay a while longer?'

This was something Brian had not expected. Wendy's request caught him unguarded.

'Well, I . . . er . . . I *suppose* I could,' he stammered. 'Are you sure you really want me to?'

'I'm so tired Brian. All this . . . it's too much to take in. Please don't go. Like you said earlier, we need each other more than ever don't we?'

'I couldn't agree more Wen,' replied Brian, wiping his eyes with the back of his hand. 'Of course I'll stay.'

Wendy was obviously relieved. She led Brian into the lounge and sat beside him on the sofa. He put his arm around her shoulder.

'This is nice,' she murmured as she snuggled up next to him. 'I'd almost forgotten how this felt. I never thought I'd hear myself say this again but at the moment it feels like you're the only person I can trust.'

Brian smiled, blissfully unaware that, within a few hours, their renewed closeness would be tested to its limit.

8

'Well, I'm blowed, if it's not the Reverend Winston Palmer!'

Duty sergeant Ray Smith grinned and put his pen and paperwork to one side as the reverend approached the reception desk.

'Ah Raymond!' replied the somewhat flustered vicar, 'I'm so relieved you're here – a friendly and familiar face indeed.'

Smith chuckled.

'Familiar eh? Not so sure about that Winston. I haven't exactly darkened the doors at St Mary's lately have I?'

The grey-haired reverend, who looked far older than his 52 years, managed a wry smile.

'I guess you've been busy doing the Lord's work here instead,' he replied, adding: 'I need to speak to you Raymond about a very delicate matter. Is there perhaps somewhere here where we could chat in private?'

'Er, I guess so Winston. I'll just see if one of my colleagues can take over at the desk for a while.'

Smith disappeared into the main office and returned a couple of minutes later accompanied by a fresh-faced junior constable.

'You'll be okay for a while Michael. Just give me a shout if you need me.'

The constable nodded and Smith guided the reverend into a small side room featuring four rather battered old wooden chairs, a sink, a small table and a fridge with a tatty low-level cupboard upon which an electric kettle and some tea, coffee and sugar jars were placed.

'Sit yourself down Winston,' said Smith. 'Can I make you a cuppa?'

Palmer shook his head.

'I'd rather just get this over with if you don't mind Raymond.'

Smith looked at his friend. He seemed worried.

'What's up Winston?'

The clearly emotional Palmer cradled his head between his hands. Smith rose from his chair and put his arm around the reverend's shoulder.

'Come on Winston, it's me. You know you can tell me anything.'

Palmer nodded. He looked up towards the ceiling and took a deep breath.

'Like I said, I'm glad it's you on duty tonight. It's all rather a mess, I'm afraid. Actually,' he added, 'I think I would like that cuppa after all.'

Smith got up and filled the kettle with water. He switched it on and opened the small cupboard. He opened the door and withdrew a battered old biscuit tin and removed the lid. He shook his head and cursed, then remembered he was in the company of a man of God. He turned and blushed.

'Sorry Winston. I was gonna offer you a Hobnob but it looks like my colleague Roger's scoffed the last ones already – they're his favourites.'

He sat down again to face the reverend across the table.

'What d'ya say, shall we make a start while the kettle boils?'

Palmer nodded.

'You remember that dreadful murder down by the canal? That girl – Gemma, wasn't it?'

'How could we ever forget it Winston? It was a dreadful case – and we're no nearer to finding out who did it than we were at the time.'

'I was asked in to come in and give a statement. Did you know that?'

'Yeah.'

'Well, now I think I should tell someone that my statement wasn't exactly accurate. It was an oversight mind. I was never intending to be misleading.'

'Okay.'

'I was interviewed by a detective. Shepperton I think his name was. Him and another guy. Clarke was it?'

'That's it. Detective Constable James Clarke. He and DCI Shepperton have been leading the murder inquiry.'

'They were very interested in a man who sometimes works for me. A chap by the name of Brian Brown – or BB as we called him. They wanted to know if he had been working on my garden that evening and what time he left.

'You'll remember the heatwave that August. It had been incredibly hot for weeks. That's why BB tended to start work later in the day, when it was a little cooler, and carried on until it became too dark to continue. My wife Samantha would regularly take out jugs of chilled lemonade to him which he always gratefully accepted.

'I always liked BB. He was a very good worker too. I trusted him completely – and that's what I told the detectives when they asked me about him – but now . . .' he sighed, 'I'm really not so sure.'

'Why so?' asked Smith.

'I told the detectives that BB rarely left the vicarage until around nine o'clock that summer. It really was getting too dark by then to do much else outside. That was true but now I realise I may have overlooked something. Most evenings BB would take a break for half an hour or so. He'd go into the old barn for a rest. I didn't think anything of it at the time. It was only after I spoke to my daughter Christine a couple of days ago that I became uneasy.

'Christine's a student at Oxford. She's studying medicine but she was at home with us over that summer holiday period. She always seemed to get on well with BB. She would often join him in the barn for a chat. She said he was very interested in her studies and how, he told her, in his earlier days he'd considered studying medicine too but nothing ever came of it.'

The kettle began to whistle.

'Hang on a sec Winston.'

Smith got up and popped a teabag into each of the cracked and stained mugs then added the water and milk.

'Sugar?'

Palmer nodded.

'Thanks, just one.'

Smith placed the mugs on the table and sat down again.

'Carry on.'

'Christine,' said Palmer, 'she's always been such a happy and carefree girl.'

He smiled.

'She's been the light of our lives but, these days . . . well, she's but a shadow of herself. Samantha and I tried so often to get her to open up, to tell us what's wrong but until a couple of days ago we were getting nowhere.'

'So,' asked Smith, 'what's changed?'

'It seems,' said Palmer sorrowfully, 'that it wasn't only Christine's studies that BB was interested in.'

'You mean he was carrying on with your daughter?'

'It seems so. She admitted to me a couple of days ago that she and BB had had feelings for each other, even though she was only just 18 years old at the time. She's years younger than him. He must be at least in his mid-forties.'

'So you reckon that's the real reason Brown was going into the barn?'

'If I'd have thought so I would never have permitted it,' insisted Palmer. 'He was old enough to be her father. Suddenly, she left Somersley. She headed back to Oxford with no explanation. It was obvious at the time she was very upset but she wouldn't say why. But now she's told me what happened.

'She found out that BB was separated from his wife and was living with another woman. Had Christine known that she would never have put herself in such a position. I guess she was just flattered that a more mature man had shown an interest in her.

'It was only after Christine explained to me that I realised that, on the night of the murder, Christine had not been around at the time and BB might not have been in the barn after all as I originally believed. I mean, he *could* have been elsewhere, couldn't he?'

'Not only that,' replied Smith, 'it's worrying that he seems to have a penchant for younger women too.'

Suddenly the reverend fully appreciated the possible consequences of his revelations.

'Oh dear! What if I've got it wrong? I do remember seeing BB leave that evening, I guess at around nine o'clock or thereabouts. Naturally I'm furious that he misled my daughter but that doesn't mean he had anything to do with the murder of that young girl, does it? Okay, I am angry at him but it's a big step up from that to suggest he might be responsible for someone's murder.'

Smith realised Palmer may be about to search for some reason to retract what he had shared.

'Tell me Winston, why did you feel the need to come here if not to share what you've been suspecting? It's clearly a scenario you feel may be possible – that Brown was at least nearby when the girl was killed and that you cannot confirm that he was taking a break in your barn at the time.'

Palmer, now most flustered, stood up.

'I'm so sorry Raymond. I've wasted enough of your time. I shouldn't have come. A bad idea. It's just me making something out of nothing. Best to just let it be. Yes, yes, best to just let it be.'

Smith took a final swig of his tea. He put down his mug, having come to a decision.

'You know Winston, I'm afraid I can't not act on what you've just told me. We have to tell DCI Shepperton. There's no alternative 'cos if Brown *wasn't* in the barn that evening we'll need to establish *exactly* where he was at the time of the murder.'

9

Brian woke up early the next morning. He hadn't slept well. Throughout the night he'd been thinking about Bradley. Surely he hadn't really killed Heather. Brian still harboured hope that, one day, hopefully very soon, she would turn up unharmed.

Wendy shared that hope. She was still asleep, her head resting on his knee. Brian twisted his head from one side to the other in an effort to relieve the stiffness in his neck.

The sofa had not been the most comfortable resting place but he appreciated the opportunity to begin building bridges with his wife. He stroked her hair gently. Wendy rubbed her eyes and looked up at him. She smiled then stretched. She sighed.

'God, is that all it is?' she said, looking at her watch.

'D'ya fancy a coffee?' asked Brian.

'It's six o'clock!'

'Yeah, but my mouth feels like the bottom of a parrot's cage!' replied Brian.

'Charming! Go on then. You know where everything is.'

Brian stood up and stretched.

'That flippin' sofa never was comfortable,' he said. 'I told you at the time that we should've bought that brown leather one instead.'

'Oh shut up and put the kettle on,' said Wendy. She curled up again on the sofa as Brian made his way into the kitchen.

Ten minutes later he returned to the lounge carrying a tray bearing two cups of tea and a few Bourbon biscuits on a plate. Wendy sat up and stretched again.

'You're right, we should've bought the leather sofa.'

Brian sat down next to her and passed her the biscuits. Wendy took one and promptly dipped it in her tea.

'Really?' said Brian in mock disgust. 'Dunkin' a Bourbon? How common can you get?'

Wendy giggled then realised it was the first time she'd done so for a very long time. Waking up next to Brian had felt surprisingly good. After everything that had happened it was somewhat reassuring to rediscover some sense of normality, albeit in the wake of one the most distressing situations that any parent could ever endure.

They sat for a while chatting in general terms but the elephant in the room could not be avoided. Wendy had killed a girl and was struggling with her conscience.

'I should've turned myself in Brian. I should've . . .'

She was interrupted by a loud banging on the front door.

'Whoever's that at this time in the morning?' asked Brian. He got up and pulled back one of the curtains.

'It's Shepperton and Clarke,' he said.

'Oh my God, they've come for me!' gasped Wendy. 'What am I gonna do?'

The door was banged again.

'Mrs Brown, it's the police! Open the door!'

Trembling, Wendy got up. Brian squeezed her hand, then Wendy, shaking like a leaf, made her way into the hallway. Nervously, she partially opened the door.

'Mrs Brown, we need to speak to your husband. We've been to his place and he's not there. Please don't tell me he's not here, 'cos his car is on your driveway.'

'He, he isn't . . . he's not here!' said Wendy in a panic as she began to shut the door. However, Clarke was swift to place his foot between the door and the frame. Brian then called out.

'Wen, it's okay. Let 'em in.'

Shepperton pushed the door fully open then he and Clarke made their way into the lounge to find Brian pacing anxiously around the room.

'You both seem very edgy, fully dressed too,' observed Clarke, who added: 'Anything you'd like to share with us?'

'It's been a very difficult time for us,' said Brian. 'Surely you can understand that? My wife and I have been under an enormous amount of pressure these past few months.'

'Well,' said Shepperton, 'at least she can relax 'cos it's you we want to speak to. I take it you won't mind accompanying us back to the station?'

'Er, yeah, okay. What's all this about? And why so early in the morning?'

'Some information has come to light,' replied Clarke, 'and we'd be very interested hear what you have to say about it.'

'Couldn't you just ask me here, now?'

A grim-faced Shepperton made it clear that was not an option.

'If you'd just come with us now Mr Brown – voluntarily of course.'

'Or,' suggested Clarke ominously, 'we could make it more official.'

The colour drained from Brian's face. He glanced towards Wendy.

'What's going on Brian?'

'I really have no idea Wen,' he replied, shaking his head. He squeezed her hand. 'Try not to worry, just wait here. I won't be long.'

'I really wouldn't be too sure of that,' said Shepperton as he took Brian by the arm and led him towards the front door before escorting him outside and assisting him into the rear seat of a waiting police car. A distraught and confused Wendy watched anxiously as the vehicle disappeared from sight. All sorts of thoughts began to run through her mind. If there had been any news of Heather – good or bad – surely Shepperton would have wanted to inform them both at the same time. And simply by their attitude, it had been obvious the detectives had been in no mood to offer any form of comfort to parents who were so worried about the welfare of their missing daughter.

No, this had to be a far more serious matter. The manner in which they spoke to Brian suggested they believed he knew more about Heather's disappearance than he had been letting on but Wendy had seen first hand how badly affected he had been since that dreadful August night.

She recalled seeing Brian weeping and how she had observed how much he had aged in that period of time. If the police thought he'd had any involvement in their daughter's disappearance or Gemma's murder well, they were off the mark.

Then there was an obvious concern. What if the police suspected that she had killed Sarah Mitchell? Would they be grilling Brian to find out what, if anything, he knew? If so it would only be a matter of time until they would come back to arrest her.

Every minute seemed like an hour with no news from the police or from Brian. Throughout the day Wendy paced around the house trying without success to remain calm and rational. By mid-afternoon she was at her wits' end. She went into the hallway to telephone the police station.

'Somersley police station. How can I help?'

'It's Wendy Brown. Your detectives took my husband in early this morning and I haven't heard anything. What's it all about?'

'I'm sorry Mrs Brown, I'm not at liberty to divulge that information over the 'phone. I suggest you call in at the station later in the day. We should be able to put you in the picture later on.'

'Well, can I just speak to him? Can't you just put him on the 'phone for a moment?' she pleaded.

'I'm really sorry but he's being interviewed as we speak. Like I say, call in at the station later today or this evening. I'm sorry Mrs Brown but I can't tell you any more at this stage.'

'Oh, for God's sake!'

Exasperated, Wendy slammed down the receiver.

'Try not to worry,' Brian had said as he was about to be led away but Wendy had noticed he appeared like a rabbit in headlights at the time. She had known him since they were teenagers so she was fairly sure there was no way he could have hidden the fact he had been really scared.

The day dragged on and on. By eight o'clock she decided not to wait any longer. She would go to the police station as advised. Fortunately her colleague Felicity had lent her the use of her car until she could replace her own. Wendy started it up and headed to the far side of the town. Ray Smith was, yet again, on duty at the reception desk.

'Good evening Mrs Brown.'

'Is it?' she replied. 'I'm not so sure about that. I want to speak to my husband. I was told to come here tonight.'

Smith looked rather puzzled.

'Er, he's not here Mrs Brown. He left at least a couple of hours ago.'

'Ridiculous,' she replied, 'he would have 'phoned me. You must be mistaken.'

'Sorry Mrs Brown but I called a taxi for him myself. He was picked up . . . oh I dunno . . . around five thirty, maybe six o'clock.'

Wendy was astounded.

'Where did he go?'

'He asked to go back to his cottage.'

Wendy was seething. How dare he not call her! He must have known how worried she had been. And why didn't he come back directly to her home?

Without another word to Smith she turned around and stormed out of the building. Smith screwed up his eyes as he heard the tyres of her car squealing as she drove off. Ten minutes later she screeched to a stop outside Brian's home. Getting out of the car she slammed the door loudly behind her and strode towards Brian's front door and banged on it as hard as she could.

She looked to her right. The cottage was in darkness but she could have sworn she had seen a light in the downstairs room when she arrived. There was no answer so she began to bang loudly on the front door again.

'Brian! BRIAN! I know you're in there! Open the door! I'm not going anywhere until you do!'

She was sure she could see some movement through the window of the darkened room. Once again she hammered on the door.

'I mean it Brian! I'll keep on banging until you open this door!'

Eventually she heard footsteps and noticed a chink of light from behind the door. She stood back as she heard the key in the lock. The door partly opened. Nervously, Brian peered back at her.

'Well? Are you gonna let me in or not?

Brian feebly nodded and opened the door wider. Wendy burst in before he could change his mind.

'Just what the hell is going on?' she demanded. 'I've been going out of my mind with worry. Just one 'phone call! Was that too much to ask?'

'I'm . . . I'm sorry Wen, I just . . .'

His voice drained away and he sank to his knees in front of her, his face between his hands.

'Oh God Wen! It's all such a mess. A terrible, terrible mess!'

He began to sob and rock. Wendy, however, was in no mood to watch Brian's display of self-pity.

'Oh get up for God's sake! Get in there and tell me what's going on. Is there any news of Heather?'

Brian shook his head pitifully. He stood up and gestured to Wendy to go into the lounge. She sat down on one of his rather tatty armchairs then demanded to know what had happened at the station.

'I'm so sorry Wen. I can't tell you.'

'Well, I'm not going anywhere until you do!'

Even in his highly emotional state Brian could tell it would be futile to argue. He had never seen Wendy so determined to get her own way.

'It's embarrassing Wen. I don't know how to tell you. I really don't. It's just that I did something really stupid. Really unkind.'

'Not for the first time then,' snapped Wendy with obvious reference to the day Brian had walked out on her and Heather to live with Stella and Gemma.

'I know, I know. I guess I deserved that. Trouble is Wen, I've done something just as bad, if not worse.'

Wendy listened in almost disbelief as her husband revealed his affair with Christine while he had been working at the vicarage.

'Oh my God, you're disgusting. How old was she?'

'I dunno. About 18, 19 maybe 20 I guess.'

'You were old enough to be her father!'

'She *was* an adult,' offered Brian by some way of excuse.

'So why are you telling me this? And what's it got to do with Heather?'

'It's more to do with Gemma and the time she was killed. Reverend Palmer has revised his statement. Now he can't confirm I was at the vicarage when Gemma was killed. But I *was* there, I swear it Wen, you've gotta believe me!'

'What did Shepperton and Clarke say?'

'As far as they are concerned, I'm a suspect again. That said, they didn't have enough to hold on to me. They've let me go and told me to stay in the neighbourhood.'

'You idiot! Why were you carrying on with that girl in the first place? Have you no self control?'

Brian looked incredibly sheepish.

'I couldn't help it. Me and Stella – we were going through a sticky patch. We rowed quite a bit. Christine, she was just a really nice girl. Friendly. We got on. It felt good to have someone like her to chat to. It's just that, after a while, things got a bit out of hand. I'm not proud of it but, I swear, that's the truth.'

'So you were with her when Gemma was killed. She could be your alibi.'

Brian shook his head.

'No, we stopped seeing each other a week earlier. We had words and she stormed off back to uni in Oxford.'

'Why, what happened?'

'Oh God!' he groaned. 'I knew you'd ask me that! This is the worst bit. She turned up in the barn. She was absolutely beaming. I asked her why then she told me . . .'

His voice tailed off once more.

'Told you what?' demanded Wendy.

Brian began to weep again. He began to shake from head to foot.

'Told you what?' repeated Wendy impatiently.

Brian mumbled.

'What? What did you say?'

Brian sobbed.

'She told me she was pregnant and that I was the father.'

Wendy was astonished. Even by Brian's recent low standards, this was a new depth.

'So when were you gonna tell me you've got another child?'

'I haven't,' he blubbed. 'I told her there was no way I was gonna be a father again. I told her she'd have to get rid of it. That's when she stormed off. I haven't seen or heard from her since.'

'Well, I can't say I could blame her for that!' declared a furious Wendy. 'That girl and her baby will be far better off without you!'

'I don't even know if she had the baby,' replied a shame-faced Brian. 'Surely if she had, the reverend would have told Shepperton. Anyway,' he pleaded, 'how would I even know if it was mine? I reckon she must've got rid of it so her father didn't find out.'

'How can you be so callous! I can hardly believe what I'm hearing. In fact – I've heard enough. I'm outta here!'

Wendy stood up, her face crimson with rage, then headed towards the door.

'Wen, Wen stop! Please don't leave me like this! What am I gonna do?'

Wendy turned and sneered at her pathetic husband.

'I don't know and I don't care. You disgust me!'

As she slammed the door shut behind her she could hear Brian calling out after her.

'At least I haven't killed someone!'

Beyond furious, Wendy spun around, poked her finger through the cottage's letterbox and screamed back at him.

'Well I've only got your word for that. I swear if I find out you had anything to do with what's happened to Gemma or Heather I swear I'll hunt you down and I'll kill you myself!'

10

The following morning Wendy was woken by the sound of a car starting up on her driveway. She pulled back the bedroom's net curtains and spotted Brian reversing his car onto the road. As he was about to pull away he glanced up to her bedroom window, obviously having seen her but not acknowledging her presence. He drove off, much to Wendy's relief. She had been dreading a further scene on her front doorstep.

Thoroughly miserable, she ran a bath and laid some fresh clothes out on her bed. Still not ready to return to work, the day ahead was clear and she had no idea at that moment how to fill the time. Staying indoors all day though was not an option. That's when her mind would torment her the most. She needed to keep herself occupied.

The incident with Sarah and the disposing of her body was rarely far from the forefront of her mind. In fact, those images tormented her. At the end of the day she had to face the unpalatable fact that she was a killer, albeit an accidental one. However, Brian's suggestion that it could have been more than accident kept spinning round and round in her head, making her doubt herself. Had she, in a moment of madness, thrust the knife into Sarah's side to prevent her from ruining her career?

As she laid soaking in her bath she contemplated wandering around the town centre. Under normal circumstances this was something she would have enjoyed but then she recalled the last time she had done so.

The publicity surrounding Heather's disappearance and the fact she was a long-standing local school teacher ensured she was a well-known face and, as a result, so many people, well-meaning as they had been, had stopped her either to offer sympathy or to enquire if there had been any further developments. No, she thought, she couldn't cope with that today.

She laid back and completely submerged herself in the warm bath then sat up, having come to a decision. She needed to get away – well away from Somersley, if only for the day. A change of scene would do her good. Once dried and dressed and after a hearty breakfast she left the house and got into the car, started up and began to drive with no particular destination in mind.

The weather for the time of year was glorious, sunny and still reasonably warm with clear blue skies. A nice day like this, she decided, would best be spent at the coast. Brighton maybe? Yes, Brighton would be good. It would also give her the chance to give her recently-purchased second hand Vauxhall Viva a good run. She started up then headed through the side roads until she reached the junction for the M3.

Now heading southwards on the motorway Wendy wound down the driver's window and put her foot to the floor resulting in the wind blowing through her hair. After all the stress she had been experiencing, this was a brief feeling of freedom and she savoured every moment.

Sadly, her momentary exhilaration was soon over as she approached the end of a long tailback. Having come to a grinding halt she heard the approaching sirens of police vehicles squeezing their way between the lanes of traffic. Two traffic cars and an ambulance came past and slowly weaved their way into the distance.

Two hours later she had barely moved an inch. Eventually a traffic report on the car radio explained the hold-up. A three-vehicle collision just south of Junction 10 had completely blocked the carriageways. The motorway was expected to be closed for some time and traffic was to be diverted off the motorway at Winchester.

Wendy cursed under her breath. There was little point in trying to make it to Brighton now. Slowly but surely she reached the junction. Thoroughly cheesed off she decided to head back home. As she arrived back in Somersley Wendy turned into Church Road and noticed that the car park outside St Mary's was deserted. She pulled in, intending to make the most of an opportunity to sit quietly and undisturbed in the church. A chance to unwind from a stressful and unsuccessful journey. A lapsed Christian, Wendy had often visited the church for moments of quiet contemplation but this would have been the first time she had done so since Heather's disappearance.

Having entered via the heavy wooden door of the porch Wendy walked into the nave, her footsteps echoing throughout the building. She selected her usual pew at the front and sat down, relieved to put all the chaos of the M3 behind her.

The thickness of the walls ensured it was considerably cooler in the church but not cold. Rays of sunlight streamed through the huge stained glass window of the chancel, lighting up the pew upon which she was sitting. It was, thought Wendy, as if God was shining His spotlight directly on her – a sinner. God knows everything. He sees everything thought Wendy. She put her hands together in prayer and tearfully whispered: 'Oh Lord, forgive me. Guide me to the right path.' She repeated the words over and over again then sat with her head in her hands, weeping quietly.

How long she had remained there, she could not say but it had been for a considerable time. She looked at her watch. Five o'clock. Might as well just go home. She stood up, turned and made her way back along the nave. As she opened the main door she came face-to-face with the Reverend Palmer who was about to enter the church and who appeared to be just as shocked to see her as she was to see him. It was the reverend who spoke first.

'Mrs Brown! Er, gosh.'

He shuffled awkwardly. Wendy noticed his obvious embarrassment.

'It's okay Reverend,' she said. 'I understand. You had to do what you had to do.'

'That's very charitable of you,' he replied with more than a hint of relief. 'There was no malice, I can assure you. I just thought it was important to ensure my earlier statement was corrected. I must say I never thought your husband was capable of such a heinous crime, but . . .'

Wendy interrupted him.

'Well, Reverend, let's face it, he wasn't as squeaky clean as either of us thought, was he?'

Palmer looked surprised.

'You know?'

'About Christine? Yes, he told me last night. I was shocked. Disgusted in fact. From now on I want nothing more to do with him.'

Palmer looked at Wendy.

'You've been crying,' he observed. 'How about we go into the church room? I'll put the kettle on.'

He gently placed his hand on her shoulder and guided her back into the church. A few minutes later he handed her a cup of tea and sat opposite her across a trestle table.

'I'm so sorry for what Brian has put your family through,' she said. 'I can't imagine how much he has hurt you all.'

'That's hardly your fault, is it?' replied Palmer, 'but you're right, it's been an extremely stressful period.'

'How's Christine?'

'Very low. Very low indeed. My wife and I had no idea why she left for Oxford so suddenly. We kept asking her to come home so we could talk. We were so worried about her. We tried again and again over the following weeks to get to the bottom of it but without success. She just didn't want to come home or to confide in us. It was only a few days ago that she came home and admitted to us what had happened.'

'And the baby?'

Palmer welled up.

'Like I said, we had no idea Christine was pregnant. She told us that when she first returned to Oxford she was considering an abortion but then she changed her mind. She had the baby in April, a little girl. She named her Mariam.'

'Oh what at a beautiful name. It's very unusual.'

'It's the Greek translation for Mary Magdalen in the Old Testament,' explained Palmer.

'I see,' said Wendy. 'I remember teaching Christine. She was such a beautiful girl so I'm sure her baby must be just as gorgeous,' said Wendy.

'I wouldn't know,' replied Palmer, shaking his head sadly. 'We've never seen her. Not even a photo. Christine gave her up for adoption soon after she was born. It's broken our hearts to be honest. We never even knew she existed until the other day. Christine is still grieving. The only good thing is that she can now resume her studies.'

Wendy reached across the table and squeezed Palmer's hand comfortingly. Teary-eyed, he smiled at her.

'I'm so pleased you came here today and that we've had this chance to chat,' he said. 'It must have been the Lord's will.'

11

Wendy woke up particularly early. The sun was streaming through a narrow gap between her bedroom curtains, illuminating her room and making her squint. She stretched and yawned. For once, she had slept well but, somehow, she still felt tired.

Beneath her duvet she was warm and comfortable so she resisted the urge to get up straight away. Eventually the need to visit the toilet demanded she had to clamber out of bed, the cold air making her shiver. Hurriedly she put on her thick woollen dressing gown and made her way across the landing to the bathroom.

Shortly afterwards she went downstairs and switched on the central heating. As the boiler fired up she filled the kettle and popped a slice of bread into the toaster. She switched on the portable television on the worktop and tuned in to the BBC news bulletin. The main story featured government plans for a new identity card scheme aimed at clamping down on football hooliganism.

Totally uninterested in all forms of sport, Wendy switched channels but could find nothing of interest. She turned off her television and switched on the radio, just in time to hear the tail end of *Orinoco Flow* by Enya.

Wendy found herself humming along as she retrieved a jar of marmalade and a bottle of milk from her refrigerator. As she spread the marmalade onto her toast the kettle boiled. Wendy poured the boiling water into her mug and removed the top off the milk bottle but, in doing so, released the pungent smell of sour milk.

'Urgh!'

Wendy cursed under her breath and poured the milk down the plughole. It was no use, she realised, she needed to go shopping

– something she had been putting off owing to the cold and windy conditions of the past few days. Once the central heating had kicked in Wendy went back upstairs to have a soak in the bath.

It was only half past eight when she emerged from her front door and got into her car. A few minutes later she arrived at the local supermarket and parked up. She retrieved some shopping bags from the boot and collected a trolley from the rack just outside the store.

As she separated her trolley from the others in the rack she turned round and, in doing so, bumped into a young man who had been waiting behind her to collect a trolley from the same rack.

'Oh, I'm so sorry!' said Wendy without looking up. The young man gasped. The moment Wendy made eye contact with the young man her blood ran cold.

'Bradley!'

Bradley was equally surprised to see Wendy. He immediately panicked and turned to hurry off.

'I don't want any trouble!' he called out as he began to flee.

'Wait! Bradley wait! Come back, we need to talk!'

But Bradley was in no mood to hang around and hurried as fast as his lame leg would carry him back towards the cycle rack in the car park. Wendy though had little trouble in catching up with him. As he was fumbling around for his padlock key Wendy grabbed his arm. Bradley stared at her with an unmistakable look of fear in his eyes.

'It's okay Bradley,' said Wendy reassuringly. 'I only want to talk to you. I'm not gonna hurt you.'

'You, you, you're scaring me!' whimpered Bradley as he cowered in front of her.

'Look, it's okay Bradley,' Wendy repeated. 'Come on, let's grab a coffee somewhere. How about that cafe over there? I'll pay. After all, it's high time we had a chat and cleared the air, don't you think?'

Wendy reached out to Bradley's arm and gently guided him in the direction of Mandy's Cafe, a less than salubrious premises adjacent to the supermarket. Bradley sat down at the table nearest to the window, shaking nervously. Wendy sat opposite him and caught the attention of a young waitress.

'Two coffees, please.'

The waitress, chewing gum and wearing a coffee-stained apron, grumpily scribbled Wendy's order on a tatty notepad and walked off without uttering a word. A minute or so later she returned, carrying two badly-stained white mugs and a sugar dispenser. Again, without a word, she laid them on the table and walked away.

'She's nice, isn't she?' said Wendy sarcastically in an attempt to make Bradley feel more at ease. Bradley nervously smiled. He picked up his mug and took a sip, then grimaced. The coffee was piping hot.

'Best to leave it a while to cool down Bradley,' advised Wendy. 'In the meantime we can have that chat. Perhaps you'd like to start by telling me why you told the police you'd killed Gemma and Heather. I don't believe for one moment you ever laid a hand on either of them. Whatever made you say such things? I just can't understand it.'

Bradley gazed back at her, deep in thought and obviously struggling to come up with an answer. He avoided making eye contact with Wendy, his eyes darting from one part of the cafe to the other.

'Come on Bradley,' urged Wendy, 'you can tell me.'

'I, I think I was a bit drunk,' he stammered.

Wendy shook her head.

'No Bradley,' she replied firmly. 'You'd had plenty of time to sober up by the time you were interviewed so that won't wash. Not at all. So I'll ask you again, why did you make up such dreadful lies?'

'It wasn't my fault Mrs Brown. It was Trevor Turnbull's fault, not mine!'

'Trevor Turnbull?' said Wendy. 'I remember him. A horrible, spiteful boy. He was always getting into trouble at school. I know Heather went out with him a couple of times but I made it very clear I didn't approve so she stopped seeing him.'

Bradley nodded in agreement.

'He doesn't like me Mrs Brown. He scares me. He's always calling me names and making nasty jokes about my leg.'

'I can imagine,' agreed Wendy. 'So how was it all his fault? What did he do to you?'

Bradley began to weep. Wendy passed him a paper serviette. Desperate for information, she was determined to keep him calm in the hope he might open up. She was convinced the lad had not had anything to do with Gemma's murder or Heather's disappearance but maybe, just maybe, he knew something. Would that something turn out to be a piece of vital information? Wendy decided that it had to be worth a try. Bradley dried his eyes and took another sip of his coffee. It was still too hot.

'Come on Bradley, talk to me,' urged Wendy gently. She reached across the table and squeezed his hand. Her gesture seemed to do the trick. Bradley took a deep breath and looked her straight in the eye.

'I'm so sorry,' he blubbed. 'I never meant to cause any trouble. I loved Heather. I would never have hurt her.'

'Then why did you say such terrible things Bradley?'

'It was Turnbull's fault. Teasing me. Upsetting me. I hate him. When he heard Heather had been helping me with my homework he started calling out in front of all the other kids. He was saying I was trying to get into her knickers and that I was wasting my time. He reckoned no girl with any sense would want to be with a cripple like me.

'He said he'd done it *loads* of times with Heather and that she was just a slut. I told him to shut up. I told him that Heather was nice and that she was pretty but he humiliated me in front of everyone and they were all laughing at me.'

'That's terrible Bradley. What did you do?'

'I ran away.'

He began to sob. Wendy rose from her chair and walked around the table to sit next to him. She put a comforting arm around his shoulders. After a few moments Bradley continued.

'Heather was kind. When I came over to yours that night we were going through my homework. That's when I told her what had happened, what Turnbull had said. She told me not to listen to him. She said I had a good heart and that any girl would be lucky to have me. That's when she kissed me. No girl had ever kissed me before. It was nice.'

Wendy smiled. She could imagine her daughter comforting her friend. That's just the sort of girl she was – caring and kind.

'What happened then Bradley?'

'We did my homework and then I went home. I was very happy. The next day at school Turnbull started on me again but I didn't care 'cos Heather had kissed me.'

'Did you tell Turnbull?'

Bradley appeared shocked that she had even thought he might have done so.

'Oh no, Mrs Brown. It was *private*! A gentleman *never* tells. I heard that somewhere.'

Wendy smiled again but, frustratingly, she was no nearer finding out why Bradley made his false confessions. She decided to press him further. His response both shocked and reassured her at the same time.

'Turnbull said I must be the only boy in the class who hadn't done it with a girl. He's done it loads of times. I know 'cos he told me so. When I told Heather that night she cuddled me and said that if I wanted to try, she wouldn't mind. I said no. I didn't want to make a baby but she said it would be okay 'cos she had a pill. A girl she knew got them for her.'

Wendy gasped. So Heather was on the pill! She'd had no idea.

'So . . . so . . . did you – you know?'

Bradley managed a smile.

'No! No, of course not Mrs Brown! I was much too scared.'

Wendy breathed a huge sigh of relief, then Bradley added:

'But we did do it the next night.'

'Bradley!'

'Oh, don't worry. It's okay Mrs Brown, she didn't force me.'

'That's not at all what I was thinking Bradley! Of course she didn't!'

'We often did it after that,' said Bradley, puffing out his chest proudly. 'I liked it. I liked it a lot.'

Stunned, Wendy just gazed at Bradley, not knowing at first how to respond. She thought back to the comments made by Sarah – that Heather had gained a reputation of being a girl of easy virtue. She thought she and her daughter had enjoyed the closest of relationships – that they shared every secret – almost as if they were sisters rather than mother and daughter. Now, she wondered, if she had really known her daughter at all.

'Are you okay Mrs Brown?' asked Bradley, 'you don't look well.'

Wendy took a gulp of her coffee.

'I'm fine, Bradley,' she replied unconvincingly. 'Tell me more.'

'What do you want to know?'

'Everything Bradley. I want to know everything.'

'I told Heather I loved her.'

'Really? What did she say?'

'She smiled.'

'Did she tell you she loved you too?'

'No. She just smiled.'

'Did anyone else know about you and Heather?'

'Only Maureen. Heather told her. Maureen's her best friend.'

'Maureen knew?'

'Yes, then Turnbull found out,' said Bradley.

'Who told him?'

'I dunno but he started saying bad things about Heather. I reckon he was still angry that she'd dumped him. That made Heather sad. Then, one day, she told me she couldn't help me any more with my homework and that we couldn't have any more cuddles. When I asked her why she told me she'd just found out that she was pregnant.'

Wendy gasped. So Heather *was* pregnant!

'Oh my God!'

'Are you alright Mrs Brown? . . . Mrs Brown? You've gone a funny colour. Didn't Heather tell you?'

'No Bradley, she certainly did not! I can't believe this!'

Wendy began to weep. Now it was Bradley's turn to put a comforting arm around her shoulder.

'I never believed I'd ever be a dad,' he said. 'I was so excited but Heather wasn't. She said she was gonna get rid of the baby.'

'What did you say?'

'I didn't want her to but she wouldn't listen to me. She told me she'd made up her mind and that there was nothing I could say to make her change her mind. I was very sad. Then Turnbull found out.'

'What? Turnbull again?' gasped Wendy. 'How did he find out? Who told him?'

'He'd heard Heather telling Maureen. Heather had been crying. That's when Turnbull came up to me at break time. He started teasing me again. Calling me and Heather names. Bad, nasty names. He told me that if a girl ever told him she was gonna get rid of his kid he'd kill her but at least Heather would be okay 'cos I was just a stupid crippled weirdo who wouldn't have the bottle to do it. He said I wouldn't have the guts to do it 'cos I was a coward.'

'Oh Bradley, what a horrible boy! He must be sick in the head to bully you like that.'

Bradley nodded.

'Yeah, that's why I'm scared of him. He's very, very scary.'

He sat there, looking pitiful. Upset as she was that he had made her daughter pregnant, Wendy recognised Bradley's inability to grasp the normal concepts of society. He was simple – incredibly simple – and that made him particularly vulnerable and susceptible to manipulation by anyone with bad intentions.

He had loved Heather, that much was beyond any doubt. The poor lad, she knew, had had a poor start in life. His mother, who had given birth to him illegitimately, had turned her back on

Bradley the moment he was born, cruelly claiming she had no wish to raise a cripple.

As a result Bradley had been reluctantly raised by his maternal grandparents who rarely showed him any form of affection. No wonder, thought Wendy, that Heather's kindnesses meant so much to Bradley. Had anyone ever really loved him?'

'Is that why you said what you said Bradley?

Bradley nodded.

'I didn't want everyone to think I was a coward,' he admitted. 'I wanted people to think I was brave and tough. That's why I said I killed Gemma and Heather. I wanted people to be scared of me instead. I didn't wanna be scared any more.'

Tearfully, Wendy hugged him.

'Oh Bradley, you poor, confused boy! That really wasn't your best idea, was it?'

Their embrace was interrupted by the 'friendly' waitress.

'Are you two gonna have another drink or summat to eat 'cos we're filling up and need all the tables.'

Wendy flicked her a glare.

'Come on Bradley, let's get out of here.'

She stood up and put on her coat. Bradley joined her and they walked out together. By the time they reached Wendy's car she had come to a decision.

'Bradley, I'm gonna go and see Shepperton. I think it's important he knows what you've just told me. Will you come with me?'

'Oh, I dunno, my bike . . .'

'We can put it in the back of the car,' replied Wendy as she opened the hatchback. 'Look, the back seats fold down.'

'I dunno, Mrs Brown. That policeman, he's scary too. He shouted at me last time.'

'He won't this time Bradley, I promise. You'll be with me. I'll make sure he won't shout at you this time.'

Shepperton was taking a long overdue day off when Wendy and Bradley turned up at the front desk so, instead they were led into the interview room to speak to Det Con Clarke who was most interested to hear what they had to disclose. Having spoken for more than an hour, Clarke led them back into the reception room and was about to send them on their way.

'I hope this clears up any remaining misconceptions that Bradley is in any way involved in what happened to Gemma and surrounding Heather's disappearance,' said Wendy.

'Trust me, Mrs Brown,' replied Clarke, 'DCI Shepperton and I ruled Bradley out some time ago but, after what you have both told us, I imagine we will be bringing young Turnbull in for questioning in the very near future.'

'Why?' asked Wendy.

'Well,' replied Clarke, 'if Heather *was* pregnant, how can we be sure she was carrying Bradley's baby at all? Maybe Trevor Turnbull was the father instead. After all, he was boasting he'd had her loads of times, according to Bradley.

'That, in my eyes, makes Turnbull a possible suspect, particularly bearing in mind that he told Bradley that Heather should be killed for threatening to abort the baby. Maybe he was trying to get Bradley to do his dirty work for him.'

The possibility that Turnbull was possibly the father of Heather's unborn baby had not been a consideration for Bradley or Wendy who both reeled at the thought.

'It was *my* baby!' cried Bradley. '*My* baby!'

'Maybe it was son,' replied Clarke. 'Let's just see what Turnbull has to say, shall we? I think we also need to speak to Maureen Robson. I want to know why she did not inform us of the pregnancy when she was questioned. Now I'm wondering what else she isn't telling us.'

12

It was a bitterly cold and rainy Saturday evening. Maureen had spent the afternoon in Somersley town centre which was bustling with shoppers stocking up for Christmas. School had broken up for the festive period and, as usual, Maureen had left it late to begin her shopping for presents.

As a result she was tired and heavily laden with her purchases as she began a long walk back to her little car which she had been forced to leave in the car park on the far edge of town, all the other more convenient town centre parking areas having been packed when she had arrived in town shortly before lunchtime.

Maureen had been missing her best friend dreadfully and nothing anyone could say would raise her spirits. That day, back in August 1987 had, said Maureen, been the worst day of her life. Gemma, too, had been a friend, although not such a close one, yet Maureen could not get what had happened to the poor girl out of her head.

Despite these low moods Maureen had adamantly resisted her parents' attempts to refer her for some professional help. 'It's something I need to work out for myself,' she insisted.

Nevertheless, her parents did their best to support Maureen but, unbeknown to them, Maureen was finding their efforts claustrophobic. Earlier that day when her mother had suggested Maureen could do with some 'retail therapy' she was glad to get out of the house for a while. As much as her parents loved her, Maureen found their attention at times to be quite overwhelming.

With her shopping completed and her feet now aching considerably Maureen chose to take a short cut down Church Walk, a narrow, dimly-lit and rather eerie and little used passageway. The rain began to fall more heavily and Maureen's footsteps echoed loudly as she made her way along the cobblestones. She shivered and put her shopping bags down in order to wrap her scarf higher around her neck and fasten up the top buttons of her overcoat. She then picked up her bags and continued on her way.

After a few yards she became aware of someone walking behind her but took no particular notice until their footsteps seemed closer. She turned around but, puzzlingly, there was no-one to be seen. A sense of foreboding came over her but she walked on, nervously quickening her pace.

Then, once again, she heard more footsteps behind her – this time *very* close behind her. Suddenly she could hear heavy breathing then she felt someone grab her arm. A figure, in the half-light and dressed from head to toe in dark clothes and with a scarf covering their face, violently spun her around.

With only their eyes visible, the figure was a terrifying sight, staring menacingly at her. Before Maureen could scream, with one hand, her attacker roughly squeezed in her cheeks and pushed her back against a wall. Was it a man or woman? At first Maureen, in her abject panic, could not be sure.

She gasped in horror but before she could defend herself she was punched forcefully in the stomach. As she fell to the ground, gasping for breath, she dropped her bags causing her shopping to spill out over the cobblestones. Her attacker then unleashed a series of powerful kicks to her head, ribs and back. Instinctively, Maureen curled herself up into a ball, desperately trying, though without success, to protect her face.

After what seemed an age but probably no more than a minute, the vicious assault ended, her attacker seemingly now having run out of steam. Confused, winded and bleeding, Maureen looked up as the shadowy figure began to walk away. Writhing in agony Maureen spat out some blood and groaned loudly as the pain in her ribs intensified.

'Who are you?' she gasped as she laid prostrate on the wet cobbles. With the rain now teeming down, visibility in the passageway was limited and the immediate swelling around her eyes meant she was unable to make out the identity of her attacker. She called out again.

'Who are you? Why . . . ?'

The shadowy figure's distant response sent shivers down her spine.

'Just remember what I told you – the dead can't talk!'

Maureen watched as the figure disappeared into the darkness of the alley. Eventually she managed to pull herself up into a sitting position, her back against the wall. Cold rain water began trickling down her neck. She felt her face with the palms of her hands and could feel the swelling.

The rain continued to pour and an overhead guttering that had come away from its downpipe began spewing its cold, filthy water over her. With great effort she managed to shuffle over to her left but realised it made little difference – she was already soaked to the skin. As she coughed she noticed blood spraying out from her mouth and onto her coat.

Then came an overwhelming sense of dizziness. Desperate not to lose consciousness she struggled to get herself into a kneeling position then rested her elbows on the cobbles in an effort to keep her head as low as possible. Any hopes she may have had of someone coming to her aid soon evaporated. The passageway was rarely used and there was no-one in sight. She shivered. It was getting even colder.

Maureen knew she had to get to her feet and, if possible, to make it to her car which was parked less than a hundred yards away. Her first attempts to stand proved too much so it was on her hands and knees that she crawled, having no option than to leave her bags of shopping scattered across the cobbles behind her.

Eventually she found herself nearing the end of the alley which had on each side a number of waste bins and piles of binbags and, to her left, a large metal skip. Breathlessly, she propped herself up amongst the bins and began to weep. After a few minutes she decided to make one last desperate effort to reach her car.

Pulling herself up on the pile of binbags she managed to rise to her knees but as she reached for another bag, instead of aiding her to her feet it, and other bags, toppled over, spilling their contents of rotting vegetables over her head. Drenched, shivering, in pain and now covered in food waste so foul-smelling, Maureen gagged. The reflex prompted a tightening in her stomach that was so strong she could not prevent herself from vomiting down the front of her coat. Maureen wondered how things could get any worse.

Then she heard footsteps approaching. She peered down the dark alley and was about to call out for help before realising that the shape approaching her may be her attacker returning. Terrified, she quickly pulled some binbags over her in the hope she would not be spotted. The footsteps were getting nearer. From behind the bags of foul-smelling rubbish Maureen peered to see if she could make out who it was. To her immense relief it was a man walking slightly ahead of a woman.

'Look,' called out the man, 'There's even more here!'

Maureen watched as he bent down to pick up some of her shopping. She then heard the woman who sounded most concerned.

'Whatever could have happened here Reg? There must be a least two or three more bagfuls over here.'

Maureen tried feebly to call out but Reg never heard her. She watched in dismay as he walked back to rejoin his female companion. Together they began to pick up Maureen's scattered shopping and, having done so, they began to walk back along the alleyway from the direction they had come.

Once again Maureen tried to call out to them but her voice just drifted away. Despite her best efforts to remain awake, her injuries began to overwhelm her. Her eyes rolled back and everything went dark.

It was almost seven o'clock when Maureen opened her eyes. She had no idea how long she had been under the piles of discarded waste but she was relieved that the pain she had sustained in the attack had subsided sufficiently for her to pull herself into an upright position by hanging on to the large green skip.

At least the rain had now stopped and she was no longer shivering. Maybe, she thought, she had been shielded from the worst of the cold by the covering of binbags. As she staggered out of the alleyway into Church Street, which was well-lit, she could hear people in the distance chatting and laughing as they went about their way. Then she spotted a well-dressed woman approaching.

'Help me please, I need help!' cried out Maureen, pleadingly reaching out her hands. The woman looked decidedly uneasy and nervously gave Maureen a wide berth, crossing over to the other side of the road.

'Please, don't go! I need help!' sobbed Maureen but the woman quickened her pace and glanced occasionally back over her shoulder with a disgusted expression on her face.

'You should be ashamed of yourself, begging in the street and drunk at this time of the evening!' she shouted before disappearing in the distance.

With no other option Maureen was left to fend for herself. She made her way back to her car by leaning on other parked cars to support herself. Eventually she made it back to her four-year-old Mini – a recent gift from her parents after having passed her driving test at the first attempt – and, with great relief, flopped exhausted into the driving seat.

Not feeling ready to drive, she started up the engine and waited for the heater to kick in. After several minutes some warmer air began to circulate through the vents. At first this was a relief but, as the vehicle began to warm up, the obnoxious odour of Maureen's now filthy and vomit-covered clothing filled the interior.

Disgusted, she had no choice but to open her window. It was only then that she noticed a scrap of paper had been tucked behind her windscreen wiper. Battling against her pain Maureen clambered out of her car and retrieved the now soggy note. She flopped back exhaustedly into the driver's seat and, with trembling hands, unfolded the piece of paper to reveal a message scribbled untidily in black felt tip:

THE DEAD CAN'T TALK

Maureen shuddered as she read the note. Nervously, she ensured her car doors were locked and looked around to see if she was being watched but there was no-one in sight. Not wishing to hang around any longer she started up and, despite her condition, made her way home.

She parked up as near to her front door as possible and fumbled around for her key. Her hands shaking violently caused her to struggle to insert the key into its lock but, after a few seconds, she managed to do so.

The lights were on in the lounge.

'Mo! Is that you?'

'Yes Dad.'

'Well thank God for that! I was beginning to worry.'

Maureen opened the lounge door. Her father, George, was sitting in his favourite armchair reading the *Daily Mirror*. Without looking up he asked: 'It's getting late love. I was wondering where you'd got to.'

Maureen didn't answer. George heard a sob. He lowered his newspaper to be confronted by a dreadful sight.

'Oh my God, Mo,' he gasped as he dropped his newspaper to the floor. 'Whatever's happened to you?'

He got up from his chair and rushed over to her. He was about to hug her until he noticed her vomit-covered coat and instinctively stepped back. Maureen burst into tears.

'I was attacked in Church Walk.'

'Attacked? Who attacked you?'

'I dunno. It all happened so fast.'

'My God,' said George. 'Look at the state of you. Let's get you upstairs and get those filthy clothes off. Come on love, I'll run you a bath. Get yourself cleaned up and I'll phone for an ambulance and the police.'

His daughter's reaction stunned him.

'No Dad, no! she screamed. 'Don't you *dare* call the police!'

'Why not Mo? You're scaring me now.'

Maureen rummaged through her coat pocket and handed over the crumpled note.

'What's this? What's this supposed to mean?' asked her father.

'It means we say nothing – that's *exactly* what it means. Dad, I promise, if you call the cops, I'll never forgive you.'

George watched helplessly as Maureen painfully made her way up the stairs.

'Your mum's gone out for fish and chips. She'll be home soon. What am I supposed to tell her?'

Maureen stopped on the landing and called down.

'I dunno. Tell her I fell down some steps. Anything. Just don't tell her what really happened. I don't want her worried more than need be.'

'But sweetheart . . .'

'I mean it Dad. No police. You gotta promise me. No-one must ever know!'

Maureen went into her bedroom and fetched her dressing gown. Once in the bathroom she filled the bath, then stripped off her filthy clothes. She looked at herself in the mirror. Her face was badly swollen and bruised, as was her stomach and sides.

Painfully, she stepped into the bath and slowly lowered herself into the warm soapy water. She then fully submerged herself under the bubbles before sitting up. She wiped the soap from her eyes with the backs of her hands. She sat miserably in the bath with a myriad of thoughts spinning around in her head.

Shepperton had asked her to come into the station the following Monday morning, along with other friends and acquaintances of Heather's as the investigation into Gemma's murder and Heather's disappearance had ground to a halt. As a result the detective had decided to re-interview everyone who had been questioned earlier in the hope of unearthing a new lead that might kick-start the investigation.

From the moment her attacker spoke Maureen knew full well that those words and the message that had been left on her car had been no idle threat. She was worried. Had she known that Shepperton was now aware she knew far more than she had already revealed, she would have had even more cause to be concerned.

13

The prospect of spending another Christmas at home alone was thoroughly depressing for Wendy. Over the preceding three months Brian had bombarded her with telephone calls begging her to give him another chance but Wendy had held firm – insisting she wanted nothing more to do with him.

She had been relieved that, the previous Monday, when she had been called in to the police station to be re-interviewed, she had not bumped into Brian. She just could not face him at the moment. She did, however, see Maureen leaving the station.

'Oh my goodness Maureen, whatever's happened to you?'

Maureen's garbled explanation that she had fallen down some steps seemed far from convincing but it was clear the girl was in no mood to elaborate.

'Sorry Mrs Brown, I can't stop to chat. I'm in a bit of a hurry.'

Maureen was worried. It had been clear Shepperton had not believed her version of events, immediately raising a suspicion that she perhaps knew more than she had been letting on yet, despite his efforts to persuade her to open up, Maureen had insisted her injuries had been a result of falling down the concrete steps outside the town hall.

Afterwards, Shepperton had wanted to know why she had failed to mention Heather's pregnancy and what she knew of Heather's relationships with Trevor Turnbull and Bradley at her earlier interviews.

Her insistence that as Heather had told her of her pregnancy in confidence she had no wish to divulge that information. After all, she said, Heather may turn up alive and well one day. They were best friends so there was no way she would have broken her promise. Shepperton was frustrated. Yet another dead end. Turnbull, too, had to be ruled out. At the time of Gemma's death he had been on holiday in Scotland with his parents. His alibi had checked out.

Bumping into Brian had been the least of Wendy's concerns that morning. Having been summoned to the station to be re-interviewed, she was concerned Shepperton's real motive for getting her back in front of him was in case he had unearthed some incriminating evidence in respect of Sarah's murder. Had he reason to suspect she was responsible for the young girl's death?

As Shepperton invited her into the interview room her mouth was as dry as a bone and Wendy had to use every ounce of her courage not to show her nervousness.

'Please Mrs Brown, come on in and make yourself comfortable.' He pulled out a chair and politely gestured to Wendy to sit down.

Shepperton pulled out the chair on the opposite side of the table and sat down. He smiled kindly at her and opened up a loose-leaf folder and began to thumb through its contents.

'Ah, here it is!' he said, having found the page he had been looking for. 'Now then, let's get started. First of all, Mrs Brown, I'm so sorry to drag you in here again just to rake up things that you must desperately want to put behind you but, unlike a few months ago, I am now in a position to put aside a little time to review the cases of Gemma Gooding's death and your daughter's disappearance.

'I can clearly recall the distress you shared with your husband when I informed you of the need to concentrate on Gemma's murder investigation and the need to put Heather's disappearance to one side, albeit temporarily. As a father myself, I can only imagine how that must have felt.

'I have to be honest with you – both investigations have come to a dead end, hence the need to re-interview *everyone*, just in case any snippet of information may come to light – to see if there's anything we may have missed. I hope you don't mind.'

'No, no, that's fine,' replied Wendy while, at the same time, wondering if Shepperton was deploying a 'good cop' approach in the hope of catching her off-guard. However, as the interview progressed there was no indication that this had been his intention. Wendy began to relax slightly.

'Who else have you called in?' she asked.

'Well, obviously, your husband, Mrs Gooding, a good number of Gemma and Heather's schoolfriends and, of course, the Reverend Palmer to mention just a few. We were keen to speak to Heather's friend Maureen because her mother told us Maureen had come home upset on the night Gemma was killed. It took a while but that's now been cleared up. She'd broken up with her boyfriend earlier that week. We've checked it out and we're satisfied there's nothing more to it. As to her holding back information of Heather's pregnancy, I think we've cleared that up.'

'So, have you unearthed anything of use?' asked Wendy.

'I'm afraid not,' replied Shepperton, 'but don't worry, we won't give up.'

Having reviewed Wendy's earlier statement in fine detail and asking if she could now recall any other information that might be relevant Shepperton stood up and offered his hand.

'Thank you so much for coming in Mrs Brown. It's very much appreciated.'

It was with great relief a couple of hours later as she left the police station to return home that the investigation into Sarah's murder had not been mentioned at all.

-o0o-

With her only sister living in Florida and her parents long since passed away, Wendy woke early on Christmas morning expecting nothing more than to spend a lonely day in front of the television. Other than Her Majesty's televised Christmas message there was little to look forward to. Wendy felt thoroughly miserable – and even the screening of *Back to the Future,* a new movie that she'd been longing to see, had failed to lift her spirits.

After the programme ended Wendy poured herself a glass of sherry, laid out flat on the sofa and considered taking a nap. She had barely slept for several nights, the stresses of the past months having weighed heavily on her mind. Christmas should be a time of joy – a time for families to enjoy each other's company. She thought of Sarah's family – their first without their daughter. Wendy began to weep. Their unbearable torment was all her fault.

She sat up with a start as the doorbell rang. Whoever could that be? She had not been expecting anyone. She opened the front door to be confronted with the last person she would have expected to see – *that woman.*

'Hello Wendy – I'm assuming you're on your own?'

Wendy stood open-mouthed in complete astonishment, then nodded.

'I thought so,' said Stella, 'and I'm guessing you haven't eaten either?

'Just a couple of mince pies.'

'That's good, 'cos I've brought food. It's Christmas Wendy and I reckon it's about time we buried the hatchet. I hate being alone on a day like this and I guessed you do too. Can I come in?'

Still astonished and without answering, Wendy stood open-mouthed to one side to allow Stella, who was carrying a large covered tray, to pass.

'Where's your kitchen?'

'Er . . . just through there.'

Confused, Wendy followed her uninvited guest into the kitchen. Stella laid the tray on the worktop and removed the covering to reveal two roast dinners on large oval plates.

'Reckon a couple of minutes on Gas Mark 5 should do it,' said Stella with a smile. 'May I?'

Wendy, still speechless, nodded and watched as Stella put the plates into the oven.

'I wondered if you'd let me in at all,' admitted Stella. 'To be honest I couldn't be bothered to cook all this just for myself and I guessed you might be feeling the same way. At least cooking for two seemed more worthwhile and, besides, I can't bear rattling around in that house on my own – and especially on a day like today.'

'I . . . I know,' replied Wendy, having caught her breath. 'In a way, we're in the same boat I suppose. I never thought I'd hear myself saying this but I think I'm glad you've come along.'

To her great surprise, Stella stepped forward and gave Wendy a rather awkward hug.

'Thank you Wendy, that means a lot.'

Wendy noticed Stella's watery eyes.

'Tell you what,' said Wendy a few moments later, 'you get the plates out the oven and I'll pour us each a glass of sherry. I think I might even have some assorted biscuits in the cupboard. They'll have to do for dessert.'

'Sounds good to me,' replied Stella.

A few minutes later the least likely of companions were sitting side by side on the sofa with roast dinners on lap trays.

'Phew, Stella, I'm stuffed,' declared Wendy having cleared her plate. 'That was really delicious. Thank you. I'll get the biscuits.'

'Not on my count Wendy, I'm stuffed too. Maybe later eh?'

'More sherry then?'

Stella smiled.

'Yeah, why not?'

An hour later the sherry bottle had been drained. Wendy found a couple of bottles of Liebfraumilch and half a bottle of brandy in the sideboard. They too, soon disappeared as the two women reminisced over their times with their daughters. Inevitably, however, the discussion eventually got around to Brian.

'He assured me he'd left you,' said Stella. 'If I'd have known that wasn't true I'd never have got involved with him.'

'He's a such a liar,' hissed Wendy. 'To think I hated you when he left me. I assumed you'd both been carrying on behind my back. I was so hurt and upset.'

'You do believe me, don't you – that he told me he'd left you?'

'I do now. At the time I never dreamt Brian would ever cheat on me but now I realise there's very few depths he wouldn't sink to.'

'Really?' asked Stella somewhat curiously and sitting forward. 'What do you mean?'

Brian's secret lovechild was not something that Wendy had wanted anyone else to know about but, owing to the copious amount of alcohol she had consumed, she could not stop herself from telling Stella the whole sorry saga.

'That means he must have been carrying on with Christine while he was living with me!' gasped Stella. 'The swine! I know Christine,' she added 'Why she's not much older than Gemma.'

'Or Heather for that matter,' replied Wendy. She looked at Stella who suddenly looked deep in thought.

'What's up Stella? You've gone quite pale.'

Stella didn't answer. She began to shake.

'Stella! Stella! What's wrong? Is it something I've said?'

'Yes, yes. In a way. He never told me he'd been working in the vicarage gardens when Gemma was killed. He must have been just yards away from where she was found. How come the police didn't tell me that?'

'I dunno.'

'Oh God, I've just had the most awful thought,' said Stella. 'I don't want to believe it but now you've got me thinking the worst.'

Wendy sat forward.

'I was so pleased when he moved in with me and Gemma,' said Stella. 'My ex – Martin – was a brute. He knocked me around and he never had any time for Gemma. Brian seemed so different. He was gentle and kind. Not only that, he really bonded with Gemma and I was so pleased to think she had a father-figure in her life at last. They spent such a lot of time together – I guess he was missing Heather and Gemma became his substitute daughter.'

'You're right there,' agreed Wendy. 'That's what upset Heather so much. She was jealous that he didn't have time for her. She felt rejected. By the time Brian tried to build bridges with Heather she just wasn't interested any more. She didn't want to know.'

'Can't say I blame her,' said Stella. 'I know exactly how she felt. After a few months under my roof he spent more time with Gemma than he did with me. After a while though I noticed she would lock her bedroom door each evening whenever Brian was with her – and that's something she'd never done before.'

'Are you suggesting what I think you're suggesting?' asked Wendy.

'Well,' replied Stella, 'after you told me about Christine it makes me wonder. It seems he likes young women! I could never forgive myself if what I'm thinking might have happened really did. Gemma always seemed a happy girl but shortly before she died she seemed rather withdrawn.'

Stella began to weep.

'Oh Wendy, what if he did . . .?'

Wendy shuddered at the thought. Stella gazed intently at her.

'Your face Wendy – you're thinking the same, aren't you?'

Wendy didn't answer, trying instead to process the dreadful thoughts that were suddenly spinning around in her head. She recalled Brian telling her that he'd asked Gemma to speak to Heather. According to Brian, Gemma had agreed to do so.

But what if she hadn't? What if that had just been a story Brian had invented to deflect suspicion from himself? If Stella's hunch had any credibility Brian wouldn't have wanted Gemma anywhere near his daughter in case she exposed him. In such a situation, how far would Brian go to prevent her from doing so?

'Wendy?'

'Sorry! God Stella, what a thought! Do you really think Brian might be capable of such a thing?'

No sooner than the words left her mouth she realised that anyone, when backed into a corner, could be capable of committing the most horrendous of deeds. Brian had planted the seeds of doubt as to whether or not she had intentionally killed Sarah, thereby setting up a quandary that had tormented her ever since.

Having struggled with her conscience for so many weeks she had since decided not to hand herself in as she wanted to ensure she would be around to support Heather in the event she might eventually be found.

Furthermore, if she really believed Brian had been involved in Gemma's murder, she knew she should share her suspicions with Shepperton but, at the same time, she would run the significant risk that Brian could then reveal who was responsible for Sarah's death.

'We should go to the police, tell Shepperton what we know,' said Stella.

'No wait! Hang on a minute!' replied Wendy almost in a panic. 'I mean we don't know anything for sure do we? Let's not be too hasty. We need to think very carefully about what, if anything, we do next.'

Stella was unconvinced.

'We've gotta speak to Shepperton.'

Wendy pointed to the two empty Liebfraumilch bottles and the empty sherry and brandy bottles.

'Think about it Stella. If we turn up at the station tonight in the state we're both in, it's unlikely we'll be taken seriously. Anyway, it's Christmas Day, chances are Shepperton's not even on duty. He's probably assigned some junior lackey to work the Christmas shift in his place. We should at least wait until we've cleared our heads.'

Stella considered Wendy's point of view for a moment.

'Guess you're right,' she said. 'Another few hours shouldn't make much difference. 'Okay, let's wait until the morning.'

She looked at her watch.

'Oh my God, is that the time? I'd better be getting back home.'

'Seriously?' said Wendy. 'You reckon you're gonna drive home in that state? No, you'd best stay over here. You can have the bed in the spare room.'

An hour later Wendy clambered into her bed and switched off the bedside light. Sleep though was never a possibility with so many thoughts spinning around in her head. She could never have imagined when she got up that morning that *'that woman'* would be sleeping in her spare bedroom. Turns out she wasn't the ogre Wendy had imagined her to be. Under different circumstances they might even have been friends.

Wendy realised that Stella hadn't exactly had an easy life. An abusive husband and then having to raise a teenage girl on her own while holding down two part-time jobs could not have been easy for her.

Brian could be a smooth talker when he chose to be. Not only that, he was quite good-looking and, since his mid-life crisis, he liked to dress flashily. Maybe it was understandable that Stella fell for his lies that he and Wendy were no longer together.

But what about Gemma? Was it really possible that Brian had behaved so inappropriately while under Stella's roof? Was he really a pervert? Throughout their marriage Wendy had never spotted any indications of such a trait but, then again, people of such persuasions often hide in plain sight.

Then there was Christine. As Stella said, she was barely older than Heather and Gemma when she became pregnant with Brian's baby. Wendy shuddered at the thought she may have been sharing her life with a man who had such an inappropriate interest in young women.

Suddenly, a dreadful thought hit her, making her sit bolt upright in her bed. *If* that were the case, *if* Gemma had been killed by Brian to silence her, to prevent her from revealing what kind of man he really was, could he have behaved similarly with

Heather? What if he had killed Heather too? What if all his displays of grief had all been an act to cover up for what he had done?

Wendy even began to question whether or not his bid to kill himself had been an extreme attempt to deflect suspicion from himself or, maybe, the result of a guilty conscience. Either way Brian had been fortunate to survive.

Wendy realised she was sweating and shaking. If Brian had been abusing their daughter, why hadn't Heather confided in her? They had such a close relationship. Surely Heather would have said something? Or had she been too ashamed to reveal what might have been going on?

The possibility that she had failed as a mother – having not noticed what may have been going on between her husband and daughter – was too much to bear. Wendy got up and quietly, so as not to wake Stella, crept downstairs and went into the kitchen. She made herself a cup of strong black coffee and sat in the lounge with a blanket wrapped her, miserably staring at the photograph of her beloved daughter on the sideboard.

Maybe Stella was right. Maybe they should speak to Shepperton. Then Wendy recalled the time she and Brian had been called in to see him – the day Shepperton had informed them that they had put the investigation into Heather's disappearance onto the back burner in order to concentrate on Gemma's death. Brian had been inconsolable. If he had been faking his distress at that time she had to admit it had been a most convincing performance.

With this in mind, and despite her disgust of Brian's behaviour, Wendy decided it was not the right time to talk to the police – at least not until she'd had the chance to confront her estranged husband with her suspicions face to face herself.

Meanwhile, upstairs, Stella was still awake. Not normally one to drink, her head was thumping but, at least, she had come to a decision. Someone had to pay for Gemma's death. Whether or not Wendy agreed, in the morning she was going to speak to Shepperton.

14

'At the end of the day Mr Brown it all seems to keep coming back to you, doesn't it?'

'This is crazy, absolutely ludicrous!' declared Brian, glaring at Shepperton. 'Do you honestly think I'd ever have hurt a hair on Gemma or Heather's heads? I loved them both.'

Brian had been summoned to come to the police station the day after Stella had reported her suspicions early on Boxing Day. Wendy, however, had chosen not to accompany her, reasoning that, on reflection, she could not believe – or maybe did not want to consider the possibility – that the man she had married would be capable of such heinous acts.

As Stella had slept in the spare room Wendy had laid in bed with, like Stella, a thumping headache. Unable to sleep she tossed and turned, her mind in a turmoil. Through the night she reflected on the times she and Brian had sobbed their hearts out since Heather's disappearance – those times, she decided, had been genuine displays of grief. If Brian had been faking his emotions he was a superb actor.

Furthermore, she recalled how he had covered for her over Sarah's death and how he had disposed of her car to destroy any possible evidence that may have incriminated her. If he really had been involved in Gemma's death it would have been easy for him to pin the blame on his estranged wife bearing in mind he knew exactly what had happened to Sarah.

Furthermore, when Bradley had claimed he had killed the girls, Brian had been swift to suggest the lad was innocent when he could have so easily fed him to the wolves.

Wendy and Stella had risen early on Boxing Day and, over breakfast, Wendy explained why she could not find it in her heart to accompany Stella to the police station. Stella, however, remained determined to share her suspicions with Shepperton but, thankfully, as far as Wendy was concerned, she had taken Wendy's decision with good grace.

'Where is all this coming from?' demanded Brian as his patience was running out.

'We are merely following up on information that has recently come to light,' replied Shepperton as the interview entered its second hour.

'What information? Who have you been speaking to?'

'Mr Brown,' interrupted Shepperton, 'I am interviewing you, not the other way around. Please just concentrate on answering the questions I am putting to you.'

Flustered, Brian suddenly stood up, sending his chair toppling over as he did so.

'I'm not putting up with this!' he snapped. 'I've had enough. You seem to forget my daughter is missing, maybe dead. Is this really the way you want to treat a grieving father? Am I under arrest? If not, I'm out of here!'

'Please, Mr Brown, sit down. No, you are not under arrest – you are free to go whenever you wish – but you must understand we are obliged to investigate any suspicions that are raised if we are to succeed in finding Gemma's killer or what has happened to your daughter. If you really have nothing to hide you should do all you can to help us to eliminate you from our enquiries.'

Brian exhaled. He knew Shepperton had a point. Reluctantly he picked up his chair and sat down again as requested.

'Perhaps,' said Shepperton, 'you might like to enlighten me as to why Gemma began to lock her bedroom door shortly before she died and why she had been so subdued. I understand you spent quite a lot of time in that room, alone with Gemma.'

'Ah, now I get it!' said Brian. 'This must have come from Stella. She's the only other person who would have known Gemma locked her door. What's she been suggesting? That I'd been doing something I shouldn't to Gemma?'

Shepperton never replied.

'It *was* Stella wasn't it? Jeez, how could she even suggest such a thing? That's disgusting! That's not why Gemma locked her door. It was nothing like that at all!'

Shepperton sat forward.

'Is that so? Perhaps then Mr Brown, you might be able to explain, then maybe we could clear this up.'

Brian shook his head.

'Sorry Shepperton, I can't. I made Gemma a promise. She confided in me and I swore I'd never tell a soul.'

Shepperton was in no mood to compromise.

'You need to realise you are a prime suspect in a murder Mr Brown. Breaking your alleged promise to Gemma can't hurt her now but, if you cannot provide me with a believable reason for Gemma's behaviour leading up to her death you can understand why we need to take certain suspicions raised against you far more seriously. It's in your interest to provide me with any information that can eliminate you from our inquiry so that we can concentrate on other leads. The ball's in your court now.'

Brian looked Shepperton in the face.

'I can't, I can't . . .' he replied. 'I promised Gemma.'

'If, as you claim,' said Shepperton, 'you had no part in Gemma's death Mr Brown, I assume you would want the guilty party to be brought to justice,'

'Yes, of course.'

'Help us then,' urged the detective. 'Tell us all you can. That's the only thing you can do for her now. Tell me why Gemma suddenly began to lock her door, why she was so subdued before she died.'

Brian appeared a broken man. He placed his head in his hands and agonised how to respond. After a considerable period of time he came to a decision. It was time to share Gemma's secret after all. Shepperton had a point – it was the right thing to do – to help the police in their quest to bring Gemma's killer to justice.

'I'm gonna need a drink first.'

Shepperton nodded. Det Con James Clarke, who had been sitting alongside Shepperton on the interview, got up and filled a paper cup with water from the dispenser in the corner of the room. He passed it to Brian. With shaking hands, Brian put the cup to his lips and took a swig. He wiped his lips with the back of his hand, composed himself, then began to talk.

'Contrary to what you may think,' he said, 'Gemma and I had a wonderfully close and innocent relationship which was such a comfort to me bearing in mind my own daughter had made it clear she didn't want any contact with me. I can't blame her for that after the way I left her and my wife to be with Stella. After a while though, I think Stella resented the closeness of my relationship with Gemma.

'Stella was a good mum but she had a tendency to be judgemental. That's why Gemma would often confide in me rather than her mother. She knew I would keep anything she told me to myself.

'I think it must have been towards the end of July that I found her in tears on the landing. I asked her what was wrong and she told me something dreadful had happened. We went into her room and she closed the door. Stella was downstairs watching TV. I sat next to Gemma on her bed. I put my arm around her shoulders and swore I would keep anything she wanted to tell me to myself.

'She was in a terrible state, sobbing and shaking. Eventually, she told me why. She was pregnant. I was shocked. She was only 16 and she was so scared. She knew she was far too young to be a mother and she'd had plans to go to college. She couldn't see how she could follow her dreams with a baby in tow. She was desperate to get rid of the baby and she begged me to help her.

'At first I didn't know what to say, though I knew it would be expensive for her to have an abortion and, because of her age, I knew there would be questions asked as to how she found herself in such a condition.

'I told her I was not in a position financially to help her. I suggested she saw the pregnancy through – to have the baby and that Stella and I would support her in any way we could but she was desperate to keep the news from her mother. She begged me not to tell Stella.

'It's true Gemma locked her door from then on – usually because I was with her and she didn't want her mum walking in and hearing what we were talking about. I spent hours in that room trying to persuade Gemma to tell me who the father of her baby was but she wouldn't tell me because he was a married man. I was disgusted that a man would take advantage of her but she was adamant that she didn't want to identify him.'

Shepperton looked at Brian.

'Rather ironic that, isn't it?' he said, 'bearing in mind what you've been up to.'

Brian ignored Shepperton's observation.

'As I was saying, Gemma was in a desperate state. Then, one evening, she beckoned me to follow her into her room. She sounded a little more upbeat. That's when she told me that she'd found a way to finance a termination. Again, she didn't want to say how. I assumed that, maybe, the married man may have agreed to put up the cash in order to prevent his wife from finding out what he'd been up to.'

Clarke, who had been silent throughout most of the interview, could hold his tongue no longer.

'For Christ's sake Brown,' he exploded, 'why didn't you tell us this when you reported Gemma missing? This is vital information. That's a man with a motive. Have you any idea at all who he might be?'

'No.'

Clarke stood up, obviously furious. Brian looked at Shepperton who was shaking his head in disbelief.

'I can't believe you've held this information back from us,' he said. 'Assuming you are telling us the truth, this is something we needed to know from the start.'

'It *is* the truth,' stressed Brian. 'I wouldn't make something like this up.'

'Quite honestly Mr Brown,' declared Shepperton, 'I'm not sure what I can believe from you at the moment.'

Clarke was at this point, poring through some paperwork.

'According to Gemma's autopsy,' he said, 'she was not a virgin but there's nothing here to suggest she'd ever been pregnant.'

Shepperton too began to pore through his paperwork.

'I thought so,' he said, speaking to Clarke. 'After Gemma had been found I called Mr Brown and Mrs Gooding in. When I told them Gemma was not a virgin they both claimed it was impossible – that there must have been a mistake. Yet here we are, all this time later and Mr Brown is sitting here telling us that Gemma had been pregnant shortly before she was murdered.'

He looked accusingly at Brian.

'In other words Mr Brown, you lied! You withheld vital information.'

'I had to,' blubbed Brian. 'I'd made Gemma a promise. She didn't want Stella to know.'

'You seem to harbour a lot of secrets Brown,' replied Shepperton, notably omitting his previous polite form of address – a point which Brian immediately noticed. Shepperton and Clarke's demeanour had noticeably hardened towards him. Brian shuffled awkwardly on his chair.

'Can I go now?' he asked with more than a hint of embarrassment. 'I've told you all I can.'

'Yeah, but don't be surprised if we need to talk to you again,' replied Clarke. 'Who knows what else you've neglected to tell us? Make sure you remain available for interview if ever we need you.'

Brian stood up, eager to leave the station as soon as he could. However, as he was about to leave the room Shepperton could not stop himself from offering a final sarcastic parting shot.

'If your daughters could see you now Brown, they'd be so proud.'

Brian swung around, a puzzled look on his face.

'Daughters? Daughters? What do you mean?'

'Christine Palmer gave birth in March. You have a baby daughter, didn't you know?'

Shell-shocked, Brian faced the detective open-mouthed.

'I told her to get rid of it! No-one told me! Why has no-one told me? I have a right to see my baby.'

'Not possible I'm afraid,' said Shepperton. 'Christine gave the baby up for adoption soon after giving birth.'

'What? How is that possible? How could she do that without telling me? Surely that's against the law?'

'Christine was quite within her rights to do so,' countered Shepperton. 'She's done nothing illegal. Anyway, that's a civil matter, not a criminal one. We have far bigger fish to fry. Not only that Brown, you have just escaped a charge of sexual contact with a minor by the skin of your teeth. Do the maths – Christine is just 18 years of age. The legal age of consent is 16. She was barely of age when you took advantage of her.'

'But she *looked* much older than that,' replied Brian defensively as if he was offering a valid excuse for his actions. 'How was I to know? I've not done anything illegal.'

'*Legally* maybe,' replied Shepperton with a disgusted look on his face. 'Morally though,' he added: 'I'll leave that to you and your conscience to decide.'

15

Sitting around at home most of the time was proving detrimental to Wendy's state of mind. She badly needed something to occupy her time, something to distract her from all that had been happening. One morning while soaking herself in her bath she decided it was time to return to work. Her mood lifted immediately as she dressed. Geraldine had telephoned the previous afternoon, suggesting she might call in for a chat after school.

Wendy had been pleased to hear from her friend and suggested Geraldine call in the next evening. Having come to a decision Wendy intended to broach the subject over coffee with her closest friend. The two women went back years and had always got on well so, throughout the day, Wendy had been looking forward to catching up with her most valued friend.

Shortly before five o'clock the doorbell rang. Wendy hurried to let in her guest and greeted her with a warm hug. It was only when she stepped back to allow Geraldine to come inside that she noticed her guest had been crying.

'Geri, whatever's the matter? Come on in.'

'I'm so sorry to barge in like this,' said Geraldine, 'but there's something I need to tell you face-to-face. I don't want you to hear it from the papers or from anyone else.'

'Jeez, whatever can it be that's upset you so much?'

'It's Harry,' blubbed Geraldine. 'He's in trouble. Big trouble.'

Wendy prayed Geraldine had not spotted her obvious relief that it was not bad news about Heather. She guided Geraldine into the lounge and sat her down.

'What's happened?'

'The trustees at the hospital have suspended him with immediate effect while they carry out an investigation,' sobbed

Geraldine. 'He came home earlier than usual last night and I could tell immediately that something really bad had happened. It was awful Wendy. I've never seen him cry before. That job means everything to him and now he's saying he might never be able to go back. He reckons he's gonna be struck off. I don't know what to do. Soon after lunch today he was taken to the police station for questioning and I haven't heard anything from him since. I'm so worried.'

Wendy put her arm around her friend's shoulder.

'What's he supposed to have done?'

'I'm not sure I can tell you. If it's true it's so awful.'

'Look Geri, you don't have to tell me anything if you don't want to. Just sit there for a mo and I'll put the kettle on.'

As Wendy waited for the kettle to boil she recalled the time Heather had disappeared – a time when everyone seemed to believe a cup of tea would put the world right. It never did, of course. She filled a couple of cups and returned to Geraldine in the lounge.

'Thanks,' said Geraldine as she wiped her eyes. 'Of course I have to tell you 'cos you'll probably hear about it soon enough bearing in mind Harry's high-profile. He's been accused of carrying out illegal abortions for payment.'

Wendy was astonished.

'But that's ridiculous!' she declared. 'Harry would never do such a thing . . . would he?'

'Apparently,' sobbed Geraldine, 'he's done it before. I dragged it out of him last night. The stupid fool! I mean, why on earth would he risk such a well-paid position just to earn a few extra quid? Oh Wendy, we could lose everything! And what if he ends up in jail? Oh, the disgrace of it all, I can't bear it!'

Wendy didn't know what to say. After all, if Harry had admitted to Geraldine what he'd done, his career – and probably his freedom – would very soon come to an end. Her heart went out to Geraldine, someone who had always been a shoulder to cry on whenever she had needed her. Somehow, she thought, this didn't seem to be the ideal time to suggest a time to return to work. That, quite obviously, would have to wait until a later date.

The women sat on the settee as, over the following hour, Geraldine poured out her heart, even revealing that her so-called perfect marriage had not been all it had seemed for some time.

'I never would have guessed Geri. I always thought you were both so happy and perfectly suited. After all, how many years have you been married?'

'Nearly 20.'

'Thought so. You were together when we first met.'

'Hmm, yes,' said Geraldine. 'What you didn't know at the time is that we had only just got back together. We split up for a while a couple of years after we married.'

Wendy was astonished.

'Really? I had no idea.'

'It's true,' said Geraldine. 'You know I've always wanted a child, don't you?'

'Yes, of course. I remember you telling me so when Heather was born. I assumed there was some medical issue that was perhaps preventing you from conceiving.'

'Not with me,' said Geraldine, 'I had tests that showed the problem wasn't with me – it was supposedly Harry. He told me he'd had a test and that the problem was down to him.'

'Is that why you split up?'

'No,' replied Geraldine, shaking her head. 'It was far worse than that. One day our neighbour's daughter came round. She was crying and demanding to see Harry. Turns out he'd been sleeping with her and had made her pregnant. See Wendy, it wasn't because he couldn't have a child with me. It must have been because he didn't want one. Another lie.

'I was furious he'd been lying to me so I chucked him out. It was only afterwards that I joined the dots. I realised how furtively he'd been behaving, making excuses for returning home late from work and so on. I reckon they'd been carrying on for months before I found out what had been happening.'

Wendy was shocked. She had never considered Harry to be the unfaithful kind. Now she realised she hardly knew him at all.

'But you took him back. Why?'

'He swore he'd never let me down again. Of course I didn't really believe him but, if I'd never got back with him I'd have lost that lovely home and the fantastic lifestyle we had owing to his income. To be honest with you, I couldn't face losing it all.'

That, thought Wendy, was typical of Geraldine – putting her perceived status above anything else. However, as shocked as she had been by Geraldine's revelations, there was one more to come – something which was about to turn Shepperton's investigation into a completely new direction. Over the following minutes, husbands – or their limitations – dominated their conversation but Wendy, who until that evening considered she knew Geraldine inside out, felt she was still holding something back.

'There's something else, isn't there? I can tell.'

Geraldine nodded.

'Yes, but before I tell you, I need a drink. Have you got any of that brandy left?'

Wendy fetched an unopened bottle from her sideboard – she'd stocked up since the heavy session with Stella. She poured out a couple of glasses and handed one over to Geraldine who downed it in one gulp.

'Okay,' she said. 'You're not gonna like this Wendy but, if I'm right I've got some information that'll blow Shepperton's socks off.'

'You have information?' gasped Wendy.

'Well, a suspicion at least,' replied Geraldine. 'I told you how Harry had been behaving when he was cheating on me. Over recent weeks I've spotted the signs again – you never truly forget once it's happened before. I could tell something was up so I confronted him after he told me he'd been suspended. I asked him outright if he'd been cheating on me again.'

'Gosh,' said Wendy. 'What did he say?'

'Well, he denied it, of course. Swore he'd learnt his lesson years ago. Said he'd never been unfaithful to me since. I don't believe him. I'm sure he's been carrying on with that pretty young PA of his. He's been coming home late, sometimes not at all.'

'Maybe he's just been very busy,' suggested Wendy.

'Yeah, sure,' said Geraldine mockingly. 'Trust me, I know a cheat when I see one. Last night, he broke down crying. That's when he told me someone had been blackmailing him, threatening to expose him over the illegal abortions.

'I knew he'd been taking money out of the account but he always made some excuse. I suspected he might be using it for hotel bills. Some nights he claimed to have worked all night. I wasn't so sure but last night he admitted the money had been withdrawn to get the blackmailer off his back.'

'Who would do such a thing?' asked Wendy. 'Do you have any idea?'

'No, at least not for sure. He told me he'd already paid what had been demanded but he was so scared that one day they'd demand more cash.'

'So what makes you think this could be linked to Shepperton's investigation?' asked Wendy.

'Think about it Wendy. You told me that Gemma had been pregnant and that she had asked Brian to help her get an abortion. What if she asked Harry to help her instead? What if, somehow, she'd found out what Harry had been up to and had blackmailed him? I mean, if that's what happened, who knows how far Harry might have gone to protect himself?'

16

To the outside world the Abbotts appeared to have an idyllic life. Both had good, well-paid jobs, a lovely home, two top of the range cars, and they had enjoyed expensive holidays – the trappings of wealth, the stuff of dreams to most people. However, little did they know it was all a facade as life behind the doors of The Willows was anything but perfect.

Trust between the couple seemed to be a thing of the past. No matter how she tried Geraldine could not erase the pictures in her mind of her husband and his lover's relationship at the early stages of their marriage. Meanwhile, Harry had, correctly as it happened, suspicions of his own that Geraldine may have been enjoying the company of another man – or men – at times during the intervening years. Prior to leaving Wendy's Geraldine admitted to the occasional fling.

'Our relationship flat-lined years ago Wendy but we all need to feel loved from time to time, don't we?' she said, while adding that, to her knowledge, Harry had no idea.

'I've had to be very careful,' she added. 'If Harry found out I could lose everything.'

It was in the early hours of the morning that Harry returned home, having been charged and bailed. Miserably, he took off his coat and scarf and hung them up on the hallway stand. After removing his shoes he crept up the stairs and entered his bedroom – he and Geraldine had, long since, been sleeping separately.

Once undressed he clambered into his bed. Sleep, however, was not an option. He laid, staring at the ceiling, wondering why he had been so reckless and dreading what the future had in store for him.

In the adjacent room Geraldine was also awake. She'd heard her husband returning but was in no mood to interact with him.

Love had long left The Willows. Money was the only reason Geraldine had remained under the same roof.

While Stella had been unable to convince Wendy to report her suspicions about Brian to Shepperton. Geraldine was a completely different animal. Mid-morning the next day she entered Somersley police station and asked to speak to Shepperton.

A few hours later a police car pulled up on the driveway of The Willows and two police officers got out and rang the doorbell. The door was answered by a haggard Harry. Unshaved, he looked a shadow of the normally immaculately turned-out gynaecologist who, until the previous day, had been practically revered at Somersley General Hospital.

'We need you to come back to the station with us Mr Abbott. There's been further developments.'

'I . . . I don't understand. What developments?'

'DCI Shepperton will explain when you get there. Please, Mr Abbott, get your coat.'

'I really don't understand why I'm back here,' said Harry as he faced Shepperton once more in the interview room. 'I thought all that needed to be said was said last night. I don't have anything to add.'

Shepperton, sitting alongside Det Con James Clarke, withdrew a packet of Benson and Hedges from his jacket pocket. He offered one to Clarke, who turned it down, then offered a cigarette to Harry who accepted. Shepperton flicked his lighter and took a deep drag, then handed the lighter to Harry.

'It was a long night, wasn't it Mr Abbott? I'm sure you must be very tired. I know I am.'

Harry took a drag and nodded.

'It wasn't an experience I'd like to repeat,' he replied – an understatement if ever there was one, adding: 'What's this all about?'

Shepperton pressed the Record button on the tape recorder sitting in front of him and introduced himself, Clarke and Harry to the tape. He then recorded the time and the interview began.

'Certain information has come to light, Mr Abbott. Perhaps you might like to begin with telling us all you know about the death of young Gemma Gooding.'

Harry certainly hadn't seen that coming. He sat open-mouthed. His face went pale. Clarke thought he looked as if he was about to faint. For a moment Harry said nothing. Then, after taking a long drag on his cigarette, he gazed directly at Shepperton.

'You're kidding me aren't you?' he said, barely able to disguise his anger. 'You mean that poor kid who got killed down by the canal? All I know is what I've read in the papers and heard on the radio and telly. What on earth makes you think I'd know anything about her murder?'

'So,' replied Shepperton calmly, 'you're telling us you never met her. That you didn't know her?'

'That's *exactly* what I'm saying Shepperton. How could you even think I'd had anything to do with it? My wife knew her. She was a pupil at Somersley Secondary. Otherwise, all I know about the girl is what my wife has told me. She reckoned she was a good kid. It's terrible, the way she died – but it was nothing to do with me. My God, you're really clutching at straws now, aren't you. No wonder you're no nearer finding out who killed her!'

Clarke, noticing Shepperton looked as if he was about to retaliate with a few choice words of his own, intervened.

'Gemma Gooding was only 16 Mr Abbott.'

'So, what about it?'

'We believe she may have been pregnant and that someone helped her abort her baby. We suspect that someone might have been you Mr Abbott. After all, from what we discovered yesterday, it appears you were the go-to-guy around here for that sort of thing.'

'Well, it certainly wasn't me!' snapped Harry.

'Tell me then Mr Abbott, 'would you like to tell me where you were on Saturday, 29th August, 1987.'

'Good God man,' said Harry, 'how the hell would you expect me to answer that? It's more than a year ago. I couldn't tell you where I was last month. I bet you couldn't either. What's so special about that date?'

'It's when Gemma Gooding's body was found,' replied Shepperton.

'This is ridiculous!' said Harry, adding: 'I've had enough of this. I'm saying nothing more until my solicitor is present!'

'Very well, Mr Abbott,' replied Shepperton who, having stopped the tape recorder, turned to his colleague, said: 'Get a search warrant James. I want Mr Abbott's home, all outbuildings, his car and garden searched with a fine toothcomb. I want no stone left unturned. I have a feeling there's a lot more Mr Abbott isn't telling us.'

'I had nothing to do with that poor girl's murder, I swear!' blurted out a panic-stricken Harry.

'Well,' replied Shepperton, 'if you have I promise you we'll soon find out.'

Later that day the search of The Willows was in full swing as officers in white overalls meticulously made their way from room to room, opening drawers, poring through diaries, and emptying cupboards systematically as their search progressed.

Other officers concentrated on the outbuildings and garden while two more began to pull Harry's car apart.

Towards the evening Shepperton arrived on the scene, hoping something of evidential value had been unearthed. He was disappointed to be informed that no items had been found to link Harry with Gemma's murder. Having put on a white suit and shoe coverings Shepperton entered the property and began to look around.

'Where's Mrs Abbott?' he asked.

'She decided not to stay,' replied one of the officers. 'She's gone to stay at a friend's.'

'Who might that be?'

'Mrs Brown, the missing girl's mother.'

Geraldine had indeed, left home the moment the police arrived to search The Willows. She turned up on Wendy's doorstep, appearing most upset.

'Oh Geri, come on in,' said Wendy. 'What's happened now?'

Geraldine explained she had spoken to Shepperton and, as a result, Harry was now at the police station being questioned.

'They must suspect something,' she told Wendy. 'Why else would they be turning our home upside down?'

'I still can't believe Harry would be involved in Gemma's murder,' said Wendy. 'I've known him too long to think he could ever do such a thing.'

'Well,' replied Geraldine, 'would you ever have believed he would get himself involved in illegal abortions?'

Wendy shook her head.

'Guess you've got a point there. I can't think why he'd risk his career like that. I mean, you're both well paid. I can't think why he'd do it.'

'Gambling.'

'Pardon?'

'Gambling – Harry's a compulsive gambler. Poker. It's driven a wedge between us for years – that coupled with his affair has made our marriage a sham. It turns out he owes thousands Wendy.'

'Oh my God Geri, I had no idea!'

'Well, it's hardly something I wanted to shout from the rooftops.'

'No, I guess not,' said Wendy. 'What are you going to do?'

'I don't know. I don't fancy going back home at the moment.'

'Then stay here with me,' said Wendy. 'You can have the spare room. Stay as long as you need to.'

Geraldine smiled appreciatively.

'You may like to reconsider that offer,' she said. 'Think about it. If Harry has been involved in what happened to Gemma and Heather, would you really want me under your roof?'

Wendy reassuringly squeezed Geraldine's hand.

'You've always been there for me Geri – through the worst imaginable times. You're my best friend. I really don't know how I could have got through everything without your support. Now it's my turn to help you.'

Their conversation was interrupted by the doorbell. Wendy peered through the curtains.

'It's Shepperton.'

'Oh God, what does he want?' groaned Geraldine.

Wendy went into the hall and opened the front door.

'Hello Mrs Brown. Is Mrs Abbott still with you?'

'Yes detective. You'd better come on in.'

Shepperton followed Wendy into the lounge. He looked awkwardly at Geraldine.

'Mrs Abbott, I'm sorry we've had to put you through all this.'

'It's okay,' replied Geraldine, albeit most unconvincingly. 'I guess you have to do what you have to do.'

'I wanted to inform you that our officers will be continuing their search through the night and into tomorrow. You may like to arrange somewhere to stay for the time being.'

'It's okay,' said Wendy, 'she's gonna stay here with me.'

Shepperton nodded.

'That's good. I'm sorry to have bothered you.'

He turned to leave. Wendy led him into the hallway and had just opened the door as her telephone rang. Shepperton turned and thanked her.

'I'll leave you to your call. Bye for now.'

Wendy closed the door behind him and answered the telephone.

'Mrs Brown?

'Yes.'

'This is Detective Constable James Clarke. Is DCI Shepperton with you? It's urgent.'

'Hang on, he's just left. Just a sec.'

Shepperton was about to get into his car as Wendy called out to him. He came back inside.

'Sorry about this,' he said as he picked up the receiver. Moments later he put it down again bearing a most serious expression.

'That,' he said, 'was very interesting.'

'Why?' asked Geraldine. 'What's happened?'

'Something has been found in your husband's office Mrs Abbott,' replied Shepperton, adding: 'As a result he's now got some *very* serious explaining to do.'

17

'Wen, have you heard the news?'

Had Wendy known it had been Brian telephoning her she would not have picked up the receiver.

'What news Brian?'

'It was on the radio. Just now. They've arrested someone. They reckon he might have had something to do with Gemma's murder.'

'Oh that. Yes I know.'

'I wonder who it could be.'

'It's Harry Abbott.'

'What? Harry? Are you sure? It can't be!'

'It is. Geraldine told me yesterday that she was gonna turn him in.'

'So you knew but you never thought to tell me?'

'Hurts, doesn't it – you know, when someone keeps things from you? I know too that your baby was adopted soon after Christine gave birth. Reverend Palmer told me.'

'When? When did he tell you that? Shepperton's only just told me! Why didn't *you* tell me?'

'I bumped into Reverend Palmer in St Mary's a few weeks ago. Now you know Brian how hurtful it is when people keep secrets from you.'

'What else did he tell you? Did he tell you where the baby is?'

'No, he doesn't know. One thing's for sure though – he's certainly not your biggest fan. I can't think why.'

'Oh come on Wen, don't be like that. This has gone on long enough. Anyway, from what I've just heard from Clarke, you and Bradley have been talking to him, telling him that Heather really was pregnant. Seems you can keep secrets from me too.

'Did you not think I should have known first? Look, I can understand why you're mad at me. I really can but it's no use carrying on like this. After all we've both done things – really bad things – that we regret, haven't we? Can't we just bury the hatchet?'

'How can I?' replied Wendy, 'when all I can think about is what you might have been getting up to with Gemma in her room – and maybe even Heather for all I know.'

'Oh for God's sake Wen! Do you honestly think that's the kind of guy I am? You've known me since we were in our teens. Surely you must know me better than that? What happened with Christine should never have happened. Look, I was both stupid and weak to get involved with her, I admit that, but you taught her. Tell me she didn't look considerably older than she really was. I bet you can't.'

Brian had a point, though Wendy was struggling to accept it.

'That's hardly an excuse Brian.'

'I know. Like I said, I was stupid and weak but I've had to pay for it. I know what you, Shepperton and the Palmers must think of me. I've put Christine through hell and now I've just discovered I've got a baby I'll never see. Trust me Wen, no-one could possibly hate me more now than I hate myself.'

'Well, that's your fault Brian isn't it?'

'Yes. Yes it is. Totally. So, what are you gonna do Wen? Are you gonna hate me for ever or can't you just give me a break? Can't we at least meet up sometime for a civilised chat?'

'I dunno.'

'Please Wen! Just a chat.'

Wendy thought for a moment.

'Okay, but on one condition – you don't tell Stella. She's been through enough.'

'Really? I thought you couldn't stand her.'

'So did I – until we spent Christmas together. That's when we found out we had more in common that we thought – in particular, we'd both been lied to and badly let down by you.'

On the other end of the line Brian was flabbergasted to learn that his wife and his former mistress had actually spent time together – and particularly on Christmas Day. How, he thought, could that ever have been possible?

'Are you still there? Have we got a deal then?' asked Wendy after a long silence.

'I'll do whatever it takes if it could patch things up between us,' he replied. 'I know we've said it before but I reckon we need each other now more than ever.'

Back at the police station Shepperton and Clarke were huddled together in Shepperton's office. Shepperton picked up his telephone.

'Has Mr Abbott's brief arrived yet?'

He had.

'Good,' said Shepperton. 'Get Mr Abbott back into the interview room ASAP.'

Moments later a pale-faced Harry, accompanied by his solicitor, Mr Mayhew, entered the interview room. Shepperton gestured to them both to sit down opposite himself and Clarke. Shepperton set the tape recorder to Record and introduced everyone present to the tape.

'Mr Abbott,' he said, 'perhaps you might like to explain this.'

Shepperton placed a pendant enclosed in a see-through plastic evidence bag onto the table.

'That's Geraldine's,' replied Harry.

'Is that so?' said Clarke, 'because it perfectly matches Gemma's missing pendant. See? It's got her initial G inscribed on it.'

'Well,' said Harry defensively, 'it seems you've forgotten my wife's name. Tell you what, I'll give you a clue, it begins with a G.'

'Very amusing Mr Abbott,' said Clarke. 'If that's the case I take it your wife will have no problem in identifying this piece of jewellery as her own?'

Harry looked at his solicitor then back at Clarke.

'Of course not. Like I say, it belongs to my wife.'

Shepperton interjected.

'Mrs Gooding purchased a pendant as a present for Gemma's 16th birthday. She bought it from Ramsey's, the jewellers in the High Street. She's just brought in the receipt and we have checked with the jewellers. They have confirmed this to be the pendant Mrs Gooding purchased for her daughter.'

Harry was about to answer but his solicitor was quick to interrupt.

'DCI Shepperton, is that really the best you can do? Are you suggesting that this pendant here is the only one of its kind? My client has told you, this is his wife's pendant. Who knows, she may even have purchased it from Ramsey's herself. You have no proof that this pendant ever belonged to Gemma Gooding.'

Shepperton looked at Clarke. He knew Mayhew had a point. Furthermore, the pendant had been examined for fingerprints. Only Harry and Geraldine's prints had been found. None of Gemma's had been identified. However, the detectives had another card to play.

'Mr Mayhew, Mr Abbott,' said Shepperton, 'you may like to know that later today this pendant will be examined by a forensic scientist. If there is any trace of this pendant having been in contact with Gemma Gooding you can expect to be charged with her murder. Do I make myself clear?'

Shepperton thumped his fist on the table in front of Harry, initially startling his suspect. Harry, however, quickly recovered his composure.

'I can assure you DCI Shepperton, you will find nothing to suggest Gemma has ever been in contact with my wife's pendant. Why, you've said yourselves that only my fingerprints and those of my wife's are on it. What possible way could you prove otherwise?'

Shepperton, this time speaking calmly, explained.

'Have you ever heard of DNA?'

Harry nodded.

'In that case,' said Shepperton, 'you will be aware that it's a relatively new process. Like a fingerprint, everyone has their own DNA. Every time you touch something you leave a trace of your own DNA. It's not visible to the naked eye but laboratory tests can reveal its presence. If Gemma Gooding has been in contact with this pendant, DNA examination will confirm it.

'As I said, it's a new scientific tool at our disposal. It was first used to prosecute a criminal case a couple of years ago and, thanks to its discovery, many previously unsolved cases have now been successfully cleared up.

'So tell me – are you still insisting this pendant is not Gemma Gooding's 'cos, believe me, if the genetic test results come back with a positive trace in a few weeks' time we will know for certain that you are responsible for her death.'

At this point the detectives ended the interview. Without any further evidence against Harry they had no option other than to let him go. Shepperton now needed to speak to Geraldine. A car was despatched to Wendy's to pick her up.

Meanwhile Harry was relieved to leave the station. Having been caught out carrying out unauthorised abortions, the last thing he needed was to be considered as the main suspect in a murder case. At least, he thought, once Geraldine sees the pendant, she could clear everything up once and for all. Unfortunately, however, Harry's confidence was about to be shattered.

'What, Mrs Abbott, can you tell me about this?' asked Shepperton as he slid the clear plastic envelope containing the pendant across the table towards Geraldine.

'Oh that! Harry gave it to me for my birthday,' she said. 'I wasn't impressed. Our marriage was on its knees and he thought some cheap piece of jewellery would help him worm his way back into my affections. I threw it back at him. I told him I'd never be seen wearing something as tacky as that!'

The detectives looked at each other.

'When was this?' asked Clarke.

'September 3rd,' replied Geraldine.

'Last September?' asked Shepperton.

'No, it was the previous year, 1987.'

Clarke's face dropped.

'Are you thinking what I'm thinking?' he asked Shepperton.

'I certainly am' said Shepperton. 'That's just five days after Gemma was murdered.'

It had been a long day. Tired, Shepperton stopped the tape. He and Clarke excused themselves and left Geraldine in the interview room with an officer while they took a break for a coffee and a brief consultation. Both were frustrated. They both felt the net was closing in on Harry Abbott but each knew that the recently established Crown Prosecution Service would not consider taking the matter further without a good deal more evidence against him.

'It's gotta be him, hasn't it?' said Clarke.

Shepperton, deep in thought, did not answer. Instead, he flicked through his notes as he paced around his office. Letting Harry walk went against every instinct he had but he had no choice.

'We need more,' he said eventually. 'But it's no good moping around here. Let's get cracking. I want everything we can find about Abbott's finances – every tiny detail. I want to know all about his career, his friends, acquaintances, business interests if he has any. I want the lot.'

'There's something else,' said Clarke. 'If Heather Brown was pregnant and wanted rid of the baby, who would she go to? Abbott maybe?'

'There could be link,' admitted Shepperton. 'I guess we'll find out soon enough. In the meantime, let's get back in there and see what else his wife can tell us.'

Geraldine was just finishing off a tasteless coffee as the detectives re-entered the interview room.

'Can't say I'm very impressed with your coffee machine,' she said as Clarke and Shepperton re-appeared. Shepperton grinned.

'Yeah, sorry about that Mrs Abbott, I know it's not the best. Shall we continue?'

Geraldine noticed Clarke getting out his notebook.

'Still taking notes, then? Why do you do that? It's all gonna be on tape.'

'Just for my own reference,' replied Clarke.

'I see you're like me.'

'Sorry?'

'You're left-handed. There's not many of us about.'

Shepperton interrupted.

'Shall we just get on with it?' he suggested with more than a little hint of impatience. Once again he pressed the Record button on the tape recorder.

'Your husband claims he has no idea where he was on the day Gemma Gooding's body was discovered. I don't suppose you could shed any light on this?'

'Well,' said Geraldine, 'I don't know where he was, but he certainly wasn't at home. He didn't come home at all that night. I remember it clearly because I was so upset when Gemma's body was identified. I knew Gemma well as she was a pupil at my school. I remember Harry telephoning me the next morning to say he'd had to work all night and I can remember telling him she'd been murdered down by the canal.'

'And you're not convinced he was working?'

'Maybe he was. Maybe he wasn't. I couldn't say for sure. Perhaps his PA could clear that up for you – they spent a lot of nights together from what I can see.'

Shepperton detected a certain tone in her reply.

'What are you suggesting Mrs Abbott?'

'Harry cheated on me early on in our marriage and he has an eye for a pretty woman. She's certainly pretty, I have to admit. Let's just say, trust has to be earned and, right now, I'm not sure how much I can trust him.'

'What's this PA's name?'

'Amanda Chapman.'

'We'll certainly be needing to speak to her,' said Shepperton.

The detectives continued to question Geraldine for the next couple of hours. Having finished, they thanked her and bade her farewell then met up again in Shepperton's office.

'Well,' said Shepperton, 'what do you think?'

'I feel sorry for her, to be honest,' replied Clarke. 'Sounds like a miserable marriage. She's just found out her husband's been caught out doing dodgy abortions, he's got 'em into debt and it sounds like he's been playing away again. Chances are he'll be on a charge of murder before too long. With her high profile she's gonna find life pretty tough going before too long.'

'Guess, you're right there,' agreed Shepperton. He yawned and stretched then looked at his watch.

'God, is that the time? I dunno about you but I'm knackered. Reckon we should both get off home and get some kip.'

Clarke didn't need any persuasion. He grabbed his jacket and began to make his way out to the car park. As he was about to put his key into the door of his car he heard Shepperton calling after him.

'Sorry James, you'd better get back in here. Looks like the boys may have found Heather Brown's body.'

'Really? Where?'

'On a piece of land next to Harry Abbott's garden. They're bringing him in now.'

18

Harry appeared most bewildered on his return to the police station in the early hours of the morning. His interview, however, had to wait until the arrival of his solicitor, Mr Mayhew, who arrived shortly after nine o'clock.

In the meantime, the body had been left where it had been found. An eagle-eyed officer had noticed through a gap in the fence that a patch of earth on an overgrown adjacent plot of land had been disturbed. This particular patch, while still overgrown, was noticeably clear of the brambles that covered the remainder of the plot. After a few moments of digging, officers soon unearthed a fully-clothed body in a shallow grave.

While there it was examined by a pathologist who, after an initial assessment, gave the go-ahead for the body to be transferred to the mortuary where, it was hoped, a formal identification and cause of death could be established.

'I have no idea how a body ended up there,' Harry insisted. 'It might have been there for years for all I know, probably long before Geraldine and I moved into The Willows.'

Shepperton frowned.

'That may be the case Mr Abbott. The body needs to be forensically examined before we can be sure it is that of the missing girl but, as my team have informed me, it appears the clothing of the body matches that as worn by Heather Brown on the day she disappeared. Because of that we have every reason to believe it is, indeed, her.'

Clarke was more forthright.

'I suggest Heather Brown came to you requesting an unauthorised abortion,' he said. 'You agreed to help her but something went wrong and she died. Then, in order to save your own skin, you buried her in that patch of land next to your garden.'

'That's absurd!' Harry shouted. 'I've dedicated my whole working life into preserving and saving lives. I'm no killer!'

'And that's coming from a man who thinks nothing of aborting unborn babies!' snapped Clarke who immediately regretted his comment.

'I'm sorry,' he added awkwardly. 'I'll take that back. I was out of order.'

'Too right you were!' responded Harry angrily. 'That just goes to show how little you understand the trauma so many pregnant women go through.'

Clarke raised his hands in the form of surrender.

'Like I said, I was out of order. I apologise.'

Harry shrugged his shoulders and turned away, seemingly unwilling to accept Clarke's apology. Nevertheless, Clarke pressed on.

'Had you ever met Heather Brown?'

'Yes, of course I have. Her parents are good friends of ours. Her mother works as a teacher in Geraldine's school. We go back years. Heather and her parents have been frequent guests at our home. That's why all this is so ridiculous. Heather's a lovely girl. I would never have hurt her – or anyone else for that matter.'

At this point Mr Mayhew interjected.

'I think DCI Shepperton, my client should be allowed to leave. He has answered your questions. Unless you intend to charge him I suggest you allow him to leave with me now.'

Shepperton shook his head.

'Mr Mayhew, are you serious? A body has just been unearthed next to your client's garden and we have reason to believe the pendant found in his home is the property of another young lady who was brutally murdered nearby. No, Mr Abbott will remain here for the time being while our investigation continues.'

While Mr Mayhew may have been testing the water, he still challenged Shepperton's assertion.

'You have 24 hours from the point of apprehension to hold my client. After that you will either have to charge or release him.'

Shepperton smiled.

'Mr Mayhew, you and I have both been in this business for a good number of years so please don't play games with me. You know as well as I do that 24 hours is the standard time limitation available to us and that, in exceptional circumstances, when someone is suspected of a more serious crime such as murder, we will be able to apply to hold on to your client for up to 96 hours before charging him. That, if necessary, is precisely what we will do.'

Harry slumped in his chair and groaned.

'Ninety-six hours?'

'Yes Mr Abbott. Though I don't expect we will have to wait that long before we are charging you with at least one count of murder. Let's just see what our forensics team uncover in the meantime.'

-o0o-

'Er, Wendy, it looks like you've got company,' said Geraldine as she spotted Brian's car pulling up outside. 'I'd better leave you both to it. I don't want to intrude. Shall I go upstairs?'

'No,' replied Wendy, 'you stay right here. I want you with me.'

She went to open the front door just as Brian was reaching out to press the doorbell.

'Hi Wen,' he said awkwardly. 'Can I come in?'

Wendy didn't reply but stood aside to allow him through. He leant forward to give her a kiss on the cheek but she turned away, leaving him feeling even more awkward than before.

'What do you want Brian?'

'You said we could chat. I thought it was about time we did. I just passed the Abbott's. There's an awful lot of police activity there,' he said as he made his way into the lounge. 'I was wondering if you'd heard anything. Do you really think Harry could have . . .'

His voice drifted away the moment he spotted Geraldine sitting on the settee.'

'Oh, hi. Sorry Geri, I didn't know you were here.'

'Obviously,' replied Geraldine. 'And, no, we haven't heard a thing other than Harry was questioned last night and released a while later.'

'How is he?'

'I don't know,' said Geraldine. 'We're not exactly together at the moment. That's why I'm staying here.'

'Oh Geri, I'm sorry to hear that. What went wrong?'

'Brian,' interrupted Wendy, 'that's none of your business is it?'

'Sorry, course not. Sorry Geri. I seem to make a habit of putting my foot in it recently.'

'And not just your foot apparently,' said Wendy pointedly.

'Oh Wen, come on, let's not start that all over again. Can't we just . . .'

Once more his voice tailed off as he spotted two figures through the lounge window.

'It's Shepperton and Clarke,' he said. 'Were you expecting them?'

'No,' replied Wendy as she squeezed past him to answer the doorbell.

'Hello Mrs Brown,' said Shepperton. 'May we come in?'

'Sure.'

Wendy ushered the detectives into the lounge, both of whom seemed surprised to find Brian and Geraldine present.

'Mr Brown, Mrs Abbott, we weren't expecting you to still be here. At the moment Mr Brown we have an officer heading to your cottage. This, however, will save him the effort.'

'I don't like the look of this,' muttered Brian to Geraldine. 'They look pretty serious.'

Shepperton wasted little time in confirming Brian's fears.

'I'm afraid we have some very distressing news – for all of you as it happens,' said Shepperton. 'In the early hours of this morning our officers unearthed a body in an overgrown piece of land next to your home Mrs Abbott.'

Wendy, Brian and Geraldine stood shell-shocked at the revelation. Wendy began to weep.

'Is it our Heather?' asked Brian.

'We can't confirm that at the moment,' said Shepperton, 'but I'm afraid we have every reason to suspect it might be.'

Wendy let out a banshee-like wail. Brian burst into tears. Geraldine just stood, appearing shell-shocked, not saying a word.

'I'm afraid the clothing found appears to match that which you described Heather wearing on the day she disappeared Mrs Brown,' said Clarke. 'And there's also this.'

He opened his briefcase and withdrew an evidence bag containing a pair of earrings.

'Do you think you could you identify these?' asked Clarke.

'I think they're Heather's,' said Brian. 'I think I recognise them. What do you think Wen?'

Wendy seemed reluctant to look. It was as if her confirmation would end any dwindling hope she had that Heather may one day be found alive.

'Wen, can you take a look?'

Geraldine walked across the room and put a comforting arm around Wendy's shoulders.

'Take a look Wendy. Just get it over with.'

Wendy turned and looked at the bag. Once again she wailed and turned away.

'Mrs Brown, we really need to know. Do you recognise these earrings?' asked Clarke.

Wendy, with her back to the detectives, nodded.

'They're Heather's.'

Brian, in floods of tears himself, embraced his wife who, in turn, embraced him. This was no time for discord.

'Thank you Mrs Brown,' said Clarke. He returned the evidence bag into the safety of his briefcase then Shepperton addressed Geraldine.

'I'm really sorry Mrs Abbott but we will soon need either Mr or Mrs Brown – or both of them – to identify the body recovered. Assuming they confirm the body is Heather's we will be charging your husband later today with her murder. Subject to the result of DNA testing we should inform you that we will probably also be charging him with the murder of Gemma Gooding within the next few weeks.'

Geraldine stood without answering, staring vacantly into space. Eventually she spoke.

'Wendy, I should go. It's not appropriate me being here. I'll get my stuff and go and stay with my sister.'

Wendy, however, was having none of it.

'No! I need you here with me. You're my best friend and you're hurting too.'

'Wen's right,' said Brian. 'You need each other more than ever now.'

'But what about you Brian?' asked Geraldine.

'He can stay here too,' interrupted Wendy. 'He shouldn't be on his own. Not now. He should be with us.'

'We're really sorry Mr and Mrs Brown,' said Shepperton. 'You too, Mrs Abbott. I know this has been a terrible shock for you all. If you'll excuse us, we'll be on our way. We'll let you both know Mr and Mrs Brown when we are ready for you to come along to the mortuary to make a formal identification.'

Brian guided the detectives to the front door.

'Are you telling us everything,' he whispered as Shepperton was about to step outside. Shepperton beckoned him to close the door behind him. The two detectives and Brian stood on the driveway where they could not be heard by Wendy and Stella.

'It looks as if Abbott didn't want to risk the body to be identified,' said Shepperton. 'He'd covered it in lime.'

'Oh God! My poor girl!' gasped Brian.

'Keep it to yourself, please,' said Shepperton. 'Sometimes we like to hold certain information back, as I'm sure you must realise.'

Brian nodded and thanked the detectives as they made their way back to their car. Brian went back inside and stood in the hallway and sobbed uncontrollably.

19

Harry had been on remand for almost eight weeks, having been charged with Heather's murder following her parent's identification of her body. Meanwhile, an uneasy truce was holding between Wendy and Brian.

Geraldine had since left Wendy's in order to stay with her sister on the other side of town after insisting it was about time she gave her friends some space to grieve. Nevertheless, she and Wendy stayed in daily contact and were there for each other whenever needed.

Both Wendy and Brian had been keen to arrange Heather's funeral but were informed her body could not be released for the time being. They were facing the same situation as Stella who had to wait for several months before her daughter could be laid to rest. A post mortem revealed that Heather had also been stabbed though it had not been possible to ascertain how many times owing to the state of her body when it was recovered.

Back at the police station, Shepperton and Clarke were still compiling evidence that they hoped would be sufficient to secure a conviction against Harry. They had unearthed a series of significant and regular cash withdrawals from Harry's bank account. Under pressure and already charged with conducting illegal abortions and one murder, Harry had little option other than to co-operate with the investigation.

With great reluctance he eventually admitted his gambling addiction and that he owed thousands of pounds to various shady individuals who were not the kind to accept cheques. He had been warned that failure to keep up the payments would more than likely result in painful consequences. That, he explained, was one of the reasons he had been tempted to conduct the illegal abortions as the cash payments he received for his services could not be traced.

In spite of this, he vehemently denied being involved in Gemma or Heather's murders. Despite Shepperton and Clarke's efforts, nothing they could say would persuade Harry to confess any responsibility for their deaths.

Amanda Chapman, it was revealed, was not only Harry's PA. They had been conducting an affair for more than three years, Harry explaining that, as his marriage had been dead in the water for some time, he and Geraldine more or less had led separate lives. His relationship with Amanda, he insisted, was hurting no-one. Amanda's husband, presumed Shepperton, may have seen things rather differently.

Under questioning, Amanda had at first insisted there had been no romantic liaisons with Harry. They just worked together. Eventually though the truth came out but, she insisted, the night Gemma had been killed, she and Harry had spent the whole night together. There was no way, she claimed, he could have been anywhere near the canal that night.

Shepperton and Clarke though were convinced she was lying and, even more so when the DNA results on the pendant came back. Gemma's DNA *had* been detected on the bracelet. The detectives informed Harry that his claim that the bracelet belonged to Geraldine no longer held water. Having consulted with the Crown Prosecution Service they further charged Harry with Gemma's murder – a move that was received with great relief by Stella who had waited so long for someone to be held accountable for her daughter's untimely and vicious death.

Having now charged Harry with both Heather and Gemma's deaths the detectives were now keen to find links that he had also killed Sarah Mitchell – a case that, so far, had led only to a series of dead ends.

Wendy, meanwhile, was in torment. Not only grieving for her daughter, her conscience was severely troubling her. Having been responsible for Sarah's death she had fluctuated between wanting to hand herself in or choosing not to in order to be there for Heather should she ever be found.

With the latter no longer an option it took all of Brian's persuasion to prevent Wendy from owning up. This, however, was not just for Wendy's protection. Brian knew only too well that, if his involvement in covering up what had happened was to be revealed, he too would be in deep trouble.

Wendy's earlier plans to return to work had been put on hold as she felt there was no way she could have concentrated sufficiently with everything else going on in her life. Geraldine, however, had decided to front it out and returned to work, telling Wendy that she felt the need to be kept busy.

This was not an easy time for her. Somersley was a small market town. Everyone seemed to know each other's business and Harry's arrest proved to be the main talking point amongst the local populace.

Meanwhile, Clarke was beginning to worry. Although he and Shepperton had been convinced they had the killer in custody, someone at the Crown Prosecution Service had since been looking deeper into the case and had begun to have doubts. Clarke's former brother-in-law – and still a close friend – had gone out on a limb to share his concerns in a telephone call.

'If I'm right James,' he said, 'I'm concerned your case might not bear up under scrutiny in court. I know how upset you were a few years back when that case backfired in London. How your Super jumped the gun and got the wrong man. I'm wondering if your colleague Shepperton may have jumped to a similar speedy conclusion.

'Alright, Abbott may not be squeaky clean but, just because he's been done on the abortions it doesn't necessarily mean he's a killer. I know the pendant was found in his office and the body was found next to his home but it was not actually at his residence. What if you and Shepperton have added two and two and made five?'

'What are you suggesting Clive?'

'I dunno really James. It all seems rather convenient to me. As far as I can tell, your case will almost certainly be challenged as being based on circumstantial evidence. I mean can you actually *prove* Abbott placed Gemma's pendant in his office? Can you actually *prove* he buried Heather's body next door to his own home? It makes me wonder.'

'Wonder what?'

'That maybe Abbott's been set up?'

20

Whether or not Harry was responsible for the deaths of the two girls, later that year he found himself in court charged with carrying out illegal abortions. It was of little surprise that he was found guilty and sentenced to five years' imprisonment. Worse still, at least as far as Harry was concerned, he was struck off by the General Medical Council – the career for which he had been so highly regarded was now condemned to the dustbin of history.

The news spread like wildfire around the Somersley district. Geraldine became convinced she could hear everyone's tongues wagging and that fingers were being pointed at her – some people even suggesting she must have known what her husband had been up to – guilt by association in its clearest form. All this piled on the pressure yet, through it all, she battled on at work, determined not to allow the clouds of suspicion and idle gossip stop her from leading as normal a life as possible.

Yet life was far from normal. The discovery of Heather's body adjacent to The Willows made it a destination for macabre-minded individuals. Eventually, the daily sight of these people staring at the house or driving by slowly in order to get a good view persuaded Geraldine to move out to live with her sister.

The straw that finally broke the camel's back was the morning Geraldine had come downstairs in her dressing gown and noticed a man trying to peer through the smallest of gaps between her lounge curtains. Enough, thought Geraldine, was enough. Once safely ensconced in her sister's home, Geraldine put The Willows up for sale.

Through it all though came Wendy's endless support. Despite the fact that Geraldine's husband was, in all probability going to be imprisoned for murdering her daughter, Wendy never lost sight of her dedication to help her friend in her hours of need –

even though many of her friends and acquaintances felt it odd, even inappropriate, that she should be doing so. Geraldine became a frequent visitor and it was during one of those visits that Wendy eventually broached the subject of returning to work.

'Are you sure that's really what you want?' asked Geraldine. 'Now you know what's happened to Heather wouldn't you rather wait until her body is released and you can lay her to rest? Why don't you wait just a little longer, say until after the summer holidays?'

'I'm going nuts just sitting around the house,' replied Wendy. 'I need something to focus on – and, to be honest – I need the money. I'll wait until the new term but not a minute longer.'

And so it was, on Wednesday, September 6th, for the first time in months, Wendy returned to Somersley Secondary School. Just as before she received a warm welcome back though many of her colleagues obviously felt awkward, not really knowing what to say regarding Heather's untimely demise. At least, thought Wendy, it would be a short week – the best way to test the water.

As it happened it was a hectic three days. The new intake of pupils certainly kept Wendy on her toes. Getting to know all those new faces had never been a problem for her before but, this time, it was only natural that her mind tended to wander to some degree. However, as the children left school on the Friday afternoon, it was a tired, though satisfied Wendy who joined her colleagues in the staff room for a coffee and chat before they all headed off home.

Heather was almost constantly on Wendy's mind which was the main reason she had been so keen to return to work. The following Tuesday would have been Heather's birthday so to be standing in front of a full class of youngsters and teaching them Elementary French turned out to be as good a distraction as any.

Ironically, though, at that very moment, a distraught mother was heading for Somersley Police Station. She headed directly to the reception desk and, in tears, asked for the detective in charge of the murder investigation. The duty sergeant, Richard Bywater, immediately sought out Shepperton who, in turn, alerted Clarke. Bywater was instructed to invite the tearful lady into the interview room where she could speak to the detectives privately.

'What d'you reckon?' asked Clarke.

'No idea,' replied Shepperton, 'but, according to Bywater, the woman reckons she might have some important information.'

The detectives made their way into the interview room where the woman was sitting, accompanied by a young Wpc.

'Good morning, I'm DCI Shepperton, and this is my colleague Detective Constable Clarke. What can we do for you Mrs . . . ?'

'Robson, Deborah Robson.'

'Ah yes, Mrs Robson!' said Shepperton. 'I thought I recognised your face. Didn't you accompany your daughter here soon after Gemma Gooding was murdered?'

'She was called in when Heather Brown was reported missing. My daughter had been with her earlier that day.'

'Ah yes, of course, I remember now.'

'Maureen's the reason I'm here. She's in a dreadful state. I don't know exactly why, but I'm convinced it has something to do with Heather Brown's murder. I'm hoping she'll talk to you 'cos she won't open up to me.'

'What about her father? Has she spoken to him?'

'What, George? He doesn't know I'm here. He'll be furious when he finds out. I think he must know something 'cos when I suggested coming here he insisted I shouldn't. He said Maureen would never forgive me if I did. I've no idea why but she's my daughter and I love her. I can't bear to see her the way she is. I'm really scared she might do something drastic.'

'Like?'

'I dunno. You hear things, don't you? I could never forgive myself if she did something to hurt herself – or worse – if I'd just stood by and done nothing. I think you'll need to insist she comes here to speak to you – you know – to find out what it's all about.'

'How old is your daughter?' asked Shepperton.

'She's 18.'

'There's a problem Mrs Robson,' said Clarke. 'If your daughter doesn't wish to come here, we cannot force her to do so unless we believe she's done anything wrong or she's withholding information. At the end of the day it's up to her whether she comes here or not.'

'But you've gotta do *something*!'

The detectives looked at one another. Shepperton was the first to speak.

'There is another option. If we came to your home, do you think she would speak to us there?'

'But George . . .'

'Does he work? Perhaps we could call round when he's not there.'

'I suppose.'

'Well,' said Clarke, 'I suggest you go home and speak to Maureen. If she's agreeable, we'll come over to speak to her.'

'Thank you. Thank you so much.'

Mrs Robson stood up and buttoned up her coat.

'No problem Mrs Robson. Thank you for coming in to speak to us,' replied Shepperton who politely opened the door to allow her out.

Shepperton and Clarke watched as she walked along the corridor towards the reception area. They were about to return to Shepperton's office when Mrs Robson stopped in her tracks, turned back to face them and called out to them from the end of the corridor.

'By the way there's something else I should have told you. Maureen insists that Harry Abbott did not kill either of those girls. She says she knows for sure that he had nothing to do with either of the murders.'

21

An hour later it was time, decided Clarke, to have a long overdue chat with Shepperton. Since speaking to Clive, Clarke had held his tongue, not wishing to get his former brother-in-law into trouble. For that reason, he offered up Clive's suspicions to Shepperton as his own.

'I'm worried Dave,' said Clarke. 'I've already been down that road with the Mabusi case in Limehouse back in '71. I just want to make sure we dot all the *i*'s and cross the *t*'s before we get into court. Not only that, we've now got the Robson girl claiming she knows Abbott didn't kill Heather Brown. I think we really need to speak to her as soon as possible – find out what she's got to tell us.'

'That's only *if* she'll talk,' replied Shepperton. He smiled and rather condescendingly tapped his colleague on the shoulder.

'Okay James,' he said, 'if that'll calm your nerves, we'll do that. To be frank with you though I don't really see the need. I reckon we've got Abbott right where we need him. Ripe for the picking. He's guilty as hell in my eyes.'

Shepperton picked up the telephone and dialled.

'Somersley 3630.'

Shepperton immediately recognised Deborah Robson's voice and could also hear raised voices in the background.

'It's DCI Shepperton here. Can you hear me, Mrs Robson?'

'Yes.'

'Can you please inform your daughter that Detective Constable Clarke and I wish to speak to her? We should be with you in a few minutes.'

'Oh no! Please don't! My husband and daughter are extremely upset that I've been to speak to you.'

Maureen had obviously overheard their conversation.

'Tell him no way! I'm sayin' nothing!'

'Did you hear that Mr Shepperton?' asked an obviously distraught Deborah.

'I did indeed,' replied Shepperton. 'I'm sorry, but that convinces me more than ever that there's a good reason that we need to speak with your daughter. We'll be right over.'

He replaced the handset and turned to Clarke.

'Come on James, get your jacket.'

Clarke and Shepperton arrived at the Robson's semi-detached home on the outskirts of Somersley just a few minutes later. The front door was wide open. The two detectives walked up the drive. Shepperton rang the doorbell and immediately became concerned when he heard sobbing from the lounge.

'Mrs Robson!'

'Go away!'

'Mrs Robson, are you okay? We're coming in.'

Neither detective was quite prepared for what they witnessed in the lounge. Deborah was on her knees, rocking back and forth, in floods of tears. With her hair dishevelled and mascara running down her cheeks, she looked up pitifully at the men who immediately noticed a large reddened bruise under her left eye.

'Oh my God!' said Clarke as he immediately knelt down next to her. 'Whatever's happened?'

Deborah tried to reply but neither Clarke or Shepperton could make out what she was saying through her sobs.

'I'll fetch a glass of water,' said Shepperton as Clarke gently eased Deborah back up to her feet.

'Where is your husband and daughter?' asked Clarke as he lowered her down onto an armchair.

'They've gone,' she blubbed.

'Where?'

'They wouldn't tell me!'

Shepperton returned holding a glass of water which he handed over to Deborah. She downed it in a couple of gulps, took a deep breath and tried to compose herself.

'Maureen went mad when I told them I'd been to see you,' she said. 'I've never seen her so angry. George too.'

'What did they say?' asked Clarke.

'George has never shouted at me before but he was absolutely furious. 'You have no idea what you've done!' that's what he said. Then Maureen lashed out at me. It was totally out of character. She was screaming that she had to get away – as far from Somersley as possible. George said he'd take her. They ran upstairs, stuffed some clothes in bags and drove off. I've no idea where they've gone. They wouldn't tell me.'

'How long have they been gone?' asked Shepperton.

'I dunno, 10, maybe 15 minutes.'

'What about the car? What is it? What's the registration number?'

'It's a blue Morris Minor. CDX 432.'

Clarke rushed outside, back to the police car. He picked up the radio handset and alerted all officers to be on the look-out for George, Maureen and the Morris.

Harry Abbott is innocent according to Maureen. Shepperton was now beginning to wonder if Clarke's reservations might actually have some merit to them. Seeds of doubt were beginning to form in his mind, a sense of uneasiness. Why would George and Maureen Robson suddenly rush off like that?

More worryingly, what did they have to hide?

22

The search for George and Maureen proved fruitless over the following few days. It seemed they had both disappeared into thin air. The detectives were keen to keep this development out of the public domain, fearing it could prove to be prejudicial to the case against Harry Abbott.

Eventually Shepperton decided to abandon the search. He had no proof the Robsons had anything of value to offer the investigation and he preferred instead to gain as much evidence as possible against Harry in order to ensure a successful prosecution against him. Time was not on his side as Harry's trial had been scheduled to commence within the next four months.

United in their grief Wendy and Brian, against all the odds, were still living under the same roof, albeit in separate bedrooms. Their hitherto bad blood had, thankfully, been set aside and life at No23 was now running as smoothly as possible under the circumstances. Obviously they both had their down days but at least, from time to time they were together and able to support each other through the most desperate of times.

The news of Heather's death had, obviously, not escaped Stella's attention and she had since been a huge support to Wendy and vice-versa. A most unexpected friendship had developed from the most traumatic circumstances.

As a result Stella became a frequent visitor which, although awkward at first owing to the fact that Brian had been hurt that she had even contemplated his relationship with Gemma might have been far from appropriate, Stella had since conceded she had been wrong and Brian, eventually, accepted her reasons for contacting Shepperton with her suspicions.

Now a far more relaxed attitude existed between the three grieving parents. All three were there to support Geraldine too –

a situation that, to the outside world must have seemed more than strange.

The ninth of October was Wendy's birthday, though she was in no mood to celebrate. The previous day Brian had been so concerned about her mental well-being that he reached out to Stella.

'Wen's really down today,' he said. 'I've gotta admit I'm worried about her. Is there any chance you could come over tomorrow night? I'm sure she'd be pleased to see you.'

Stella willingly agreed. She could appreciate exactly how Wendy had been feeling. Brian was helping with the washing up in the kitchen the following evening when Stella arrived bearing two bottles of red wine.

'Stella! What a surprise!'

'Brian called me. He told me you needed picking up a bit.'

The women hugged.

'I wish I could say Happy Birthday,' said Stella, 'but obviously it's not. I've had a chat with Brian and we thought we should all be together and try to make the most of a bad situation.'

'Oh thank you Stella,' said Wendy who then turned to Brian and gave him an unexpected hug. 'That means a lot.'

'Well,' said Brian, 'I guess those bottles are not gonna open themselves.'

Stella handed over the bottles and Brian fetched three glasses and uncorked a bottle of Chardonnay. Very soon afterwards both the bottles had been drained.

'What a shame,' said Wendy as she watched the last drops coming from the second bottle.

'I could pop down to the offy,' suggested Brian.

'Oh don't bother,' said Wendy. 'It's so cold outside.'

'So what?' said Stella. 'It's your birthday!'

Brian grinned.

'I'll get my coat.'

He disappeared, then 20 minutes later, returned carrying four more bottles.

'I couldn't decide which one to buy so I bought 'em all.'

Over the course of the evening three more bottles were consumed. 'Who fancies another bottle?' asked Brian.

'No, not for me Brian, I've had enough,' said Stella.

'Same here,' said Wendy. She looked at Stella and Brian and smiled.

'Thank you both for tonight,' she said. 'If only for a few hours you've made me feel a lot better. It's been a nice evening hasn't it? Such a shame we'll all be crashing down to earth again in the morning.'

Brian nodded.

'I think we all needed a night like tonight,' he said. 'Life's been pretty grim since we lost the girls, hasn't it?'

'Well,' said Stella, slightly drunkenly, 'I know I wouldn't say this if Geraldine was here but I can't tell you how much I hate Harry Abbott right now. I really hope they throw the book at him so he can never be released.'

Wendy nodded in agreement but Brian offered an alternative scenario.

'In a way, I think I'd rather they let him out.'

Wendy looked astonished.

'Why ever would you say that?'

She noticed Brian's eyes filling with tears.

'Because,' he explained, 'after what he's done to our girls I could get my hands on him and I could kill him myself!'

He began to sob. The mixture of heightened emotions and excess alcohol had got the better of him. Wendy and Stella embraced the grieving father.

'If you didn't do it Brian,' said Stella, 'I reckon me and Wendy would instead. That monster of a man doesn't deserve the air he breathes.'

23

While most people were preparing for Christmas Wendy and Brian were busy. At long last – in fact, as far as her parents were concerned, long overdue – the Coroner's Office had released Heather's body for burial.

Previously Wendy had returned to her teaching duties at Somersley Secondary and fortunately, so far, nothing untoward had happened to make her regret that decision. She was at work when the news came through that Heather's body was to be released and, as usual, Geraldine had been the first to offer help and support with the funeral arrangements.

Stella too proved to be an invaluable help which made Wendy feel rather guilty as she had not been there to support Stella at the time of Gemma's funeral. The situation though, Stella reminded her, had been considerably different between them at the time. Now they were friends and, unlikely as it was, an unbreakable bond had since been forged between them.

Brian, for his part, did his best to support Wendy but she soon realised that he was struggling to hold it together himself. Over the months since he had moved back into the matrimonial home many of the cracks in their relationship had been smoothed over although they still occupied separate bedrooms.

Thursday, December 7 was the date selected for Heather's funeral. Wendy and Stella conducted all the arrangements that involved the Reverend Palmer, Wendy having suggested to Brian he should stay in the background owing to his unfortunate liaisons with the reverend's daughter.

However, the man of God was swift to assure Wendy that he bore no grudge against a grieving father and he asked her to assure Brian of a warm welcome at St Mary's on what was bound to be a very emotional day. When Wendy passed on the reverend's message Brian's shoulders slumped.

'What's up Brian?'

'I was just thinking he's a far better man than I could ever be.'

He began to weep. Wendy instinctively put her arm around his shoulders and, for the first time since he'd left her to move in with Stella, she kissed him gently on the cheek.

With tears streaming down his face he turned to hug her. A long embrace ensued. Wendy, now also in tears, could feel his body shaking as he sobbed uncontrollably in her arms. If she had harboured any lingering doubts as to his involvement in what had happened to Gemma and Heather they would now have dissolved completely from her mind.

It was a cold and windy, though bright and sunny morning when the hearse and funeral cortege arrived at St Mary's Church. Newspaper reports of the forthcoming service had ensured the streets leading to the church, much to Brian and Wendy's amazement, were lined with well-wishers, many of whom threw flowers at the hearse.

Heather's coffin, made of light oak with brass handles, was laden with floral tributes. A large floral tribute alongside the coffin bore the word DAUGHTER while two more tributes on top of the coffin were from Somersley Secondary School and Heather's grandparents – Brian's parents – who lived in the south of France both of whom now, sadly, were in poor health which prevented them from attending the service.

Geraldine and Stella led Wendy up to the front pew and sat next to her while Brian remained outside the church gates in preparation for his role as one of the pall-bearers. As the organist began the first few bars of *All Things Bright and Beautiful*, Heather's coffin was carried up the aisle and laid on trestles. The service then began.

After a welcome from the reverend another hymn was sung then Geraldine walked up to the pulpit to deliver a most moving eulogy. Brian had attempted to write one himself but, having dyslexia and after screwing up several drafts, he soon realised he did not have the words to adequately express his feelings. Nor did he feel he would have the strength to deliver a eulogy in front of a packed church. Geraldine's offer to do so was met with great appreciation by both Wendy and Brian and they were greatly moved by her kind thoughts and words – all delivered and projected so clearly by someone who was so accustomed to public speaking.

The parting music, *I Will Always Love You* by Dolly Parton, was played as Heather's coffin was about to be carried out of the packed church though Brian and Wendy struggled to take in individual faces as they walked, arm in arm, behind their daughter's coffin.

From the relative comfort of the church they gasped as the cold air hit them as they emerged outside. It was only then, in the bright sunshine, that Wendy first noticed Shepperton and Clarke standing solemnly and respectfully a few yards away. Both men nodded as they caught Wendy's eye. Wendy attempted a smile in return.

A couple of moments later, after the reverend had committed Heather's body to the care of the Lord, one of the pall-bearers switched on a cassette recorder and the strains of Donna Summer's hit *I Feel Love* – one of Heather's favourite songs – filled the air.

While Wendy may have thought Shepperton and Clarke had kindly attended the funeral to pay their respects, she did not realise they also had an alternative motive. The officers were also there in an observational capacity, looking out for any possible sign that could strengthen their case against Harry Abbott. Clarke was also wondering if Maureen Robson might have been tempted to break her cover in order to attend her best friend's funeral. With nothing of value to add to their case the detectives began to walk back to their car.

'Strange, wasn't it?' said Clarke.

'What?'

'Abbott's missus reading the eulogy.'

'Yeah, suppose it was.'

'Specially bearing in mind her old man's up for the girl's murder.'

'Reckon it took guts then,' said Shepperton. 'The poor woman must have been going through hell these last few months.'

He shivered as he pulled up the collar of his overcoat. The wind, now much colder, began to gather strength.

'Come on James, Let's head off. I'm frozen. I can't even feel my toes now.'

No sooner had the last notes of Donna Summer's hit faded away, everyone at the graveside had come to the same conclusion as Shepperton – that it was time to get back into the warm. Most of the mourners headed off to the nearby Dog and Duck for the wake.

Now, for the first time, Brian and Wendy could fully take in the identities of some of those who had turned up as their faces at the church and graveside services had been much of a blur at the time. Wendy headed immediately to Geraldine and gave her the biggest of hugs.

'Oh Geri, you were marvellous! Thank you so much!'

Brian agreed.

'I don't know how you can find the words,' he said. 'I couldn't have done it. You did Heather proud. Thank you!'

'How are you both doing?' asked Geraldine.

'Well,' replied Wendy, 'I suppose it's going as well as we could have hoped so far – but to be honest, I'll be glad when it's all over, you know, when we can get back home.'

She looked around.

'Guess we'd better mingle,' she said.

Geraldine agreed but suggested they both get a cup of hot coffee first of all to thaw themselves out.

Over the next couple of hours the platters of sandwiches, sausage rolls and snacks gradually disappeared and people began to drift away. Wendy took the opportunity to chat to some of Heather's former school friends and thanked them for coming along to pay their respects. As they were leaving, Wendy turned around, expecting Brian to wave them off too but he was nowhere to be seen.

'Stella, have you seen Brian?'

'Not for a few minutes. He's probably in the loo.'

Gradually the room began to empty but there was still no sign of Brian. Wendy began to get concerned. She walked over to the doorway leading to the Gents toilets. She opened it slightly and called out.

'Brian, are you in there?'

'Sorry Wen, won't be long.'

'Okay. People are leaving, we need to say goodbye.'

'Okay.'

Five minutes later, Brian had still not reappeared. Only Stella and Geraldine remained.

'Brian, are you alright in there?'

'Sorry Wen! Got a dicky tum!'

Wendy heard a toilet flush then, a minute or so later, a hot air dryer. A man wearing a full-length overcoat came out, followed by Brian who was looking most subdued.

'You alright?'

'Yeah, I'll be okay,' he replied most unconvincingly.

'Everyone's gone now,' said Wendy, 'except Stella and Geri.'

'Yeah, sorry Wen.'

'You ready then? Shall we head off home?'

Brian nodded.

Stella said her goodbyes and left. Geraldine then drove Brian and Wendy back to No23.

'I'll leave you both to it,' she said as she pulled up outside the gate. 'You must both be tired and you'll have a lot to talk about.'

Geraldine drove away. Wendy opened the front door and they went inside. Almost immediately it became obvious Brian had been desperately waiting to get Wendy on her own.

'Wen,' he said as he grabbed her arm, 'we've gotta talk. Something's happened.'

'Okay,' said Wendy, 'just let me get my coat off first will you?'

She looked at Brian. He seemed most agitated.

'Are you alright?'

'No, I'm confused and I don't know what to do for the best.'

Wendy guided him into the lounge and urged him to sit down.

'Now then,' she said, 'are you gonna tell me what all this is about?'

'Did you see the tall bloke right at the back of the church, all dressed in black?'

'Almost everyone wore black Brian.'

'He sat in the back row. Had a thick black scarf over his face and wore a full-length black coat.'

'No Brian, I can't say I noticed.'

'Well, he turned up halfway through the wake. I was wondering who he was. Then he caught my eye and signalled to me to shush by putting his finger to his lips, then pointed towards the loo. That's why I was in there so long.'

'Who was it then?'

'I had no idea at first but, once we were in there he checked all the cubicles to make sure we were alone – and that's when he told me.'

'Told you what Brian? Come on, for God's sake. What's this all leading up to?'

'I think you should sit down too now Wen.'

Wendy, now worried, obliged.

'He only whispered. He told me Harry was innocent and that he had to reveal the truth before the trial. I asked him how he could be so sure. He told me he knew exactly who had killed Gemma and Heather and why. He said he wanted to make sure the real culprit paid the price but he insisted that, under no circumstances, could either of us go to the police because it would put his life in danger.

'He said if we go to the police we'd never know the truth. Then he said we should wait and he'd be in touch. He said we are to meet him at a specified time and place – and that we'd have to follow his instructions to the letter.

'I asked how I could trust him. He told me he'd risked his life just coming to the funeral but that it was something he just had to do 'cos Heather had meant so much to him. He insisted we should tell no-one we had seen him. He made me swear to secrecy – and that's when he revealed himself to me.'

Wendy could wait no longer.

'For God's sake Brian, who the hell was it?'

'I had no idea until he pulled his face scarf down a little. That's when I realised it wasn't a bloke at all. It was Maureen – Maureen Robson.'

'Oh my God!' gasped Wendy. 'So she's turned up at last – and right under Shepperton's nose! Where is she now?'

'I dunno. As soon as she revealed herself she kissed me on the cheek, told me she'd loved Heather and that I was to wait for five minutes. She's cut her hair short and dyed it black. Then she pulled her scarf up across her face again and ran off.'

'I saw her!' declared Wendy. 'I saw her come out while I was waiting for you outside the door. What are we gonna do?'

'Look,' said Brian. 'I trust her. Do you?'

Wendy remembered seeing Maureen, all battered and bruised, when she was leaving the police station. Had someone got to her? If so, her claim that her life was in danger seemed to have a ring of truth to it.

'Yes Brian. I trust her.'

'In that case, we should do *exactly* as she says. She looked absolutely terrified. There's no way she was faking it. If her life really is in danger, I don't want to be the one that puts her at risk. I think we should wait until she gets in touch. And remember – we tell no-one – no-one at all 'cos Maureen's life may well depend on it.'

24

'Wendy, Brian, I have something to tell you.'

It was Christmas Eve and Geraldine had called around for a coffee and chat, 'but don't worry,' she added, 'this time it's good news. I wanted to tell you Wendy before we go back to school after the holidays.'

'I'm intrigued Geri,' replied Wendy as they sat around the dining room table. 'Come on then, we could do with some good news.'

'Well,' said Geraldine, 'I hope you will be happy for me. As you know my relationship with Harry went down the toilet a long while ago and you already know that I've had one or two gentleman friends in the past. The trouble was, I couldn't chance Harry finding out in case I lost The Willows and all the financial security 'cos divorces are expensive, but now we know Harry won't be around . . .'

'That's assuming he's found guilty,' interrupted Brian.

'Oh, he's guilty alright,' replied Geraldine confidently. 'Now we know Harry won't be around I can be open about a relationship I've had over the past few months. I've been longing to tell you for weeks Wendy – but I wanted to be really sure because you know the man concerned. You're my best friend so I wanted you to be the first person I've told.'

Intrigued, Wendy sat forward.

'Crikey Geri, whoever is it?'

'It's Harvey.'

'Harvey? Oh wow!' gasped Wendy.

'Who's Harvey?' asked Brian.

'Harvey Nunn,' explained Wendy. 'He's the Art teacher at Somersley Secondary.'

'So you know him. What's he like?'

Wendy frowned.

'He's really nice Brian but . . .'

'But what?'

'Well, he's married.'

'I *knew* you'd say that,' said Geraldine, 'but the truth is Harvey and Monica have been living separate lives for the past few months. She's already moved on. She's got a new fella.'

'Oh,' conceded a relieved Wendy, 'that's okay then.'

'Guess it was meant to be then,' said Brian with a grin.

'What do you mean by that?' asked Wendy.

'Obvious innit? A Nunn and an Abbott getting together!'

Geraldine chuckled.

'I've never even thought of that!'

Wendy gave Geraldine a hug.

'Well, in that case I'm really pleased for you Geri. Everyone needs a little love, don't they?'

'Yes,' replied Geraldine as she first looked at Wendy and then Brian as if implying she thought they should give their marriage another chance. Wendy responded with a blush.

'Let's just say Geraldine,' said Brian, 'that since the funeral, I'm no longer relegated to the spare bedroom.'

Geraldine shrieked with pleasure.

'Oh, thank God for that! A new start for you both. A new start, in fact, for all of us. I really hope it works out for you.'

'Why don't you go and make yourself comfortable in the lounge Geri,' suggested Wendy, 'and I'll put the kettle on.'

As Geraldine wandered out of the dining room Wendy squeezed Brian's arm.

'It's great news Brian, isn't it?' she whispered. 'Are you sure we can't tell her our news? She is my best friend after all.'

Brian was quick to dismiss the idea.

'Absolutely not Wen,' he whispered firmly. 'We stick to the plan. We wait for Maureen to get in touch and we do exactly as she says. We can't do anything that might endanger the girl, whether Geraldine's your best friend or not. You've gotta promise me you'll not say a word.'

Wendy nodded.

'Guess you're right,' she conceded, 'though if Maureen's right – that Harry *is* innocent – I wish I could at least let Geri know.'

Brian faced her and put his hands on her shoulders, looking her straight in the face.

'Wen, please – you've gotta promise me.'

'Okay, okay.'

'Thank God for that!'

Over Christmas both Wendy and Brian were on tenterhooks. How and when would Maureen get in touch? Perhaps she wouldn't. Every time the doorbell sounded or the telephone rang they would jump out of their skins.

'I thought we would have heard from her by now,' said Wendy. 'All this waiting is doing my head in.'

'She's scared Wen. I'm sure she'll let us know as soon as she feels it's safe enough to do so.'

'If Maureen wants to sort this out before the trial she's cutting it fine,' said Wendy on Boxing Day. 'It's due to start on the 15th. My nerves are frazzled. I'm not sure how much more of this I can take.'

Thursday, January 11th dawned but there was still no word from Maureen. That evening Brian decided to have an early night.

'I'm knackered Wen. I haven't slept well for weeks. I think I'll have a soak in the bath then get into bed.'

'Good idea Brian. I'll be up shortly too.'

An hour later he was sound asleep. Wendy decided on a mug of Ovaltine before going upstairs herself. As the kettle was boiling the telephone rang. Wendy almost dropped her mug. She dashed into the hallway and picked up the receiver.

'Mrs Brown?'

'Yes.'

'It's Maureen. Has Mr Brown told you about me?'

'Yes.'

'I can't talk long, so I'll be quick. I'll come over to your's on Monday. About five o'clock. You'll need to tell Mrs Gooding to come too. I want you all together so I can tell you all at the same time. Otherwise, make sure you don't tell anyone. Not a soul. Do you understand? I'll be taking a huge, huge risk if I'm seen.'

'Who killed our girl Maureen?' blubbed Wendy. 'I really need to know. Don't you think we've waited long enough?'

'I'll explain it all on Monday Mrs Brown. I'm sorry but I need to know it'll be safe. I'm afraid you'll just have to wait.'

Finally, the nerves and her conscience got the better of Wendy. Before she could stop herself she made a confession.

'But I can't wait that long!' wailed Wendy. 'You don't understand. I've done really something terrible and I'm at my wits' end. I killed Sarah Mitchell. It was me!'

'What?'

'You heard me. She bad-mouthed Heather and then she attacked me. It was self defence!'

Wendy began to sob.

'Oh Jeez! Please, Mrs Brown, don't cry. Oh God, this is all my fault. Look, I can't talk any longer. I'll see you on Monday, five o'clock. I'll explain everything when I get there. I've gotta go now.'

The line suddenly went dead. Wendy stood in the hallway, still clutching the receiver. She began to shake uncontrollably. The landing light came on. Wendy looked up the stairs and saw Brian, in his pyjamas, staring down at her.

'Was that . . . was that her?' he asked, rubbing his eyes.

Wendy nodded. Brian hurried downstairs.

'What did she say?' he asked anxiously.

'She's coming here on Monday, about five o'clock. She said to make sure Stella's here too.'

'So, it's really happening then,' said Brian. 'Are you okay?'

'No.'

He hugged her.

'I've told her,' said Wendy, sobbing.

'Told her what?'

'That I killed Sarah.'

Brian stood back, looking aghast.

'You never did!'

'I did. I just came out. I couldn't help it.'

'Oh my God!' said Brian, 'have you completely lost your mind?'

'She said it was probably all her fault.'

'How could that possibly be Wen?'

'I dunno. I dunno Brian. I'm so, so scared!'

'You should be Wen. How do you know she'll keep a bombshell like that to herself? We'll just have to hope and pray she does or we'll both be up to our necks in it.'

Sleep was not an option as Wendy laid in bed that night. How she regretted revealing her involvement in Sarah's murder.

Brian was right. If Maureen cannot hold her tongue it wouldn't just be the end of the road for her but for Brian too as he had helped to dispose of the incriminating evidence.

Brian was up early the following morning. Like Wendy, he had barely slept.

'Surely you're too tired to work today,' said Wendy. 'You look beat.'

'I've got at least two jobs this morning and three this afternoon,' Brian replied. 'I'm not sure what time I'll be home 'cos I'm calling in at a couple of places later this afternoon to price up a couple more jobs for next week.'

He went into the bathroom to get washed and dressed. Wendy drifted off to sleep. As Brian was eating a slice of toast the telephone rang. He rushed to answer it in the hope Wendy would not be woken. A conversation in the region of 10 minutes ensued after which Brian replaced the receiver then quietly opened the front door and left home, leaving Wendy still sound asleep.

It was 11.30 by the time she woke. Rarely had she ever slept in for so long. She sat up in bed and groaned. She had a dreadful headache. As she opened the bedroom curtains the dazzling winter sun streamed through, hurting her eyes and causing her to swiftly turn away.

She looked at the calendar. Friday the 12th. Friday? Oh God, she thought it was Saturday. She should have been at school. She ran downstairs and telephoned Geraldine.

'Geri, I'm so, so sorry! I've only just woken up. I had a terrible night and I've got a splitting headache. I feel so bad to have left you in the lurch.'

Geraldine, as ever, made light of the situation.

'It's okay Wendy. It's not a problem. Felicity's kindly filling in for you today. Why don't you take a tablet or something and go back to bed? Hopefully, you'll feel a lot better tomorrow.'

'Thanks Geri. I might do just that.'

Wendy put down the 'phone and went back upstairs. She clambered back into bed but, after a while got up again, then washed and dressed. Once downstairs she took a couple of aspirins and made herself a coffee. She sat forlornly at the dining table. Why, she kept asking herself, did she open up to Maureen last night? Furthermore, what might Maureen do with that information?

Thoroughly miserable, she decided some fresh air might make clear her head. She put on her coat and scarf and went outside. She made her way to a pleasant wooded area half a mile from her home. In past times it was a place she had always enjoyed for a walk and, although it was cold, the sight of the sun streaming through the branches of the trees was one to behold.

She smiled as she recalled happier days a few years previously when she would bring her labrador Rufus up to the woods. Once there she would let him off his lead and more often than not he'd find a rabbit or squirrel to chase although he'd never actually managed to catch one.

She reached an opening in the wood. After brushing the damp leaves off a wooden bench with her hand she sat down. A myriad of thoughts began to race through her mind. Normally, a walk such as this would have lightened her mood but, sadly today, it was not to be. Suddenly she felt chilly so she got up and began to make her way back home. As she was putting her key into the front door lock she heard the telephone ringing.

She hurried inside and grabbed the receiver.

'Mrs Brown?'

It was Maureen.

'Yes.'

'There's been a change of plan. I'm coming over tonight. I'll be with you around five o'clock.'

'But Maureen, my husband's at work. He won't be back by then and I'll not be able to contact him. I don't even know where he'll be.'

'I'm sorry Mrs Brown, wheels have already been set in motion. Whether your husband is with you or not, it *has* to be tonight. Just make sure Mrs Gooding's with you.'

'But . . .'

The line went dead. Wendy looked at the hallway clock. Nearly two o'clock. Just three hours to go. She had no choice. She dialled Stella's number.

'Somersley 3647.

'Stella, it's me.'

'Oh hi Wendy. How are you?'

Wendy ignored her question.

'Stella, I need you to come over tonight. Around five o'clock.'

'Oh Wendy, I'm sorry. I can't make it I'm afraid. I've got a hair appointment at 5.30.'

'Then you'll have to cancel it Stella. This is important. Whatever happens, you *must* be here at five o'clock!'

'Oh, okay, if you say so. What's so important that it can't wait?'

'I can't tell you Stella. I'm sorry but, believe me, you can have no idea what might happen if you don't turn up.'

'Goodness Wendy, you sound like you're in a right old panic. Are you sure you're okay?'

'No Stella, I'm not. To be honest, I'm absolutely petrified. I just need you to be with me. Please don't be late and, most importantly, don't tell anyone you're coming over. *No-one at all*, do you understand?'

'Er, yeah. Okay. Should I come over now or would that be too early?'

'Yes, yes, come now! That would be brilliant. I don't want to be here on my own a minute longer.'

'Where's Brian then?'

'I dunno. Working somewhere and there's no way I can get hold of him. I just hope he gets back in time.'

'Okay Wendy. I'm putting on my coat as we speak. I'll be with you in 10 minutes.'

That 10 minutes felt like a lifetime to Wendy. The moment Stella arrived, Wendy flung her arms around her and burst into tears.

'I'm so glad you're here,' she blubbed.

'Are you gonna tell me why now?' asked Stella.

'I can't. I've been sworn to secrecy. Someone's life may depend on it.'

Stella was taken aback.

'Who's life?'

'I can't tell you Stella. I'm so sorry. You'll find out at five 'cos she's coming here to speak to us both.'

'Yes, but what about?' asked Stella who was still hoping for some kind of clue.

'All I can tell you,' replied Wendy, 'is that this person insists Harry Abbott didn't kill our girls but she says she knows who did.'

'And you believe her?'

'She's scared for her life so yes Stella, I do. Brian believes her too. I reckon in just over a couple of hours' time we might be discovering who really killed our girls.'

25

Every few minutes Wendy was pulling the net curtains in the lounge to one side.

'It's only 4.15 Wendy,' said Stella.

'I know. I'm sorry. It's just that every little sound makes me wonder if it's her.'

'Why don't you just come and sit down next to me?' suggested Stella, 'cos you're making me even more nervous.'

Wendy sat down yet moments later, there she was, peering through the net curtains once again. She looked at the clock. 4.20.

'God, is that all it is?' she said. 'The time seems to be dragging by, doesn't it?'

'Let's have another cuppa,' suggested Stella, keen to find something to occupy Wendy's mind, if only for a short while. Wendy didn't answer, being too busy peering outside.

Eventually her restlessness proved contagious. Stella also began pacing around the room and watching anxiously through the window.

The hall clock eventually began to chime. Five o'clock.

'Where is she?' asked Wendy anxiously. 'Five o'clock, she said.'

'Do you really think she's gonna turn up?' asked Stella.

Wendy sighed.

'Oh I dunno.' She looked once more at the clock. 'Maybe not.'

Once again she began to pace anxiously around the room, frequently looking at her watch. As the minutes passed her anxiety levels raised. Stella thought it looked as if she was about to explode.

The hall clock chimed 5.30.

'Well, that's it!' groaned Wendy. 'She ain't coming!'

'Er, I wouldn't be so sure about that,' said Stella. 'A car's just pulled up.'

She peered through the window trying, without success, to make out who was getting out of the passenger door of the vehicle. No sooner had the person shut the car door, it roared off down the road and out of sight. The person turned to face the house and began to walk down the driveway towards the front door. Still Stella was unable to make out who it was.

Wendy dashed to the front door. No sooner was the door slightly open, the person dashed inside, obviously being keen not to be spotted. Wendy shut the door.

It was only when Maureen lowered her face scarf that Stella realised who it was.

'Maureen!'

'Hello, Mrs Gooding. Hello Mrs Brown. Are you absolutely sure no-one knows I'm here?'

'No-one,' Wendy assured her.

'Can you close the curtains please? I don't want to be seen by anyone outside.'

Maureen was undoubtedly on edge. Wendy immediately obliged. She then gestured to Maureen to sit down.

'Now then,' said Wendy, 'are you gonna tell us what all this is about?'

'Soon,' replied Maureen. 'I'm waiting for a 'phone call first of all to let me know if it's safe to carry on. Besides, I've just called someone else. They'll be here in a few minutes.'

'Who?' asked Stella.

'Shepperton and Clarke,' she replied. 'They'll be here soon. They couldn't believe it when I called them just now. It seems they've been looking for me and my dad. I told them if they really wanted to know who killed Gemma and Heather they should get themselves over here right away.'

Barely had the words left her mouth a police car pulled up outside. Shepperton and Clarke got out and made their way up the driveway. Wendy let them in.

'Miss Robson,' he said the second Shepperton clapped eyes on Maureen, 'I think you need to come with us.'

'I don't think so,' Maureen replied, 'unless you don't want to hear what I have to say.'

'DCI Shepperton is right,' said Clarke. 'Anything you need to say can be said back at the station.'

He stepped forward towards Maureen but Stella and Wendy, in unison, stepped between them.

Wendy then turned to face Shepperton.

'What's the rush, detective? This young lady tells us she is risking her life coming here to speak to us.'

'Yes,' chipped in Stella, 'and we want to hear what she has to say.'

Both Wendy and Stella appeared determined not to back down.

'Very well,' said Shepperton. 'Ten minutes, and then she comes with us. Perhaps you'd like to begin with telling us about the argument you had with Heather and Gemma. I hear it got rather heated.'

'Who told you that?'

'Mr Trent, the manager of the Wimpy Bar in the High Street. We called him in for a second interview the other day. He said he didn't mention it in his first interview 'cos it was a couple of weeks before Gemma's murder and he didn't think it was relevant. He reckoned it was nothing more than a silly spat between two or three teenagers. We wondered if it could be more that.'

'It was nothing,' said Maureen, waving her arm dismissively. 'It was all sorted out later that day.'

'What was it about?' demanded Shepperton.

'A boy, okay? Trevor Turnbull. I told Heather he was no good. She shouted at me, told me I sounded like her mother and that I should mind my own business. Gemma backed Heather up. That's what upset me 'cos I was only trying to make sure Heather didn't get hurt. All the girls at Somersley Secondary will tell you that Trevor thinks he's God's gift. That's all it was. A few minutes later it was all smoothed over. That's all it was, I swear.'

'Okay then, Miss Robson, start talking,' said Clarke.

'Not yet,' replied Maureen. 'I'm waiting for a 'phone call.'

'Who from?' demanded Shepperton.

'You don't need to know.'

'Okay, that's enough,' said Shepperton impatiently, 'let's get going.'

'If you take me now, I swear I'll say nothing at all at the station,' said Maureen. 'It's your choice 'cos I'm not saying a thing until I can be absolutely sure that I'm safe. Besides, Mrs Brown and Mrs Gooding deserve to hear this from me directly. That's the least I owe them. '

She looked at her watch. 5.40.

'Any minute now, I reckon.'

Seconds later, as if on cue, the telephone rang. Maureen picked up, then replaced the receiver.

'Who was that?' demanded Shepperton. 'What did they say?'

'Go ahead,' replied Maureen.

She breathed a long sigh of relief and her eyes began to water. She looked at Shepperton.

'I've had to do some bad stuff,' she said. 'Really bad stuff. I need you to grant me immunity from prosecution if you want to hear exactly what happened to Heather and Gemma.'

'You know I can't promise that without having any idea of what you are about to tell us.' replied Shepperton.

'I won't say anything then,' said Maureen.

'Oh for God's sake Mr Shepperton,' said Wendy impatiently, 'give her a break or else we might never get down to the truth.'

Shepperton and Clarke walked to the far end of the lounge and conducted a short whispered discussion.

'Look, Miss Robson,' said Shepperton, 'we'll listen to anything you have tell us here on an informal basis. However, if we decide whatever you tell us now requires you to make a formal statement at the station, well that could be a different matter entirely.'

'We can't guarantee anything,' said Clarke, 'but, within reason, we will treat anything you have to tell us sympathetically if it is of evidential value. You have to bear in mind we already have Mr Abbott in custody. As far as we're concerned, we already have our man.'

'By the time I've finished, you'll realise you have the wrong man,' said Maureen. 'You have to understand, I need to protect myself. I've done bad things but they were done under duress. If you can promise me to bear that in mind, I'll take my chances.'

Shepperton nodded.

'Within reason – you've got a deal.'

'Can't we just wait until Brian gets here?' asked Wendy. 'This concerns him too.'

'I'm really sorry Mrs Brown but I've been trying to pluck up the courage for this moment for so long. I need to do it now before I chicken out completely. I need to get it over and done with.

'I think you should all sit down,' she added. 'cos I've got a lot to tell – and a lot of it, you won't like to hear – especially you, Mrs Brown and Mrs Gooding, but I swear on my life, everything I'm about to tell you is the truth – and not only that, I can prove it.'

26

'Okay, I'm gonna start right at the beginning,' explained Maureen. 'Only then will you get the full picture – and for that reason Mr Shepperton you can forget your 10-minute deadline.'

She turned to Wendy and Stella.

'As you know, Heather, Gemma, a few of the other girls and I would meet up each Saturday in town. After Mr Brown moved in with Mrs Gooding there were tensions between Heather and Gemma which was a real shame as they'd always been such good friends. That's why Gemma stopped coming along with us.

'We used to hang around in town. Sometimes we went window shopping and then finished the afternoon off in the Wimpy Bar in the High Street, other times we'd meet up with some of the boys from school down Roman Way beside the canal. Trevor Turnbull and Bradley Winterton often joined us there too. Us girls, we'd buy those big bottles of cider. Trevor usually brought along a little bit of weed.

'We just liked to hang out. Usually, we had good times but sometimes Trevor spoilt things. He'd keep making fun of Bradley and make him drink more and more cider 'cos he thought it was funny to watch get him drunk. Heather was always very protective of Bradley but that just made Trevor tease him even more.

'One day, when we were at school, Gemma was in a dreadful state. Heather was the first one who went over to console her. That was typical of Heather wasn't it?'

Wendy smiled, proud to think her daughter had put their differences aside in order to comfort Gemma.

'What was wrong with Gemma?' asked Stella.

Maureen looked at her awkwardly.

'She was pregnant,' she replied. The colour faded from Stella's cheeks.

'Who was the father?' she asked.

'Mr Nunn, her art teacher.'

Wendy gasped in astonishment.

'I can't believe it,' she said. 'Harvey Nunn and Geraldine are an item now. If this is true Maureen, Geraldine will be devastated.'

'It *is* true,' insisted Maureen. 'Why do you think she stayed on so often after school? She told her mum it was for extra art lessons but it was far more than that.

'When she found out she was pregnant Gemma was devastated. She was really scared but when she told Mr Nunn he didn't want to know. He turned his back on her. Gemma didn't know what to do. Eventually though she decided to ask Mr Brown if he could help her get an abortion . . .'

'You mean Brian knew?' interrupted a shocked Stella.

Maureen nodded.

'Yes, but Gemma swore him to secrecy. She was desperate you shouldn't know Mrs Gooding. She thought you'd go spare.'

'Well,' admitted Stella, 'I wouldn't have been happy, that's for sure but I wouldn't have gone mad at her.'

'Don't go too hard on Mr Brown,' said Maureen. 'He did his best to comfort and support Gemma. It's just that he didn't have the money to help her. When she told Heather that Mr Brown couldn't afford to help her Heather told her about Lucy Chapman and Mr Abbott. I think Lucy's mum worked for Mr Abbott as his secretary. Apparently there had been rumours that after Lucy got pregnant Mr Abbott had sorted it for her. Unofficially of course.

'Heather said Mr Abbott was a family friend and that she reckoned she could persuade him to help Gemma out. He did, but only after Gemma managed to get her hands on a couple of hundred quid to pay him.'

'But Gemma wouldn't have had that sort of money,' said Stella.

'I know,' said Maureen. 'Some of us chipped in what we could. Gemma had to nick the rest.'

Stella looked shocked.

'Who from?' she asked.

'No idea, she didn't say. She only did it 'cos she was desperate. Ironically, a few weeks later, Heather found herself in the same situation. The difference was she had some savings so she went to see Mr Abbott expecting him to help her too – especially as he was a friend of the family – but he told her the price had gone up. He said he wanted £400. Heather was very upset. She told him she hadn't got that sort of money. He just told her that he wasn't a charity and sent her away.'

Wendy sat with her head in her hands. If Maureen was to be believed her daughter and Gemma had both smoked weed, drank cider and had sex. This didn't sound like Heather at all. Although Bradley had told her about his sexual liaisons with Heather Wendy was finding it difficult to accept Maureen's version of events. Nevertheless, Maureen continued.

'Heather came round to our house that evening. We went up to my room and she told me what Mr Abbott had said. She was both fuming and scared. She wasn't even sure who the father was. I'm sorry to tell you this Mrs Brown, but Heather told me she'd been having sex with Bradley in her room when she was supposed to be helping him with his homework.'

'That's what Bradley told me recently,' said Wendy. 'I couldn't believe it at first but, in the end, he convinced me it was true.'

'The trouble was,' said Maureen, 'she couldn't be sure Bradley was the father because she'd also been getting it on with Trevor Turnbull.'

Wendy began to weep. Stella was swift to comfort her.

'I'm beginning to wonder how well we knew our girls after all,' she said. 'It's as if Maureen is describing strangers.'

Stella nodded.

'Then, unfortunately, I had an idea – a really bad one as it turned out,' said Maureen, suddenly looking more than a little uncomfortable. 'This is where I need assurances from Mr Shepperton that he won't take it any further.'

'As I've already told you Miss Robson,' reiterated Shepperton, 'I'm in no position to guarantee you anything at this stage. For all I know, all of this could be a tissue of lies and, if it's not, if everything you are about to tell us is true, I would need a very good reason not to press charges against you if you reveal something that cannot be ignored. It's up to you what you wish to reveal to us. Only afterwards could I make a decision either way.'

Maureen looked uncertain. She pondered her options and eventually seemed to come to a decision.

'You might not trust me Mr Shepperton, but I'm gonna put my trust in you. I suggested blackmail might be a possible solution to Heather's problem. I . . .'

'So, it was *you* blackmailing Harry Abbott,' interrupted Shepperton. 'His wife told us he'd been paying someone to cover up his illicit abortions.'

Maureen shook her head.

'Don't jump the gun Mr Shepperton, It wasn't Mr Abbott we were threatening to expose, it was his wife.'

Wendy gasped.

'Geraldine? That's ridiculous! She's my best friend and I can assure you she's never done anything she could be blackmailed over. She's . . .'

'Mrs Brown,' interrupted Maureen, 'you don't really know her at all do you?'

'Oh yes I do. I know her better than anyone. She has been a tower of support to us ever since Heather disappeared. We would never have coped without her.'

'Mrs Brown,' replied Maureen sadly, 'she wasn't here to support you at all. She wanted to keep close to you to cover her own back – to keep up to date with all the latest developments in Mr Shepperton's investigation so she could cover her tracks.'

'What on earth are you on about?' snapped Wendy angrily. 'How dare you talk about her like that! That's enough! DCI Shepperton, I suggest you take this young lady back to the station with you as you planned. I can't listen to any more of this nonsense.'

However, Maureen still had another devastating revelation that would rock everyone in the room.

'Mrs Brown,' countered Maureen, 'I think you should know that the person who killed your daughter and Gemma also wants me dead. That's why I had to get away so quickly.

'That person is your so-called best friend Geraldine Abbott. I know none of you will want to believe me, but I can assure you she's been playing you all for fools. She's the killer and, believe me, I can prove it!'

27

'That's a very serious accusation Miss Robson,' said Shepperton. 'You need to bear in mind that Mrs Abbott is a highly respected head teacher who has served this community well for a number of years.'

'So was Harry Abbott, but that didn't stop you arresting him,' argued Maureen

'It's a cruel lie!' shouted Wendy. 'Geraldine wouldn't hurt a fly! There's not a bad bone in her body.'

'I think we've heard enough here,' said Shepperton. He began to stand up but Clarke grabbed his arm.

'Hang on a bit Sir. Let her speak. I want to hear what else she has to say.'

Clarke had harboured reservations about the credibility of the charges against Abbott since his conversation with his former brother-in-law and he had no wish to suffer the reputational damage his former Super had endured back in 1971.

'I can back up everything I tell you,' Maureen insisted. 'Like I said, you won't like it, but it's the truth.'

'I don't understand,' said Stella. 'Harry was the one with the secret. Blackmailing Geraldine makes no sense. Why would you expect us to believe that?'

'Because we had something on her,' replied Maureen, 'and I reckoned she'd be the easier one to manipulate. As it turned out, I was wrong.'

'This is nonsense,' hissed Wendy.

Maureen ignored her and carried on.

'It was all my idea,' she said. 'I'd been struggling with my history revision so I went into the school library after hours to find a book I thought might be useful. I sat down behind one of the book racks and started to take notes. School had finished for the day but I had a test the next morning. I guess no-one could have seen me where I was sitting. Then I heard voices. It was Mrs Abbott and Mr Nunn. They came into the library.

'It was obvious there was something going on between them. They had no idea I was there, hearing everything they were saying. He told her he loved her and that he was prepared to leave his wife to be with her. She said she'd love nothing more but if she left her husband he'd divorce her and she'd lose everything. That's when the idea popped into my head. Now I wish it hadn't 'cos of everything that's happened since.

'I really wanted to help Heather so I spoke to Gemma and she agreed it was a good idea. We put it to Heather. At first she thought it was crazy but eventually we persuaded her that it was her only option.

'The next day Gemma slid an envelope under Mrs Abbott's office door with a note telling her that if she didn't pay £200 her secret would be revealed – that was the extra money Heather needed to pay Mr Abbott. We weren't being greedy – we could have fleeced her for the whole amount.'

'How very charitable of you,' murmured Shepperton.

'The trouble was, the next day, Heather realised she wasn't pregnant after all. She'd had her period. I decided we should abandon the blackmail. Heather agreed but Gemma insisted we shouldn't let Mrs Abbott off the hook – she'd never liked her and, because Mr Abbott had helped her out she kinda had a misplaced loyalty to him – even though he'd made her pay him for the privilege.

'Eventually she persuaded Heather and me that we should carry on as planned. Now I wish I'd never thought of it in the first place. From that point on everything's spiralled out of control. Gemma's note instructed Mrs Abbott to leave the money in the waste bin alongside the gate of the bridleway near the canal 'cos it was a remote and quiet spot. The trouble was Mrs Abbott must have spotted Gemma slipping the note under her door.

'My guess is, she had to make sure that Gemma was a problem that had to go away – permanently. That evening we all crouched down in the bushes and waited to see if Mrs Abbott would turn up at six o'clock – that was the time the note instructed her to be there.

'At first we were quite excited when we spotted her. She was holding a brown envelope and she did as instructed – she popped it into the waste bin and left – or so we thought. We waited a few minutes then Gemma checked to see if the coast was clear. She went over to the bin and picked up the envelope but, when she opened it, she discovered it was empty. She turned to face us and ripped the envelope open so we could see there was no cash inside.

Then Heather and I noticed some movement in the bushes behind Gemma but, before we could warn her, Mrs Abbott jumped out and started slashing at her with a knife. Gemma screamed then fell to the ground but Mrs Abbott didn't stop – she just kept stabbing and stabbing Gemma like she was in a frenzy.

'It was terrifying. Heather screamed. Mrs Abbott looked up and spotted us. She stepped over Gemma and began to run towards us. She was still holding the knife. Heather and I turned to run away but there was a chain link fence behind us so we were cornered. I was the nearest so she tried to stab me but Heather saved my life by pushing me to one side but the knife caught her instead. It went deep into her chest.'

'I don't believe you,' said Wendy angrily. 'You're a fantasist. Geraldine's a family friend and I know she'd never do such a thing!'

'I'm telling the truth Mrs Brown,' insisted Maureen. 'Heather fell to the ground. I believe she died instantly. Then Mrs Abbott turned to me. She had blood on her hands and on her dress but she didn't seem at all concerned about Gemma and Heather.

'I thought she was gonna kill me there and then. She could have 'cos she had me cornered. I started to cry and I was pleading for my life. She just sneered at me then stood there as if she was thinking what to do next.

'I begged her to let me go. I promised her I wouldn't tell a soul – that she could trust me to keep my mouth shut. I said I couldn't blame her for what she'd done – that it had all been Gemma and Heather's idea and that I'd tried to talk them out of it. I said anything I could think of that might stop her from attacking me too.

'She told me to shut up 'cos she was thinking. After a while she said 'I'm not gonna kill you – not yet anyway. You've got work to do.' She opened her shoulder bag and took out some kinda gun and pointed it at me.

'That's when she made me drag Gemma's body into the long grass by the towpath. I was so scared. Gemma's blood was over my hands and skirt. I couldn't stop crying. Then she leant over Gemma and removed her pendant. She put it in her pocket. Some kinda sick trophy, I reckon.'

Clarke nudged Shepperton and whispered.

'How would she know about the pendant? That info was never released.'

Still unconvinced, Shepperton merely shrugged. Stella began to sob.

'Don't listen to her Stella,' said Wendy. 'She's making it up as she goes along. You know Geraldine almost as well as I do. Surely you can't believe all this nonsense!'

'That's the trouble Wendy,' she replied. 'I'm beginning to think I do.'

'I'm not telling you all this just to upset you,' said Maureen. 'You need to know the truth. You need to know my part in all this too. I can only hope you'll forgive me when I've told you everything. This is not some sick, twisted joke, I can assure you.

'I feel terrible about what has happened and, like I said, it was my stupid idea that set the ball rolling. A lot of this is my fault but I cannot live the rest of my life in fear. I know I won't be safe until Mrs Abbott is behind bars.'

Wendy sat glaring at Maureen.

'You might fool the others but I'm sorry Maureen, you can't fool me. Nothing you can say will convince me that Geraldine has been involved in all this in any way.'

Maureen shrugged.

'I might as well shut up then,' she said.

'No,' said Stella. 'Keep going.'

Clarke nodded.

'Might as well carry on now we've got this far,' he said. Shepperton, like Wendy, still seemed unconvinced but Maureen took Clarke's lead and continued.

'Mrs Abbot told me to go back to fetch Heather's body. She was still pointing the gun at me. We were about to go back when we noticed some kids walking along the towpath. They sat down real close to Gemma's body and started smoking and larking around.

'Mrs Abbott told me to keep quiet then told me she'd had a change of plan.

'She seemed excited. She made me drag Heather's body in the opposite direction to a spot behind the trees where she'd parked her car. She unlocked the boot and told me to put Heather inside. I tried but I couldn't lift her. Mrs Abbott said she'd take Heather's legs but warned me that if I tried anything she'd shoot me there and then.

'Between us we managed to get Heather into the boot. I was exhausted. Then she pointed the gun at my head and told me to get into the boot with Heather. I said I couldn't do that. I told her that I get scared in confined spaces and there was no way I was going to get in there with Heather's body but she insisted and I was left with no choice. I climbed in and she shut the boot.'

'What kind of car did she drive?' demanded Shepperton.

'It was a Granada I think,' replied Maureen.

'What colour?'

'Oh I dunno!' snapped Maureen. 'Green maybe. I wasn't paying much attention to the car at the time.'

Clarke nudged his colleague.

'Mrs Abbott drives a green Granada.'

'Yeah, but a lot of people probably know that already,' replied Shepperton. 'This kid's still gotta convince me that she's not wasting our time.'

His comment riled Maureen.

'I am not a kid! I'm taking a huge chance here so have some respect!'

'He didn't mean it,' Clarke assured her in an attempt to keep her talking. 'Would you carry on please Maureen?'

Maureen glared angrily at Shepperton. Clarke was hoping she wouldn't clam up.

'Please Maureen,' he said, 'keep going.'

He smiled reassuringly at her and was relieved to notice his effort had not been in vain. Maureen took a deep breath and continued.

'I heard her get into the car and start up. It was a very bumpy ride until she reached the roadside. After that it was only a short drive before she stopped. I heard her shut her door and walk away.

'I thought she was just gonna leave me in there with Heather. I started to scream and kick the boot lid in the hope someone might hear and rescue me. I screamed and screamed and kicked and kicked until I was almost out of breath.

'Eventually I heard someone approaching so I started screaming and kicking again but, sadly, it wasn't a passer-by, it was Mrs Abbott. I don't know how long she'd left me in there but it was dark by the time she let me out. She still had the gun in her hand. In the other she had a spade.

'We were in a plot of land next to her house. She handed me the spade and ordered me start digging a hole. The ground was hard and it took me ages. She just stood watching me then, when I'd finished, she made me lift Heather out of the boot. She took Heather's legs and we laid her in the hole.

'Then she told me to bring over a bag laying in the grass nearby. It was heavy and there was some white stuff in it. She told me to spread it over Heather's body.'

'Bloody hell!' gasped Shepperton.

His reaction startled both Stella and Wendy.

'Miss Robson,' he said, 'I'm beginning to think I might owe you an apology.'

Wendy and Stella looked confused.

'Mrs Brown, Mrs Gooding, there was a degree of information we held back from the public. I have to tell you that Heather's body was covered in lime. There's no way Miss Robson could have known that if she had not been there at the time. That was a closely-guarded piece of information that we'd held back.'

'See, I told you I could prove it,' declared Maureen, 'and there's more.'

'Why would she cover my daughter with lime?' asked Wendy. 'Why would anyone do that?'

Shepperton looked at Clarke, unsure as to whether they should pile on the agony by explaining. Stella, however, helped them out.

'Lime speeds up decomposition Wendy,' she explained. 'It's a method some killers use to try to hide the identity of their victims. I've seen it on those crime programmes on the telly.'

At this point, the stress of listening to Maureen's version of Heather's last moments, her death and burial overcame Wendy. She was close to fainting.

'I think we should stop for a while,' suggested Stella, 'it's all too much for her. I'm struggling too. I'm finding it hard to reconcile Maureen's description of Gemma's behaviour with the daughter I thought I knew.'

'Okay, let's take a 10-minute break,' said Shepperton. 'James, perhaps you could fetch Mrs Brown a glass of water?'

Fifteen minutes later Shepperton deemed Wendy had recovered sufficiently to allow Maureen to continue.

'Mrs Abbott began to laugh, almost hysterically. She was waving the gun around in the air and had an almost crazy look on her face. She started saying 'This'll make you pay Harry!' She said it over and over again. I don't know why. Then she told me to dig another hole. I thought there's no way I was gonna dig my own grave so I refused. I told her she'd have to shoot me 'cos I wouldn't do it.

'She shouted at me and told me to do as I was told but I still refused. I was really scared but suddenly she just smiled at me and told me I was brave. She handed me the gun and began to laugh almost crazily. That's when I realised it wasn't a gun at all, it was just one of those novelty cigarette lighters.'

Wendy and Brian exchanged glances.

'The lighter!' he said.

Shepperton looked intrigued.

'What about it?' he asked.

'It was a birthday gift from Brian and me, years ago.'

'I was desperate,' continued Maureen. 'I was sure she would kill me too. I mean, why wouldn't she? Then I had an idea. I told her that way before Gemma and Heather got involved, I'd told one of the girls from school that, I had plan and that I'd be setting Mrs Abbott up. She demanded to know who I'd told but I refused. I told her that if anything happened to me, it wouldn't take a genius to work out who might be responsible.

'She thought about it for a while then said I could go but I was to remember something – the dead can't talk. If she suspected I'd said anything she swore she'd hunt me down. She also said, if anything went wrong and she was arrested she wouldn't hesitate to implicate me. She'd say I'd dug the grave and that I helped her to kill Heather.'

'What happened next?' asked Clarke.

'What do you think? I ran. I ran as fast as I could. I ran and ran and ran all the way home. I was absolutely petrified and I have been ever since. I'm always looking around to see if Mrs Abbott is behind me. Believe me Mr Shepperton – that woman is plain evil!'

'Then, just before Christmas last year you might remember that you asked me to come to the station. You said you wanted to re-interview anyone who might be able to help with the investigation. You remember I told you I'd fallen down the steps outside the town hall?'

'Yes,' replied Shepperton.

'Well, it was obvious you didn't believe me. I don't blame you. Mrs Abbott had attacked me in Church Walk the previous day. She warned me to keep my mouth shut. She left this under the wiper on my car.'

She dipped into her pocket and handed Shepperton the crumpled note. Shepperton opened his briefcase and withdrew a pair of gloves and a small evidence bag.

'I'll take that if you don't mind,' he said. 'We'll need to check that forensically.'

Maureen handed the note over to him. Shepperton immediately placed the note into the bag and sealed it.

'Now do you believe me, Mrs Brown?' asked Maureen.

Wendy didn't answer. Up until the last few minutes she had been convinced Maureen had been spinning a tissue of lies against her best friend. Now the thought that Geraldine had been by her side from the moment Heather had disappeared made her feel sick to the stomach.

How could Geraldine have possibly acted in such a cruel way without her realising? Wendy wondered if her best friend had even gained some twisted, perverted form of pleasure as she watched her suffer. Maureen's claim that Geraldine had been excitedly exclaiming that Harry would pay could have been a result of his infidelity, the embarrassment arising from his conviction and his gambling debts.

'My dad didn't believe me either,' said Maureen, 'but eventually, he persuaded me to tell him the truth. He said I'd have to tell the police but I was convinced Mrs Abbott was watching my every move – I know that sounds daft, but I was imagining she was around every corner, day and night. I told dad there was no way I was gonna go to the police but then my mum came to see you Mr Shepperton.

'I freaked out when she told me you would be coming to speak to me. I lashed out at her. I've never done anything like that before but I was so scared. That's when dad and I left Somersley and went into hiding.'

'Where did you go?' asked Shepperton.

'I'm not saying,' replied Maureen. 'Not until I'm absolutely sure Mrs Abbott's been locked up somewhere. Even my mum doesn't know where we went.'

'Stella,' said Wendy almost inaudibly. 'Can you believe all this?'

Stella nodded.

'Geraldine's taken me for a fool, hasn't she?'

Stella squeezed Wendy's hand.

'I think she's taken all of us for fools,' she said.

Wendy sobbed.

'I've been so stupid! Things are starting to add up now.'

'What do you mean Mrs Brown?' asked Shepperton.

'Geraldine told me about Harry's affair. It wasn't the first time he'd cheated on her. She told me she'd been seeing Harvey Nunn but she wasn't prepared to divorce Harry 'cos she'd lose out financially. I can't see how Maureen could have known that if she hadn't heard her talking in the library.

'I reckon she was trying to set Harry up. She must have placed the pendant in Harry's office as an act of revenge. She must have been hoping he'd be locked up for good so she wouldn't lose out.'

'It's rather ironic then,' said Stella, 'that she had no clue that Harry was conducting illegal abortions on the side 'cos he's since been locked up anyway.'

Wendy turned to Maureen.

'I'm sorry Maureen. I didn't want to believe you.'

'But you do now?'

'Yes,' replied Wendy reluctantly, 'I do now.'

'I'm sorry too Mrs Brown. I hope you can forgive me. You too Mrs Gooding.'

The women tearfully nodded.

'What about you Mr Shepperton, Mr Clarke?'

'Mr Abbott's trial is due to begin in court in a couple of days. If we can corroborate everything you've just told us Miss Robson, you've really put the cat amongst the pigeons.'

'I know, but do you believe me?'

Shepperton looked at Clarke, then back to Maureen.

'Yes, Miss Robson. I think it's safe to say we both believe you.'

Maureen sighed with relief.

'Thank goodness!'

She instantly burst into tears, her obvious relief leaving everyone in the room finally convinced of her version of events.

'What now?' asked Stella.

'Well,' said Shepperton, 'Miss Robson will need to come down to the station with us to make a formal statement.'

Maureen looked at him, tears streaming down her face, her eyes puffy.

'But what about Mrs Abbott?' she asked. 'Are you gonna arrest her?'

'We'll have to bring her in,' admitted Shepperton.

'What about me?' asked Maureen. 'Am I in trouble?'

'I promised I'd consider that after you'd told us everything,' said Shepperton. 'Assuming we can verify all you have told us I think I can assure you that you will not be facing any prosecutions.'

'And you'll keep me safe?'

'If it turns out we can establish evidence that Mrs Abbott was involved in the murders we will ensure you come to no harm. I think now we need to locate Mrs Abbott and bring her in for questioning.'

Wendy looked at her watch.

'She always works later on a Friday night but she should back at her sister's by now. She's the landlady at The Golden Boot in Burberry.'

'She'll certainly be in for a shock when your lot turn up,' said Stella.

'Oh, I don't think so,' said Maureen. 'I 'phoned her just before I came over here.'

'What?' gasped Shepperton.

'I called her. I've spent all this time terrified of her. I rang her and told her she was right – the dead can't talk – but that the living can. I said I was with Mr Shepperton and that I was gonna tell him everything so she couldn't scare me any more.'

Shepperton and Clarke groaned simultaneously.

'What's wrong with that?' asked Maureen. 'After all I've been through it felt good to turn the tables on her at last.'

'I think the detectives are concerned you've given Geraldine the chance to get away,' said Stella.

'Oh God,' said Maureen. 'I didn't think of that! I must be so stupid! I'm so sorry.'

'Get to the car quickly James,' instructed Shepperton. 'Get on the radio. We need cars to The Golden Boot and to the school. We'll have to hope we can find her at one or the other. If not, we'll need to alert all cars to look out for her green Ford Granada.'

'Okay,' replied Clarke. He hurried outside to the car but, within seconds, he returned.

'No need to search,' he said. 'Just had a radio call. Geraldine Abbott's been found already.'

'Where?' asked Shepperton.

'In her office at the school,' replied Clarke, 'but that's not all. She's dead – and she's left a note. The school caretaker called it in 10 minutes ago.'

28

'My God!' exclaimed Stella as Wendy shut the door. 'What did you make of all that?'

The women watched through the lounge window as Shepperton and Clarke accompanied Maureen to their car.

'I believe her,' admitted Wendy. 'but at first I just wanted to slap her. Saying all those dreadful things about Geraldine. She was the last person I would have suspected. All that time she was supposedly supporting me, lending me a shoulder to cry on. I told her so many things – deeply personal stuff – that I would never have shared with anyone else. Now I feel such a fool.'

'Well,' declared Stella, 'I'm glad she's dead. I can't get those pictures of Gemma's last moments out of my head. If everything Maureen says is genuine, our poor girls had the most horrendous deaths.'

The tearful women embraced. Each knew exactly how the other felt. A shared grief – the kind of grief only a bereaved mother could understand. Unlikely as it was, the women now shared a bond and it was this feeling that prompted Wendy to make an admission.

'Stella, I need to tell you something. I've done something terrible and I can't keep it a secret any longer. It's doing my head in.'

Stella looked puzzled. Wendy, however, now felt an overwhelming need to unburden herself.

'Brian is the only other person to know this,' she said. 'I wanted to hand myself in to the police but Brian insists I shouldn't. I need to know what you think. If you think I should, I'll hand myself in to Shepperton.'

'Jeez Wendy,' replied Stella, 'as if we haven't heard enough today already.'

'Yeah. Sorry, but this is something you'll need to know. I'd rather you find out from me than anyone else.'

Over the next few minutes Stella sat, completely astonished, as Wendy described the events leading up to Sarah's death and how Wendy had left her body in the long grass at Roman Walk.

'Say something Stella,' pleaded Wendy as her new-found friend gazed into space.

'I, I don't quite know what to say,' she replied. 'I mean, I've never had someone tell me they've killed someone. I know you wouldn't have intended to do it – you must have been terrified but, apart from that, I just dunno what to say. It's such a lot to take in.'

'Yeah,' agreed Wendy. 'I know.'

Eventually Stella seemed to have come to a decision.

'I think you should go to Shepperton and tell him everything. Sarah's mother deserves to know the truth. Think about how our lives have been torn apart by not knowing what happened to our girls. That poor woman will be going through hell, just like we were. She needs to know how her girl died.'

Wendy nodded in agreement.

'Will you take me to the station?' she asked. 'I just want to get it over and done with.'

Stella gave her a supportive hug.

'Yes, of course. I'll come in with you if you like. I can tell Shepperton that you were under an immense strain when it happened. He'll understand. He has to, surely?'

'I wouldn't bet on that,' said Wendy. 'Can we go now?'

'I think we should wait a while though,' replied Stella. 'Brian needs to hear what Maureen told us and told that Geraldine is dead. He needs to hear it from us, don't you think?'

'Yes, but on the other hand, he won't want me to tell Shepperton 'cos he helped me to cover it up.'

'Well, don't tell Shepperton about his involvement then,' advised Stella. 'Only tell him what you need to. At the end of the day, you don't need Brian's permission to do the right thing.'

Wendy managed a slight smile.

'I guess you're right Stella. As soon as we've told Brian everything, you can take me to Shepperton.'

She looked at the clock. 7.10.

'Speaking of Brian, where is he? It's pitch dark out there. I would have expected him home at least a couple of hours ago. I mean, you can't do much gardening at this time of the year can you? I wonder what's keeping him?'

Stella noticed car headlights outside.

'I guess he can tell you himself in a moment,' she said. 'He's just arrived.'

Wendy raced into the hall and opened the door. As Brian stepped indoors she flung herself into his arms.

'Thank God you're back!'

Brian grinned.

'Well, it's a long time since I've had such an enthusiastic welcome home Wen!'

Then he noticed her tear-stained face and Stella watching them from the lounge doorway.

'Brian, Maureen's been here. She's told us everything that's happened. Harry didn't kill our girls. Geraldine did.'

Wendy expected Brian to be just as astonished as she and Stella had been. Neither woman expected his response.

'Yeah, I know!'

29

'You know? How could you possibly know? Maureen has only just told us.'

Brian, with a broad smile on his face, suggested they all sit down in the lounge.

'I've got such a lot to tell you both,' he said.

Stella and Wendy, both puzzled, followed him into the lounge. They sat side by side on the settee while Brian sat facing them on the armchair opposite.

'I was about to leave for work this morning when the telephone rang. At first I couldn't make out who was on the other end of the line but he was asking for me. His voice sounded muffled, as if he had his hand or a handkerchief over his mouth. You were still sound asleep upstairs.

'He wouldn't say who he was but he insisted I speak to no-one, not even you Wen. He said I was to drive right away to the recreation ground, to park there and to walk towards the cricket pavilion.

'He said no-one should follow me. If I wanted to know exactly what happened to Heather I should do exactly as he said. I told him a man had already been arrested for Heather's murder and the trial was about to begin. Anything I'd need to know would come out during the trial.

'He said he knew about Harry Abbott but he could prove Harry was innocent and that he also knew who the real killer was and he insisted that he could prove that too.

'I thought it was a crank call but then he mentioned the pendant. Shepperton and Clarke had told us not to mention it to anyone. As you both know, it was information kept from the public. That gave the caller the credibility he needed to persuade me to meet up with him.

'I drove straight to the recreation ground. I sat on the bench outside the pavilion as instructed and waited. A few seconds later I noticed two people approaching me. It was Maureen and her father George. Over the following hour or so they told me everything that had happened – the blackmailing, Gemma and Heather's killing, how Geraldine forced Maureen to bury Heather, the lot. Maureen was in a dreadful state. Absolutely terrified that Geraldine would, somehow, get to her.

'George explained he was prepared to go to any lengths to protect his girl. I said I could quite understand that. Then he said he had come up with a way to ensure Maureen's safety and to avenge Gemma and Maureen's deaths. He asked if I wanted to help them.

'To me, that was a no-brainer. Geraldine had to pay for what she'd done. She needed to face justice but, as George said, the sort of justice that only we could administer.'

'So all this happened early this morning?' asked Wendy. 'Where have you been all day?'

'Planning.

'Planning what?' asked Stella.

Brian gazed at both women with a steely, yet satisfied, look on his face.

'Vengeance,' he replied, 'vengeance.'

'Oh my God!' declared both women in unison.

'What have you done?' asked Stella.

'Well, ladies, it all panned out like this . . .'

30

Two and a half hours earlier:

It was almost five o'clock and everyone, pupils and staff, apart from Geraldine, had gone home. Following Maureen's telephone call she was in a panic. Should she front it out or run? She was pacing around her office when Brian entered, startling her. She looked up over her horn-rimmed spectacles.

'Brian! What are you doing here?'

No sooner had she asked the question she noticed his agitated state. Brian bore an almost manic expression as he began pacing around her office.

'Brian, what's the matter?'

'I've done something. I've done something t-t-terrible!'

He clasped each side of his head with his hands.

'Come here, sit down,' said Geraldine in an attempt to calm him down. She took his arm and, very gently, guided him to the chair on the opposite side of her desk. She put her arm around his shoulder and stroked the back of his head as she cradled him against her ample bosom.

'Now then Brian, whatever it is you've done I'm sure we can sort it.'

Brian shook his head and sank to his knees.

'It's too late!' he wailed. 'Much, much too late! The damage has been done!'

Geraldine knelt down on the floor, bringing her face level with his.

'Come on Brian,' she urged. 'Talk to me. You can tell me anything in absolute confidence.'

Brian paused for a moment, then took a deep breath.

'I'm on my way to see Shepperton,' he said. 'I can't go on like this – all the lies – I'm gonna hand myself in.'

'For what Brian? Whatever are you talking about?'

'Wen must have told you sometime, hasn't she? About my psychosis? My delusions?'

'No, Brian, it's never been mentioned.'

'It's been happening on and off for years but last night I woke up and realised what I'd done. I need your help Geraldine. I can't hand myself in until you've helped me.'

Geraldine was at a total loss to understand what Brian was trying to tell her. Patiently she decided to allow him time, without pressure, to explain.

'You know I can't write – I can barely spell my own name – but you, you're good with words – look at the way you wrote Heather's eulogy for us. You did it so well.'

Geraldine smiled.

'It was nothing Brian. I just spoke as I felt, that's all.'

'I need you to write a letter to Wendy – a letter from me. I want to dictate what's happened so she can understand. After I hand myself in I won't get the chance to tell her. Please Geraldine, will you help me?'

'What is it you want her to know?'

Brian remained on his knees and began to rock.

'I need to tell her that it wasn't Harry who killed the girls. It was me!'

Geraldine gasped, hoping Brian wouldn't notice her relief and began pacing around her office. She fumbled among the items on her desk.

'Did I hear you right? Say that again.'

'It wasn't Harry who killed the girls. It was me!

'But that's ridiculous Brian. Shepperton's already got enough evidence against Harry. It couldn't possibly have been you.'

'But it was, Geraldine. *I* did it. Harry's totally innocent! His trial is due to start any time now. That's why I have to hand myself in but first, I need you to help me write that letter.'

Now it was Geraldine's turn to pace around the office.

'Well say something then,' said Brian. 'Are you gonna help me or not?'

Geraldine continued to pace around her office, seemingly at a loss of what to say or do. Eventually she sat down at her desk and looked directly at Brian.

'Tell me why you reckon you killed the girls,' she demanded.

'It came back to me in the night,' he explained. 'Flashbacks. Real clear flashbacks. I could clearly remember sticking the knife into Sarah and . . .'

'Whoa! Whoa! Wait a minute!' interrupted Geraldine. 'Sarah? Are you telling me it was *you* who killed Sarah Mitchell?'

Brian nodded.

'Yeah. I still can't remember why, but the murder itself – well, it's come back to me as clear as day now. Sometimes I get these urges you see. Afterwards I took her body down to Roman Walk and left it there in the long grass. There were other flashbacks too – Gemma and Heather. Those weren't so clear but, obviously, I must have killed them too.'

Geraldine appeared stunned at his revelations.

'I can hardly believe this,' she exclaimed. 'I guess you have no choice then. You'll have to speak to Shepperton.'

Brian nodded, but added: 'Yes, but not until you help me write to Wendy.'

Geraldine, seemingly reluctant, opened her desk drawer and took out a writing pad and a pen.

'Let's just get this over with then,' she said. 'What do you want me to write?'

Brian seemed to ponder over a suitable choice of words then began to dictate his confession to Wendy.

'I think we should start with *'Dear Wendy'*, he said. 'Yeah, start with that.'

Geraldine began to write and Brian continued to dictate.

'It is with a very heavy heart that I write this to you. I want you to know I've loved you over the years and I hope that some day, you might find it in your heart to forgive me for the terrible things I have done, though I very much doubt you will ever be able to do so.

'I can no longer live with my conscience. It's time to come clean. For reasons that I cannot explain, I need you to know that it was not Harry, but me who killed Gemma and Heather. I also killed Sarah.

'I am so sorry for deceiving you these last few months, for looking you in the eye and hiding the truth from you. I do not ask for, or deserve your pity. Only God can forgive me now. I am so, so sorry.'

Geraldine stopped writing and looked up at Brian.

'Is that it?' she asked.

'I think that's enough,' he said. 'Did you get all that?'

Geraldine nodded. Brian stood up.

'Thank you. Tell Harry I'm sorry will you? Tell him I'll explain it all to Shepperton. I'll go and see him now.'

Geraldine put down the pen, barely able to hide her glee.

-o0o-

'So Geraldine's note was dictated by you,' said a gob-smacked Wendy afterwards.

'Yep,' said Brian proudly. 'Genius wasn't it? It's there in black and white, in her own handwriting – a full confession for killing all three girls.'

Stella looked uneasy.

'Brian,' she said, 'Wendy's just told me about Sarah.'

'Can't say I'm surprised,' he replied calmly. 'It was only a matter of time until she cracked. She keeps saying she wants to hand herself in – to own up – but now, there's no need. As far as Shepperton will be concerned, Geraldine did it – she's admitted it in her suicide note.

'Wen,' he added, 'don't you see, you're in the clear. You kept saying Sarah's mum needed to know what happened to her girl. Now she'll know – Geraldine killed her.'

'But it's not the truth,' said Wendy.

'Maybe not,' replied Brian, 'but it's our kind of justice, isn't that right Stella?'

'Brian's right,' said Stella. 'What good would it do for you to confess now? If Mrs Mitchell believes Geraldine killed Sarah, that's good enough for me.'

'You mean you'd cover for me?' replied Wendy. 'I couldn't ask you to do such a thing.'

'You haven't asked Wendy. Leave it be. Geraldine killed Sarah. End of story. Like I said, that's good enough for me.'

'That's settled then,' declared Brian triumphantly.

He grinned.

'I should have got an Oscar for my performance,' he said puffing out his chest proudly. 'I must have been very convincing. Can you imagine how she felt when I suggested that I'd been the killer all along? Okay, it'll be a while before Harry's released, but he will be one day and he'll know he's been set-up. She probably saw it that Harry would believe I'd been the one setting him up.'

'I have to say, Brian,' said Stella, 'it was, as you say, genius. Was it all your idea?'

'No, not entirely,' he admitted. 'George had plenty of ideas, I just polished up the edges really. The cleverest part of it all was a suggestion from Maureen.'

'What was that?' asked Stella.

'Maureen said it was common knowledge that Geraldine always worked late on a Friday evening. A few minutes before I entered Geraldine's office, she had a telephone call – from Maureen. She told Geraldine that she was fed up of hiding and that she was about to see Shepperton, and that she'd be telling him everything. The dead can't talk,' she told her, 'but the living can – so you don't scare me any more!'

'No wonder Geraldine was at sixes and sevens when you went into her office,' said Stella. 'She must have been bricking it!'

'So Maureen knew *exactly* what she was doing when she 'phoned Geraldine,' gasped Wendy. 'It wasn't a mistake, it was all part of the plan!'

'Exactly!' said Brian, 'and it worked perfectly. Geraldine suddenly realised that if I'd admitted to the killings, it didn't matter what Maureen was telling Shepperton at that very moment 'cos he wouldn't believe her. As far as Geraldine was concerned, I was dictating my own confession.'

After the tensions of the last few hours, Wendy allowed herself a rather satisfied chuckle.

'Yeah,' she agreed. 'Genius!'

Stella, however, remained silent, deep in thought.

'Penny for them, Stella,' said Wendy.

'Maybe I'm a bit dim,' said Stella. 'There's something I don't quite understand. Why would Geraldine kill herself? As far as she was concerned, it was Brian's confession and he was gonna send it to Wendy.'

'Yes, but Brian presumably hadn't signed it,' suggested Wendy.

'Of course I didn't,' said Brian.

'In that case,' said Stella, 'she would have expected Brian to have taken the note with him, not leave it with her in her office. Do you see what I mean?'

Wendy, puzzled, looked to Brian for an explanation. He responded by appearing flustered. He stood up and began to pace around the lounge.

'What aren't you telling us, Brian?' asked Wendy.

'Yes, Brian, there's something else, isn't there?' demanded Stella.

'You remember that conversation we had when we thought Harry was the killer?' he replied. 'How we said we'd kill him ourselves if we could have got our hands on him?'

'Yes,' said Stella.

'And you both meant it, didn't you?'

Both women nodded.

'That's exactly what George, Maureen and I felt about Geraldine,' said Brian. 'She needed to pay the full price for what she'd done to our girls. No mercy!'

'Oh my God Brian, are you saying what I think you're saying?' asked Wendy.

He nodded.

'Look, we all know that when Sarah died it was an accident Wen. A tragic accident. Just think what Geraldine has put us all through, what she did to our girls and how Sarah's death came as a result of the stress you were under because of Geraldine.

'Geraldine didn't deserve to live. She had to die and I made sure of it.'

Stella and Wendy were stunned.

'What happened Brian? What *exactly* happened?' asked Stella.

'She asked me if I wanted to sign my confession,' he replied. 'I made an act of dropping my pen on the floor behind her. She thought I was picking it up but, as soon as I was behind her, I took a plastic bag out of my pocket and pulled it over her head and held it tightly. She was struggling to breathe and began thrashing around.

'She tried grabbing her telephone but I pulled her back. She kept trying to reach it but I was too strong for her. Then the bag split and she started to call out.

'Brian! Brian! she cried, Why are you doing this? I told her to shut up. I mean, what a stupid thing to ask. Why wouldn't I have wanted her dead?

'I put my hand over her mouth but she was still reaching out for the telephone. Then, suddenly, she went limp. She was dead.

'Her desk had been kicked over so I stood it up again and put everything back in place. Then I put her arm on the desk and used a paper knife I bought this morning to cut her wrist so it looked like a suicide. I bought a real fancy knife 'cos I thought that was the kind Geraldine would have purchased, what with her being such a fancy cow. I left the note on her desk and the knife in her hand and left.

'Maureen said the caretaker, Mr Merritt, always checked the premises before locking up each night so we knew it wouldn't be long until the alarm was raised. George was waiting for me down the road in his car. I got in and told him that he and Maureen needn't worry about Geraldine any more.

'He hugged me with relief and we drove off. George stopped by the telephone box on the corner of Angel Street and rang here.

When Maureen answered he just said 'go ahead', that was our code to let her know it was safe to talk to Shepperton. Maureen knew all along that Geraldine was already dead when she was speaking to you.'

'Oh, I dunno,' said Wendy, 'this is all getting too messy. We'll never get away with this, and I can't stop thinking about Sarah's mum.'

Brian was quick to reassure her.

'Look Wen, I think it's safe to say we're all glad Geraldine's dead. I am right, aren't I?'

Stella and Wendy both nodded in agreement.

'Well,' said Brian, 'so will Sarah's mum. She's bound to be. When the police tell her they have a confession, I'm sure she'll feel just as glad as we are that Geraldine's dead.'

'I'm worried about Maureen,' said Stella. 'Shepperton will need her to make a statement. What if she slips up?'

'No need to worry about her,' said Brian confidently. 'She's got a wise head on young shoulders. All she needs to do is tell the truth – tell Shepperton exactly what happened from beginning to end – apart, of course, from the bit where she told him she'd telephoned Geraldine while I was waiting outside her office.'

'Fingerprints!' said Wendy.

'Not a problem,' said Brian. 'It's been really cold today. I was wearing gloves all the time.'

He stood up and smiled confidently.

'Trust me ladies,' he said, 'our nightmare is over at last. We can all relax now.'

31

Shepperton and Clarke dropped Maureen off at home on their way to the school, instructing her – and her father – to come to the police station the following morning to make formal statements. George had been waiting outside, out of his wife's sight and anxiously pacing up and down, counting the minutes for his daughter to return. The moment the detectives dropped her off Maureen raced into her father's arms.

'How did it go?' he asked.

'Exactly as we planned,' she replied.

'And they weren't suspicious?'

'Well, they were at first but, by the time I'd finished, I managed to convince them I was telling the truth.'

'Well, my dear, you were, weren't you?'

Maureen nodded.

George looked towards their front door. The curtains were drawn but the downstairs lights were on.

'Are you ready for this?' he asked.

'I guess so,' replied Maureen. 'I wonder how she'll react?'

'There's only one way to find out,' replied her father as he put his key into the lock.

'Hello! Debs we're back!' he called out as he stepped into the hallway.

The kitchen door was immediately flung open and a relieved Deborah rushed towards them. George opened his arms but his wife ran straight past him and flung her arms around Maureen.

'Oh thank God you're safe Mo!' she sobbed. 'I've been going out of my mind. Where have you been all this time?'

'We've been at Uncle Gary's place,' replied Maureen. 'He said we could stay there while he was away working on the rigs.'

Maureen was referring to George's brother who lived near Aberdeen. At the time George and Maureen had fled Somersley George had no idea where he was heading but, as long as it was far from home, he didn't care too much. His only concern was to keep Maureen safe. As they headed north Maureen had the idea to telephone her uncle to see if he could offer them refuge.

Deborah continued to hug Maureen, so relieved she was to have her home again.

'I'm so sorry Mum, I didn't mean to hit you. I panicked. I was so scared when you said the police were coming.'

'It's okay, I'm just glad you're home but I can't understand why you didn't get in touch.'

'We couldn't love,' said George. 'We . . .

'I'll deal with you later!' interrupted a furious Deborah as she glared at her husband.

'Leave it Mum,' pleaded Maureen. 'I don't know how I'd have coped without Dad. It's 'cos of him I'm safe.'

'Safe? What do you mean? I don't understand. Safe from what?'

'Oh Mum, it's such a long story. I'm sorry, but we couldn't risk telling anyone where we were – not even you. Let's just sit down together then Dad and I can tell you everything.'

Deborah could hardly believe her ears as her husband and daughter revealed all that had gone on. Both George and Maureen had been dreading the moment they needed to reveal the circumstances surrounding Geraldine's death but, by that point, it was pretty clear that Deborah would have happily killed Geraldine herself after learning what the murderous head teacher had put her daughter through.

To George's immense relief his wife now seemed to appreciate the reasons for their sudden enforced disappearance and, now furnished with all the gory details, and understanding the danger

Maureen had been facing at the time, she was happy to forgive her husband for keeping her in the dark. She gave George a hug.

'I'm so glad you're both back home,' she said. 'You must be exhausted. How about I cook you a nice hot meal – a roast dinner perhaps?'

'That sounds great love,' said George, 'but it's getting a bit late for that. Don't work tonight. What do you reckon Maureen? Shall we go out and celebrate the end of your nightmare?'

'Ooh yes!' replied Maureen enthusiastically. 'How about The Dog and Duck?'

Deborah seemed stunned to think that, just hours after scheming to kill Geraldine, they could even consider such an option.

'Wouldn't you both rather just stay at home?' she asked.

George looked at Maureen, then at his wife.

'See that girl?' he said. 'She's been going through absolute hell since Gemma and Heather died. I reckon if she wants to go to The Dog and Duck, that's the least she deserves, don't you?'

Deborah managed a smile.

'I guess I can't really argue with that,' she conceded. 'I'll get my coat.'

As the Robsons were setting off to The Dog and Duck Shepperton and Clarke were at the school standing in Geraldine's office. On arrival Shepperton glanced at the slightly blood-stained note on her desk.

'Looks like she's saved us a lot of work,' he said. 'I have to admit, when we had so little to go on after Gemma's murder, I was beginning to wonder if we'd ever get to the bottom of this business. If someone had told me then that Geraldine Abbott had been involved in any way I'd have thought they were potty.'

He sighed, mostly with relief, that this long-running investigation was, at last, over. Now, he thought, the media pressure for a resolution would subside. Life in and around Somersley could return to its relative normality.

Clarke, however, remained silent, deep in thought.

'Something's not right here,' he said.

'What do you mean?'

'Look,' replied Clarke pointing to the cut on Geraldine's wrist, 'I'm no forensics expert but I would have expected to see blood spread over a far wider area than this. You've attended enough murder scenes Dave. How often have we seen blood half way up the walls? Apart from this pool on the desk, there's very little else.'

Shepperton's initial relief instantly vanished. Clarke was right. If Geraldine had been alive when her wrist had been cut, her blood, under pressure, would most likely have spurted out as her wrist was cut whereas, in this instance, it had not. The only explanation, in his view, was that Geraldine's wrist had been severed *after* her death. He groaned.

'I might have known it wouldn't have been as straight-forward as it first appeared James. We'd better call in the full team, get this room sealed off until the forensics guys have given it the full works.'

'I'll get on to it right away,' replied Clarke who, looking at Geraldine's lifeless body slumped over her desk, noticed something else.

'That's another thing Dave. Look, she's holding the paper cutter in her right hand.'

'Yeah. So?'

'Don't you remember? When the pendant turned up, we called Geraldine to the station and she identified it as one her husband gave her for her birthday. I was taking notes at the time and she observed that I was left handed – she said she was too. Why, if she wanted to cut her wrist, would she hold the knife in her right hand? It's highly unlikely in my view that she would have done so. I'd bet my pension this ain't no suicide Dave. It's a murder.'

32

Deborah sat by the bar, holding her drink, deep in thought. She was far from convinced that this outing to The Dog and Duck had been a good idea. The thought that her husband and daughter had been complicit in a murder just a few hours earlier was, naturally, proving difficult to process.

She watched as George and Maureen laughed, drank and played pool, seemingly carefree. How could they do that? Just over an hour previously, back at home she had listened in abject horror as Maureen had described Gemma and Heather's killings and how her beloved daughter had been first made to clamber into Geraldine's car boot with Heather's body and then made to dig Heather's grave.

What ghastly emotions must Maureen have been going through at such a time? It hardly bore thinking about and, of course, in between those two shocking incidents, came the attack in Church Walk which must have been an absolutely terrifying experience.

Her poor girl must have been close to breaking point.

No wonder she had needed to get away – far away – from Somersley after learning that Shepperton was intending to visit their home. Maybe then, it was understandable that Maureen and George needed this opportunity to let off steam. Best, thought Deborah, to let them get on with it.

On arrival George had ordered three baskets of scampi and chips, a pint of beer for himself, a lager shandy for Deborah and a pint of cider for Maureen, all of which had been thoroughly enjoyed. By the time the bell signalling closing time had rung, George and Maureen in particular had imbibed a considerable amount of alcohol. As they walked back to their car in the pub's car park, Deborah took her car keys from her handbag.

'It's alright Debs, I'm fine,' said George. 'I'll drive.'

'Oh, I don't think so,' said Deborah. 'You've had far too much to drink.'

Maureen laughed.

'Oh don't fuss Mum! He's just happy, that's all.'

'Yeah,' slurred George, 'and with good reason. THE WITCH IS DEAD!'

'Shhhh! Keep your voice down Dad!' said Maureen with a giggle.

George pushed past his wife to open the driver's door and sat down behind the wheel before Deborah could say more. Maureen sat beside him while a reluctant and concerned Deborah got into the back of the car. George started up and began to drive.

The area around The Dog and Duck benefited from good street lighting, so much so that George did not realise he had not turned on his headlights.

'Slow down a bit love,' said a worried Deborah from the back of the car. 'There's no rush.'

George laughed and continued on at speed.

It was pouring with rain. Marvin White, an articulated lorry driver from Somersley, was returning to his base after a long day's work on the road. As he stopped at the T-junction with Sydney Street he looked both left and right and, believing the road to be clear, he proceeded to pull out.

At the time George was approaching the same junction and, as he passed the final street light, he suddenly realised that he could see nothing except the side marker lights of Marvin's trailer directly in front of him.

'DAD LOOK OUT!' screamed Maureen.

George braked as hard as he could but it was too little, too late. There was a sickening crunch as the Morris disappeared under

Marvin's trailer, ripping off the car's roof on impact and instantly killing everyone inside.

33

Wendy and Brian were woken by a repeated ringing of their doorbell on the following Sunday morning. Brian groaned, sat up and rubbed his eyes. He glanced at the clock on the bedside table. 6.45.

'Who, in God's name can that be at this time of the morning?' he said. He clambered out of bed and pulled back a curtain. Wendy, sleepily, sat up. Brian turned to her.

'It's Shepperton and Clarke!'

'Oh my God!' replied Wendy. 'They must know something! What are we gonna do?'

She began to weep. Brian knelt on the bed, his hands on her shoulders.

'We've gotta keep calm Wen. Understand? Play it cool. Don't let 'em see you're freaking out!'

The bell rang again – and again. The detectives were, undoubtedly, becoming impatient.

'I'll go,' said Brian. 'You wait up here.'

He put on his dressing down and hurried downstairs.

'Alright! Alright! I'm coming!' he called out when he reached the bottom stair. 'What's the rush?'

He opened the door. Shepperton and Clarke stood side by side on the doorstep.

'Brian Brown,' said Shepperton addressing him solemly, 'I'm arresting you on suspicion of the murders of Gemma Gooding, Heather Brown, Sarah Mitchell and Geraldine Abbott. You do not need to . . .'

'What?' interrupted Brian. 'Are you mad?'

Ignoring Brian, Shepperton continued by reading Brian his rights.

'This is crazy!' replied Brian. 'You're mad! Why would I kill two girls I loved? You're making a big mistake Shepperton – a big, big mistake!'

'What's going on?'

All three men looked up the stairs to see a concerned Wendy standing in her dressing gown on the landing.

'They're accusing me of killing our girl,' said Brian.

Wendy gasped.

'But that's ridiculous!'

Clarke was in no mood for further discussion.

'I suggest that you go upstairs and get dressed. We're taking you down to the station to be interviewed. I'll come up with you.'

Brian glared at him.

'I'm quite capable of dressing myself thank you very much.'

Clarke, firmly, repeated: 'I'm coming up there with you.'

Five minutes later, Brian, now in handcuffs, was led to the detective's car. On the opposite side of the road, bedroom curtains were beginning to tweak as neighbours wondered what was going on.

Wendy, in tears, called out to Shepperton.

'How long will he be? When will he be back?'

Shepperton stopped and turned to face her.

'I'm sorry Mrs Brown, but I very much doubt he ever will be!'

Half an hour later Brian was once again in familiar surroundings – the interview room at Somersley police station.

'Wait here,' instructed Shepperton curtly as he left Brian in the company of a young officer.

'We'll let him sweat in there for a while,' said Shepperton to Clarke, 'then we'll see what he has to say for himself.'

Brian had already refused to say anything until his solicitor Eugene du Beke arrived. However, it was deemed that the appointment of du Beke would be inappropriate as his wife was a colleague of Geraldine Abbott and was, indeed, a close friend of the deceased head teacher.

Arrangements were made for an alternative solicitor to represent Brian – a Mr Randolf Solomon – who turned up a few minutes later, rather put out that his regular Sunday morning on the golf course would need to give way to the more serious matter of assisting Brian to prove his innocence. On arrival he was shown into the interview room where, alone, he was able to speak to his client.

'I don't know what's going on Mr Solomon,' said Brian. 'Somehow they've got it into their heads that I'm some kinda mass murderer.'

'Are you sure there's nothing I should know about before the interview gets underway?' asked Solomon, 'because, if there is, now is the time to put me in the picture.'

'There's nothing, nothing at all,' declared Brian, omitting the facts that he knew Wendy and been responsible for killing Sarah and his own involvement in Geraldine's demise.

'In that case, I suggest a 'no comment' interview,' advised Solomon. 'It's the detectives' responsibility to prove your guilt, not yours to prove your innocence. I suggest we let them know we're ready to commence. The sooner we get this over and done with the sooner you can get home to your wife and I can join my friends on the golf course.'

Solomon's final comment did little to inspire Brian's confidence in his legal representative.

'I'm sorry to spoil your golfing morning,' said Brian with more than a hint of sarcasm in his voice, 'but, if you hadn't already noticed, I'm in a bit of a fix here! I hope you'll give this your full attention 'cos if you don't God only knows what will happen.'

Solomon apologised for his flippant remark.

'You're quite correct Mr Brown. I can assure you of my complete and utter attention. Now then, if you are absolutely sure there is nothing more I need to know, I suggest we call the detectives in. I assume you agree?'

Brian nodded. Solomon banged on the door.

'We're ready!'

As Shepperton and Clarke entered, Solomon whispered to Brian.

'Remember what I said. If it gets tricky, just answer 'no comment', okay?'

Brian nodded. Shepperton and Clarke sat on the chairs on the other side of the table. Shepperton looked at his watch and started the tape.

'It's Sunday the 14th of January 1990 at 8.27am. Present are myself DCI David Shepperton, Detective Constable James Clarke, Mr Brian Brown and his legal representative Mr Randolf Solomon.'

As per usual, Clarke withdrew a notepad and pen from his jacket pocket. For the time being he was to leave the talking to Shepperton who, obviously, was keen to get the interview under way. Facing Brian he began.

'Brian Brown, you are here on suspicion of the murders of Gemma Gooding, Heather Brown, Sarah Mitchell and Geraldine Abbott. Do you have anything to say?'

'Yes,' said Brian, 'you're mad!'

His response resulted in a nudge and frown from Solomon.

'Just answer my question,' demanded Shepperton.

'I had absolutely nothing to do with any of the killings,' said Brian.

'Very well,' replied Shepperton, 'but I have to tell you that, since the discovery of Mrs Abbott's body on Friday evening, certain information has come to light that suggest quite the opposite.'

He nodded to Clarke who opened his briefcase and took out an evidence bag containing a paper knife.

'Do you recognise this?' asked Shepperton.

Brian shook his head.

'Oh, I think you do,' said Shepperton. 'It's the knife that was used to cut Geraldine Abbott's wrist, an injury that resulted in her death.'

'Like I said, I don't recognise it,' insisted Brian. 'It's a paper knife. There must be millions of 'em. How could I possibly say with any certainty that I recognise this particular one?'

'Ah,' said Shepperton, 'a paper knife you say? Well, Mr Brown, I can tell you that this is not an ordinary paper knife. No, not at all. This is a *Japanese* paper knife.'

'Okay,' said Brian, 'it's a Japanese knife. So what?'

'It means it's a rarity in this country,' explained Shepperton. 'I'm informed they're made from hand-forged Damascus steel.'

'You may find this very interesting DCI Shepperton,' interjected Solomon, 'but what exactly are you getting at?'

Shepperton puffed out his chest as if he was about to conduct a *coup de grace* but, in fact, what he was about to reveal fell a little short of that.

'As I said, Mr Solomon, these knives are rare. There are only a few suppliers locally. Our enquiries found only four outlets within a 20-mile radius of Somersley. The nearest is Whybrows

Stationery which, I'm sure you know, being a local man yourself, is but a hundred yards from this police station.

'One of my officers visited the store yesterday afternoon and spoke to Mr Whybrow who clearly remembered selling a Japanese paper knife on Friday morning. When shown this knife he immediately recognised it and, when he looked up his records, he was able to show that it had been paid for by card – Mr Brown's credit card in fact.'

The colour drained from Brian's face. He hoped against hope that Shepperton or Clarke would not notice but he was to be disappointed.

'All school staff, with the exception of Mrs Brown, were interviewed yesterday afternoon,' continued Shepperton. 'Not one of them could recall seeing such a knife in Mrs Abbott's office.'

'Why would they?' asked Brian. 'It's just a knife.'

'A *Japanese* paper knife,' replied Shepperton correcting him, the detective clearly revelling in having Brian against the ropes.

'Now then, Mr Brown,' he said, 'are you still sure you do not recognise this knife? Are you suggesting Mr Whybrow is mistaken even though a rare *Japanese* paper knife was purchased using your credit card from his store on Friday morning?'

Backed into a corner, Brian was obliged to come up with an answer.

'Okay, okay, I did purchase a knife very similar to that one on Friday,' he admitted.

'And where is that knife now, Mr Brown?'

'I lost it,' replied Brian feebly.

'Hmm, how unfortunate,' said Shepperton. 'Why did you feel the need to purchase an expensive, rare Japanese paper knife Mr Brown?'

Brian looked to Solomon for assistance. Solomon mouthed 'no comment'. However, Brian considered such a response would signal a degree of guilt and chose to ignore Solomon's advice.

'I, er, I . . I needed it to cut paper,' he replied feebly.

Shepperton grinned.

'In that case Mr Brown, it was a very wise purchase.'

He handed the knife back to Clarke who put it back inside his briefcase.

'Did you know that Japanese paper knives are specifically designed for use by right handed people?' he asked.

'No, of course I didn't know that.'

'Mrs Abbott was left handed. Did you know that Mr Brown?'

'Course not!'

'It just seems strange to me that an educated lady like Mrs Abbott, a left handed lady, would purchase an expensive Japanese paper knife specifically designed for a right handed user.'

'Well,' replied Brian, 'she probably didn't know that.'

'Possibly,' agreed Shepperton, 'but I doubt it. I think this is the same knife you purchased on Friday afternoon, the same knife used to kill Mrs Abbott!'

Shepperton brought his fist down hard onto the table to emphasise his point. Brian just stared at him, refusing to be intimidated.

'That's rubbish Shepperton, and you damn well know it! Anyway, you've got Geraldine Abbott's handwritten confession and Maureen Robson's account of everything that happened. I can't for the life of me think why you believe I'd ever harm my own daughter or Gemma. As for Sarah Mitchell, I didn't even know the girl.'

Solomon rose to his feet.

'I think we're done here DCI Shepperton. My client has admitted purchasing a knife from Mr Whybrow's shop but, unless you can categorically prove it to be the exact same knife as that which cut Mrs Abbott's wrist, I can see no good reason why you need to detain him any longer. As he so rightly says, you have Mrs Abbott's confession and Miss Robson's account of how those poor young ladies met their untimely ends.'

'Exactly!' declared Brian with renewed vigour. 'Maureen knows exactly what happened. I was not involved in any way. Ask her, she'll tell you the same!'

'I wouldn't rely on Miss Robson's testament too heavily if I were you Mr Brown,' said Clarke.

'Why shouldn't I?'

'Cos she's dead. She and her parents were involved in a road traffic collision late last night. They're all dead.'

Brian stood gawping like a goldfish.

'No! No! You're lying!'

Shepperton shook his head.

'Sadly not,' he said, 'especially as I had intended to arrest Miss Robson this morning.'

'Why? Why would you want to do that?'

'It's my belief,' said Shepperton, 'that her elaborate account of the murders was merely a ploy between yourself and Miss Robson to frame Mrs Abbott. I believe that between the two of you, you dreamt up some ludicrous account in order to set her up.'

'I have to admit,' said Clarke, 'Miss Robson was most convincing. By the time she'd finished talking she'd persuaded us both that she'd been telling the truth.

Shepperton nodded in agreement.

'That's because she *was* telling the truth! You really are mad, aren't you?' raged Brian. 'Give me one good reason why Maureen and I would want those three girls dead.'

'I'm sure we'll find out after a bit more digging,' replied Shepperton. 'I think we'll take a break now as there are a couple more potential witnesses we need to speak to.'

'Like who?' demanded Brian.

'I've asked your wife and Mrs Gooding to come to the station. They should be here any moment. A break will give you and Mr Solomon here a chance to get your stories in sync.'

'We want to see Brian,' insisted Wendy when she and Stella arrived at the police station, 'because you've made an awful mistake.'

Roger Everett, the duty sergeant, raised his hands.

'I'm really sorry ladies but that won't be possible. He's just been interviewed and now he's speaking with his solicitor. I can't let you through, I'm afraid.'

'Well, when can we see him?' asked Stella.

'I very much doubt you'll be allowed to. DCI Shepperton's asked me to show you both through to Interview Room 2. You can ask him for permission to see Mr Brown then but I can't make any promises.'

Everett guided the two women to the vacant interview room. They sat down and waited for Shepperton and Clarke to make an appearance.

'I hope they don't . . . ' began Wendy.

'Shhh,' interrupted Stella. 'Walls have ears. I've seen it on the telly.'

Seconds later, the detectives entered the room, each of them holding paper cups of coffee.

'Mrs Brown, Mrs Gooding, thank you both for coming in. Can we get you both a cup of tea or coffee?'

'No thanks,' they replied in unison.

'We want to see Brian,' said Wendy. 'He's done nothing wrong.'

'That, I'm afraid,' replied Shepperton, 'is a view we do not share. Your husband has an awful lot of explaining to do if he's gonna convince us of his innocence.'

Rather ironically, bearing in mind a few weeks earlier she had reported her suspicions of Brian to Shepperton, Stella was now insisting the detective had the wrong man.

'Speak to Maureen again,' she said. 'She'll tell you Brian is innocent.'

Both women were shaken to the core when Shepperton explained why that was no longer a possibility.

'So it was them?' sobbed Wendy. 'You're telling us they were the ones killed in the crash that was on the TV news?'

Shepperton nodded.

'That's so awful!' said Stella. 'As if that poor girl hadn't gone through enough.'

Clarke spoke up.

'I'm not so sure about that. Now we have evidence that all is not quite how Miss Robson wanted us to believe.'

Wendy, puzzled, asked why.

'I'm afraid Mrs Brown, we are now examining the possibility that your husband and Miss Brown may have colluded with each other in order to frame Mrs Abbott for the murders.'

'That's ridiculous!' declared Wendy.

'Absolutely!' said Stella.

Both women insisted that, as the police were now in possession of a confession in Geraldine's own handwriting, it was an absurd theory.

'The poor girl's only been dead a matter of a few hours and already you're trying to blacken her name. That girl went to hell and back. Dead or not, she certainly doesn't deserve this!' said Wendy.

'Come on Wendy, let's go. We can go, right?' Stella asked Shepperton.

'Of course,' he replied, 'but I would have thought you would both have wanted to assist us with our enquiries if you truly believe Mr Brown is innocent.'

'What's the point?' seethed Wendy, 'you've both obviously made up your minds!'

The women angrily picked up their coats and stormed out of the room.

'That went rather well,' said Clarke facetiously.

'I think we've kept Brown waiting long enough now James, don't you?' said Shepperton.

Clarke grinned. The detectives re-entered Interview Room 1. Once again Shepperton set the tape in motion and resumed their interrogation.

Meanwhile, Wendy and Stella were making their way towards the exit. As they were passing the reception desk they noticed Sgt Fletcher attempting to deal with a very tearful, angry young lady who was accompanied by a stout older lady holding on to a toddler.

'I'll tell you once again. I want to see Brian Brown and I want to see him NOW!' shouted the younger woman.

'I'm sorry Madam but, as I've already told you, that's just not possible. He's being interviewed as we speak.'

'I don't care. Take me to him!'

'You don't understand Madam, there's nothing I can do about it. Mr Brown will not be receiving any visitors apart from his legal representative for the foreseeable future.'

The woman, exasperated, banged her fist on Everett's counter.

'I'm not going anywhere until I see Brian! Do you understand? I'm not going anywhere!'

Everett did his best to calm her down, but without success. The woman was absolutely seething. Stella and Wendy looked at each other in amazement.

'Who's she?' whispered Stella.

'I haven't the foggiest,' replied Wendy, 'but I'm gonna find out.'

She walked over to the woman and tapped her on the arm.

'Excuse me, could you tell me who you are and why you want to see Brian?'

The woman spun around. She glared at Wendy.

'What's that got to do with you?'

'He's my husband.'

'Oh yeah, like hell he is!'

'What?'

'His missus is dead! She died in a car crash more than five years ago.'

'There must be some mistake,' said Wendy. 'Who told you that?'

'He did, of course.'

'But I *am* Brian's wife,' insisted Wendy.

'Yeah, what's your name then?' said the woman sneering at Wendy.

'I'm Wendy. Wendy Brown.'

The woman's expression changed to one of puzzlement.

'Is this some kinda sick joke?' she asked.

'This *is* Wendy Brown, she's Brian's wife,' chipped in Stella. 'Who are you?'

'Sasha McRae. Brian's my fiancé.'

Stella and Wendy exchanged disbelieving glances.

'That, that isn't possible,' said Wendy. 'You've must have the wrong Brian Brown.'

'The one whose daughter got murdered?' said the woman. 'No, I don't think so!'

'How did you know about Brian's arrest?' demanded Wendy. 'It hasn't been made public yet.'

'My dad's a civilian member of staff here. He 'phoned me this morning. That's why I rushed down here. There's no way Brian could have killed anyone. He's far too kind and gentle. That's what I love about him.'

'If that's true, why did you split up?' asked Stella.

'It was when his daughter Gemma was killed. He said he couldn't give our relationship the commitment it needed until he'd sorted his head out so I agreed to give him some space.'

'But Gemma wasn't his daughter!' said Stella. 'She was mine! Are you telling us he was seeing you when he was with me?'

Sasha looked bewildered.

'He wasn't with anyone, just me. Brian wouldn't cheat. I know that for sure. Anyway,' she added, disapprovingly looking Stella up and down, 'I don't really think you're his type!'

Stella was about to respond with an opinion of her own but Wendy got in first.

'When did you first meet him?' she asked.

'I dunno. Five or six years ago I guess.'

The older lady, holding the hand of the toddler, came over to see what was going on.

'What's happening love?' she asked.

'It's this one here Mum,' she replied, pointing angrily at Wendy. 'Silly cow's insisting she's Brian's wife.'

'Well,' said her mother as she looked down her nose at Wendy, 'she's looking pretty good for a dead woman isn't she?'

'You cheeky cow!' shouted Wendy. 'I *am* Brian's wife!'

'Yes she is!' shouted Stella.

Stella's raised voice scared the little girl. She began to cry. The older woman picked her up and tried to comfort her. The commotion was interrupted by Everett.

'Ladies! Ladies! Quieten down will you?'

He placed himself between Wendy and Sasha. He then turned to Sasha.

'This lady here,' he said pointing to Wendy, '*is* Brian Brown's wife.'

Sasha and her mother looked astounded.

'Seriously?'

Everett nodded.

'Yes, seriously. Now I don't know what's going on here but I suggest you all calm down and find somewhere else to discuss this in a more civilised manner. Okay?'

'This doesn't make sense,' said Sasha. 'None of it does.'

'It's happened again, hasn't it Stella?'

'Certainly looks like it,' she replied.

'What's happened again?' demanded Sasha.

Wendy looked at her and smiled sympathetically.

'What?'

'Sasha, we all need to calm down. There's stuff you need to know,' said Wendy.

'Would you and your mum come with us?' suggested Stella. 'Perhaps we could go and get a coffee somewhere?'

Sasha and her mother were thrown by Wendy and Stella's sudden change of tone. Sasha looked to her mother for guidance.

'Perhaps we should hear what they've got to say,' the woman suggested. Stella thought she noticed a degree of uneasiness in Sasha's demeanour as if, perhaps, she was beginning to think there might be a grain of truth in what they had been claiming after all.

Sasha rather reluctantly agreed. Her mother suggested a little coffee shop on the opposite side of the road. Much to Everett's relief, the warring parties left the police station and, a few minutes later were sitting around a table in the coffee shop.

'We need to tell you something Sasha,' said Stella, 'but please, let's not have another shouting match in here. It seems you've had a similar experience to me and Wendy.'

'Such as?'

'We've all been deceived by Brian. You need to know that Brian was not a widower when he met you Sasha. At the time he was very much married to Wendy. Later, he left Wendy to be with me after having told me that he and Wendy were leading separate lives. I believed him, but it was a lie – one of many.'

'He was, in fact,' chipped in Wendy, 'cheating on me and Stella while he was with you.'

'I think I believe them,' said Sasha's mother. Sasha's face began to crumple.

Wendy reached across the table and gently squeezed Sasha's hand.

'You *have* to believe us,' she said. 'My husband is a compulsive liar. I hate to say this Sasha but, just like he did with us, he's taken you for a fool.'

As the truth finally dawned, Sasha burst into tears.

'I never trusted that man,' hissed her mother, 'but she wouldn't listen. Always knows best, that's my Sasha!'

'I'm not so sure this is the best time to dwell on that, do you?' said Stella. 'Your daughter's just had the most awful shock.'

'That's right,' agreed Wendy, 'and I know *exactly* how she feels!'

'We both do,' said Stella as she passed Sasha a serviette to wipe her eyes.

'I'm sorry,' blubbed Sasha, 'for shouting at you both.'

'It's okay, we understand,' replied Stella. 'It's all a bit of a mess, isn't it?'

The little girl began to cry again. Sasha's mother rummaged around in her bag and retrieved a bottle of milk. She caught the attention of a waitress.

'Do you think you could warm this up please for the little one?' she asked.

'Sure, no problem,' said the waitress as the bottle was handed over to her.

'She's a beautiful little girl isn't she?' said Wendy. 'How old is she?'

'Eighteen months,' said the proud grandmother as she fondly stroked the little girl's hair.

'She has the most lovely eyes,' Wendy noted. She looked towards Stella. 'She's really beautiful isn't she?'

Stella didn't reply. She just stared intently at the child.

'I do hope,' she said to Sasha, 'that you're not gonna tell us this is Brian's child.'

Sasha tearfully nodded.

Wendy's blood ran cold. Sasha was an attractive girl who looked as if she was no more than in her early twenties – just Brian's type.

'Oh my God Stella! He's done it again!'

This time it was Wendy's turn to burst into tears. Stella hugged her as a distraught Sasha and her mother looked on.

'I told you he was no good,' said her mother curtly, apparently ignoring Wendy and Stella's advice to go easy on her daughter in order to make her point.

'I insisted she has my surname,' said Sasha, 'cos I wanted her to grow up with the McRae name, but Brian chose her first names. He adores her.'

'What's her name?' asked Stella.

'Grace. It's Grace . . .'

Wendy interrupted her.

'It's Grace Mary isn't it? she cried.

'Yes,' replied a surprised Sasha, 'how did you know?'

'Oooh, how could he? How could he do that?'

'What do you mean? How did you know that?'

'I lost my first baby when she was just three days old,' sobbed Wendy. 'Brian wanted to call her Grace Mary after his late grandmother. Now he's named his latest baby after our dead one! How low can he get?'

She sobbed uncontrollably, prompting the waitress to return with Grace's warm milk. She looked awkwardly at the women sitting around the table.

'I'm so, so sorry,' she said nervously, 'but my manager is concerned that you are all upsetting our other customers. He'd be grateful if you could all drink up and leave as soon as possible.'

'Tell him not to worry,' replied a furious Wendy, 'cos I'm off.'

She turned to Stella.

'I'm going back to the station. I want to tell Shepperton what a swine he's been interviewing. If he thinks Brian is the killer, I'm not gonna persuade him otherwise. As far as I'm concerned he can rot in hell!'

34

'Tell me about Sarah Mitchell.'

Brian looked at Shepperton blankly.

'What about her?'

'Why did you kill her?'

Solomon was swift to object.

'DCI Shepperton, I must object! My client has already told you he has no knowledge of this young lady. He has also informed you that he did not even know her.'

'I am well aware of that Mr Solomon,' replied Shepperton. 'It's just that I don't believe him.'

He thought for a moment then continued.

'Where were you on Friday, September 16th, 1988?'

'Hmm, let me think,' said Brian. 'Ah yes, that was the day I washed my hair in the morning.'

Brian's flippant response angered Shepperton. He banged his fist on the table and leant forward, his face just inches from Brian's.

'I'm conducting a quadruple murder investigation here Brown. I haven't got time for your stupid games! Just answer my question!'

'What do you expect Shepperton?' replied Brian equally angrily. 'How the hell do you expect me to remember that? I haven't a clue where I was or what I was doing that day.'

'Perhaps I could jog your memory,' offered Shepperton. 'That's the day Sarah Mitchell was killed. Strangely enough, soon afterwards, your wife's car was reported stolen. It was found burnt out on Blyton Common. I understand you drive an MBG GT sports car, is that right?'

Brian nodded.

'Yes, that's what I thought,' said Shepperton. 'That wouldn't have been much use to you that day, would it?'

'What on earth are you on about?'

'Well,' replied Shepperton, 'I reckon it'd be pretty difficult to fit a body into the boot of your little sports car. Impossible, I reckon, I think you put Sarah Mitchell in the boot of your wife's car and, having disposed of Sarah's body down Roman Walk, you drove on to Blyton Common and set your wife's car on fire to eliminate any evidence that may have been of forensic use.'

'You really are mad, aren't you?' replied Brian who, inwardly, was squirming. Shepperton's theory was not a million miles from the truth. He felt the palms of his hands sweating. He hoped the detectives would not notice his increasing nervousness.

The plan to trick Geraldine into writing a confession had, thought Brian, gone like clockwork. A couple of days previously he had been confident he had avenged Heather and Gemma's deaths and had established a smokescreen that would shield Wendy from any suspicion over Sarah's demise. Now, here he was, sitting in a dusty interview room, being challenged by detectives and facing the growing prospect of facing a charge of multiple murder.

He decided he had no choice. He had to keep calm and front it out. He kept reminding himself that Shepperton and Clarke had no evidence to link him to Heather, Gemma and Sarah's murders – after all, he was completely innocent of all three killings. All Shepperton and Clarke had were theories. No court in the land would find a man guilty without any viable evidence. With that in mind, he found himself more at ease.

'I did not kill Sarah Mitchell and I did not steal my wife's car. We were separated at the time. She will tell you I was nowhere near Somersley that day.'

Sadly for Brian though, the detectives had more up their sleeves. This time it was Clarke who was the bearer of bad news.

'Your wife and Mrs Gooding returned here shortly before we resumed this interview,' he said. 'They had some very interesting information. Trust me, Mr Brown, neither of them were very happy. Strangely, this morning, they were both adamant we had the wrong man – they insisted you were innocent and that we need look no further than Geraldine Abbott as the person responsible for killing all three girls. Yet, there they were, just over an hour later, telling us they could no longer be so sure of your innocence.'

'Actually,' chipped in Shepperton, 'they went a little further than that. Apparently, they now believe you to be a compulsive liar and a serial womaniser with a penchant for young ladies. Do the names Sasha and Grace Mary McRae mean anything to you because, according to your wife and Mrs Gooding, they should.'

This revelation sent Brian reeling. He turned to Solomon and whispered in his ear.

'My client requests a short break,' he said.

'I thought he might,' replied Shepperton with a wry smile. 'Half an hour, okay?'

'Did you see his face?' chuckled Shepperton as he and Clarke retired for a coffee break in his office. 'It was as if his whole world was crumbling right in front of him.'

'No less than he deserves,' said Clarke. 'He seems to wreck the lives of every woman he meets. I'd take a politician's word over his.'

Shepperton laughed.

'Well, that really is saying something!'

He then adopted a more serious demeanour.

'We haven't got enough on him though have we? We need something concrete. Something he can't wriggle out of.'

As if by magic, Shepperton's hopes were instantly given a massive boost as Sgt Everett popped his head around the door.

'The guys at the school have found something of interest Sir. Trust me, you're gonna love this!

35

Solomon looked at his watch and frowned.

'Half an hour, Shepperton said. What's keeping them?'

He banged on the door. A young constable opened the door.

'Yes Sir?'

'Where are DCI Shepperton and DC Clarke? We've been waiting in here for more than an hour.'

'They're in DCI Shepperton's office,' came the reply. 'Apparently there's been a development. They're not to be disturbed.'

'Well, tell them I haven't got all day!' snapped Solomon.

'I'm so sorry to have kept you waiting,' came a voice from down the corridor. It was Shepperton. He and Clarke re-entered the interview room. They sat down and Shepperton reset the tape recorder. Brian noticed they both bore rather smug expressions.

'Now then,' said Shepperton, but he was immediately interrupted by Solomon.

'Before we recommence my client wishes to tell you something.'

He nodded to Brian who cleared his throat and prepared himself to make a damning statement.

'I did not kill any of the girls,' he said, 'but I do know who killed Sarah Mitchell and why.'

Shepperton and Clarke were taken aback. This had come most unexpectedly. They sat forward in anticipation of what Brian was about to reveal.

'I've never killed anyone,' said Brian. 'Nor would I ever hurt anyone, but sometimes love makes you do things that are totally out of character.

'There was an incident at the school while my wife was teaching. Sarah Mitchell's sister made some joke about Heather. My wife was furious and slapped her. A few days later Sarah Mitchell attacked my wife in our home. My wife stabbed her in self defence. You were right Shepperton. I used my wife's car to dispose of Sarah's body – but that's all, I swear.'

He sat back on his chair, waiting to see the detective's reaction. Stella and Wendy had dropped him in it. Now, in order to save his own skin, he'd thrown his wife under the bus.

Shepperton and Clarke exchanged glances.

'Come on then,' demanded Brian, 'I've just told you who killed Sarah. Say something!'

'Okay,' replied Shepperton. 'We don't believe you. Your wife and Mrs Gooding were right. You wouldn't recognise the truth if it was staring you in the face.'

'I don't understand,' said Brian. 'You can check it out yourselves. Ask Sarah's sister, she'll tell you.'

'I don't think that'll be necessary, Mr Brown,' said Clarke. 'We already know who killed Sarah. We have a confession.'

'Yeah, Geraldine's,' said Brian. 'I know she's admitted it. Wendy was her best friend. I reckon she found out what Wendy had done and, because she felt guilty about killing Heather, she must have admitted to killing Sarah too to save Wendy's skin. Maybe it was her way of making up for what she'd done to Heather.'

Shepperton frowned.

'Your wife and Mrs Gooding – and Miss McRae – all tell us that you've treated them as fools, Brown. Don't even think about trying that with me. Let's move on from your fantasy world and get back to real life.

'You and your wife and Mrs Gooding were the only persons who knew about the discovery of Gemma's pendant in Mr Abbott's office. Apart from us only you knew about Heather's body being covered in lime. I believe you shared that information with Maureen Robson as you concocted your story about the murders in order to set up Mrs Abbott.'

'You believe this! You believe that! You're the one living in a fantasy world Shepperton, not me! I've admitted disposing of Sarah's body. That's all you have on me. There's no way on earth you can connect me to the murders and you know it! What ever makes you think I'd kill my own daughter and Gemma? I loved them both!'

'You're a man of many secrets Brown,' countered Shepperton. 'Christine Palmer and Sasha McRae to name but two. Who knows how far you would go to protect those secrets? I mean, look at you. You didn't hesitate to throw your poor wife under the bus just now, did you? I'm wondering how low you could go. Did Heather and Gemma find out that you're a serial baby maker?'

'Or,' suggested Clarke, 'maybe there was an element of truth in what Mrs Gooding told us a while back – that she suspected you of behaving inappropriately with Gemma in her bedroom. Maybe Gemma told Heather what you'd been up to, after all, you do seem to like young girls, don't you Brown?'

'As you know Brown,' said Clarke, 'we re-interviewed everyone a few weeks ago – including Mr Trent, the manager of the Wimpy Bar. He recalled an argument between Heather, Gemma and Maureen Robson. Said it got pretty heated. So, it seems you and Miss Robson may both have had motives after all, doesn't it?'

'You're sick!' shouted Brian. 'Both of you!'

Shepperton grinned. Clarke too.

'What's so funny?' demanded Brian.

'Oh,' replied Shepperton with an air of casualness, 'I was just thinking how ironic it would be if you were to end up in the same prison as Harry Abbott. I wonder how he'd react to being locked up with the man who tried to set his wife up for a triple murder and then killed her too. I wouldn't like to be in your shoes if that ever happened.'

This time it was Solomon's turn to bang his fist on the table.

'That's enough! You are baiting my client and you have no evidence whatsoever to link him to any murder. I find your attitudes quite unprofessional.'

Shepperton held up his hands by way of apology.

'You're quite right Mr Solomon. I apologise.'

He turned to Clarke.

'I think we're ready now, don't you?'

Clarke smiled and nodded.

'I'll get it.' He stood up and left the room and returned a minute later carrying a cardboard box. He placed it on the table between Shepperton and Brian.

'What's that?'

'This,' said Shepperton, tapping the lid of the box, is all we need to put you away for a long, long time.'

He opened the lid and lifted out a tape recorder.

'For the benefit of the tape,' he said, 'I am showing Mr Brown and Mr Solomon a tape recorder recovered from Geraldine Abbott's office. This tape recorder has been identified as that used by Mrs Abbott to dictate letters to her PA, Mrs Emily Hudson.'

Clarke unravelled the lead and plugged it into a wall socket.

'I think Mr Solomon, you should find this very interesting.'

He waited for the red light to change to green. Brian sat bewildered, then Clarke pressed Play.

'Did I hear you right? Say that again.'

'It wasn't Harry who killed the girls. It was me!'

Shepperton stopped the tape and puffed out his chest triumphantly.

'I suppose you're gonna try to convince us now that that's not you in conversation with Geraldine Abbott?'

'Yeah, it is me, but it's not as it sounds!' replied Brian. He was now sweating profusely and in a complete panic. Geraldine had grabbed the opportunity to outsmart him by recording their conversation. No wonder she'd asked him to 'say that again'.

'Well,' replied Shepperton, 'it sounds pretty incriminating to me. What do you think James?'

'I think that's probably all we need,' replied Clarke casually.

'Nah,' said Shepperton who was now revelling in Brian's discomfort, 'let's hear a little more.'

He pressed Play.

'But that's ridiculous Brian. Shepperton's already got enough evidence against Harry. It couldn't possibly have been you.'

'But it was, Geraldine. I did it. Harry's totally innocent! His trial is due to start any time now. That's why I have to hand myself in but first, I need you to help me write that letter.

There was a pause.

'Well say something then. Are you gonna help me or not?'

'Tell me why you reckon you killed the girls.'

'It came back to me in the night. Flashbacks. Real clear flashbacks. I could clearly remember sticking the knife into Sarah and . . .'

'Whoa! Whoa! Wait a minute' Sarah? Are you telling me it was you who killed Sarah Mitchell?'

'Yeah. I still can't remember why, but the murder itself – well, it's come back to me as clear as day now. Sometimes I get these urges you see. Afterwards I took her body down to Roman Walk and left it there in the long grass. There were other flashbacks too – Gemma and Heather. Those weren't so clear but, obviously, I must have killed them too.'

'For God's sake stop the tape Shepperton!' cried Brian. 'You don't understand! When Maureen told me what Geraldine had done I wanted to make sure she'd be locked up for good. I was trying to trick her into writing a confession. Surely you can see that?'

Shepperton shook his head.

'I don't think so Brown. We believe that when you entered Mrs Abbott's office you intended to make it appear that Mrs Abbott had killed herself. You wanted us to believe she killed those girls, not you, and that's why you and Miss Robson concocted your elaborate cover story.

'Let's listen to a little more, shall we?'

'I can hardly believe this. I guess you have no choice then. You'll have to speak to Shepperton.'

'Yes, but not until you help me write to Wendy. I think we should start with 'Dear Wendy'. Yeah, start with that.

'It is with a very heavy heart that I write this to you. I want you to know I've loved you over the years and I hope that some day, you might find it in your heart to forgive me for the terrible things I have done, though I very much doubt you will ever be able to do so.

'I can no longer live with my conscience. It's time to come clean. For reasons that I cannot explain, I need you to know that it was not Harry, but me who killed Gemma and Heather. I also killed Sarah.

'I am so sorry for deceiving you these last few months, for looking you in the eye and hiding the truth from you. I do not ask for, or deserve your pity. Only God can forgive me now. I am so, so sorry.'

'Is that it?'

'I think that's enough. Did you get all that? Thank you. Tell Harry I'm sorry will you? Tell him I'll explain it all to Shepperton. I'll go and see him now.'

Brian was now beyond desperate.

'You've gotta believe me Shepperton. I was only trying to trick her. I thought a confession in her own handwriting would help you guys. You know, make it easier to secure a conviction.'

'How very considerate of you Brown.' said Clarke facetiously.

'But it's the truth! You can't blame me for wanting her locked up for good can you? She killed my girl!'

Clarke shook his head.

'No she didn't Brown. Geraldine Abbott's not killed anyone. It was you all along.'

'No!'

Brian looked to Solomon for support but the solicitor just shrugged his shoulders. It was a hopeless case.

'You fully intended to make it appear that Geraldine Abbott was the killer,' insisted Clarke, 'and, when you entered her office on Friday you had every intention of killing her.'

'Oh Clarke, you've got this so, so wrong!'

The detectives smiled. Brian may have believed that was the end of the recording but there was more to come.

'Listen to this, Brown,' said Clarke, 'and you'll understand why we don't believe you.'

He pressed Play.

'Brian, do you want to sign your confession?'

'Okay. Oops, sorry, I've dropped my pen.'

The detectives and Solomon listened in horror as the rustling sound of a plastic bag was pulled over Geraldine's head. This was followed by the sound of items falling from her desktop as she struggled frantically for survival. Geraldine could clearly be heard gasping. Then came a loud crash as her desk tipped over during the struggle. Afterwards there was an indistinguishable sound which was, in fact, the plastic bag tearing.

Geraldine let out a long gasp.

'Brian! Brian! Why are you doing this?

'Shut up!'

The struggle continued for two more minutes then all was silent apart from the sound of Brian gasping for breath. A few moments later came the sound of Brian tidying up Geraldine's office followed by a retching.

'Guess this bit's where you sliced her wrist Brown,' commented Clarke.

It was pointless to argue. Brian knew he was a beaten man. He put his head in his hands and sobbed uncontrollably.

Shepperton stood up, a solemn expression on his face.

'Brian Brown, I'm charging you with the murders of Gemma Gooding, Heather Brown, Sarah Mitchell and Geraldine Abbott.'

Brian was a broken man as Shepperton continued to read him his rights.

'I did not kill those girls!' wailed Brian.

'Well,' replied Shepperton, 'thanks to Mrs Abbott, we now know you did. We've got you now Brown and all this proves something else.'

'Such as?'

'That the dead CAN talk!'

Other paperback novels by Ivan Sage available from Amazon

Rage
Dirty Business
Evil Amongst Us
The List
The Ring
A Mandate to Kill

Printed in Great Britain
by Amazon